THE MESSIAH STONES

THE
MESSIAH
STONES

IRVING BENIG

Fawcett Columbine • *New York*

A Fawcett Columbine Book
Published by Ballantine Books

http://www.randomhouse.com

Library of Congress Catalog Card Number: 96-96592

Cover design by Carlos Beltrán
Cover illustration by Annika Nelson

ISBN: 0-449-91090-3

This edition published by arrangment with Villard Books, a division of Random House, Inc. Villard Books is a registered trademark of Random House, Inc.

Manufactured in the United States of America

First Ballantine Books Edition: November 1996

10 9 8 7 6 5 4 3 2 1

For my father

"God finds a way."

—old saying

Acknowledgments

I am indebted to my agent, Barbara Lowenstein, whose vision gave me faith; to my publisher, David Rosenthal, who accepted that faith; to my editor, Craig Nelson, whose clarity gave me courage; and to Marcia Potash and Eileen Cope, who opened the door. Most of all I am grateful to my daughter, Stephanie, a light of my life.

Contents

THE MESSIAH STONES

Tel Aviv, Israel
January 26, 1955

Dear Barbara,

I have not written these last few days because, except for a few hours' sleep, we have been constantly working on this latest dig. We have made a momentous discovery that goes beyond anything we anticipated. I don't know how to begin to describe our find, since we have really just begun to absorb its full significance. The discovery itself was as if by accident, or by an ordained providence that goes beyond the scope of any present understanding.

As you know, we have been centered on an area in and around the Jordanian portion of Jerusalem. The Jordanians have ravaged most of the ancient Jewish holy places in the old Jewish quarter, as well as desecrating the Jewish cemetery on the Mount of Olives. Much has happened in the last war, Jewish tombstones that were centuries old have been uprooted and used for new paths, and for barracks and latrine walls for the Arab Legion near Bethany. The Jordanians have been here for a few years now, but I must admit that for the most part they have not interfered with our operation. It is occasionally difficult to deal with them, but since they have little or no interest in our work, we are left alone. Lately, though, things have heated up, since everyone has been following the scroll discoveries made by the Bedouins in the desert in Qumran. This has stirred up a lot of interest! Like most other things in this life, though, their fascination is purely monetary— any artifact found in these parts is sure to be worth something, they reason, so why not put a heavy price on finding it?

About two months ago, I wrote telling you about a discovery we made in Site 4. Our main interest up to then had been domestic, and for the most part we had little luck—some cooking utensils, a few jars but no scrolls, that sort of thing. Our main objective was to unearth an item of some significance, but after a few weeks it was becoming apparent that, like most of our work, this was a blind alley. Then, out of the blue—or was it providence again?—we found it: a magnificent huge block of stone from the wall of Second Temple in Jerusalem. And here it was in Shiloh, twenty miles away! There was no doubt that this was Herodian: the chiseled lines, the classic contours, the length of the massive block and its weight are unmistakable clues to its origin.

King Herod's greatest architectural triumph was the enlargement of the Temple Mount, where King Solomon had originally built the first temple on Mount Moriah. Herod used more than ten thou- sand workers for this marvel, and upon its completion the Jerusalem Temple became one of the true wonders of the ancient world. The Romans conquered the Israelis' ancient kingdom and destroyed the Temple in 70 A.D. During the siege and conflagration, the Temple went up in flames. Block by block—bear in mind that these are huge stones weighing many tons—the Temple was destroyed. Years later, the name "Jerusalem" itself was erased from maps when the emperor Hadrian renamed the city Aelia Capitolina and built a temple to Jupiter on the site of the Jewish temple and a second temple to Venus over Calvary.

Over the years, little has remained of the Temple, except for one wall—actually an outer wall beyond a courtyard, which the Jews call the Western Wall. (This has also been sometimes mistakenly referred to as the Wailing Wall, probably because of the way pious Jews worship in front of it, in fervent prayer that looks like wailing.) But given the exigencies of this latest war between the Israelis and their Arab neighbors, the Jews are forbidden to pray at the Wall. Site 4—which is our latest dig—is not in Jerusalem, but in Shiloh, as I said, about twenty miles northeast of Jerusalem in what was called Samaria in the time of Christ—which, according to the work Dr. Anderson has done, should have been the location for a wealthy merchant's villa, our main archaeological interest. We never found the villa; instead, we found a block of Temple Wall. What is absolutely extraordinary about this, Barbara, is at its heart a very simple but truly amazing question: Why is it there? Beyond this question are others, such as how did it get there, and who brought it there? We have excavated an area the size of a football field and have as yet found no other stone or object to indicate a clue. Aside from one small unexcavated portion located at the extreme eastern tip of our dig, we have so far found nothing to indicate its history.

Please imagine how incredibly difficult it must have been two thousand years ago to tow this huge block of stone, weighing tons, miles and miles across rough roads, if indeed there were roads at all. And beyond that, the country was in a state of war! The Jews were being killed by the thousands—almost half a million alone are reported to have been taken to Rome as slaves. The Roman soldiers were everywhere, enforcing martial law. Yet, in the midst of this carnage and chaos, in the midst of the destruction of an entire nation by the weight of the Roman Empire, one block of the Wall gets transported to a site unrelated to its origin and many miles away! Were the Jews trying to hide it, to save it? Is there something else here? Was someone stealing it? Did the Jews in fact take it, or the Romans?

As the years go by, I am constantly amazed by how little we really know of the past. Perhaps it's my professional bias, but I don't think we have progressed very far. Somehow, if the ghosts that roam this land could tell us their tales, as the ghost in Hamlet says, a tale would unfold that would scare you to death!

4:00 A.M.
February 28

As it turned out, Barbara, I did not send this letter, but took it with me instead to Dr. Anderson's house. He is giving it to a young student who will mail it home from Tel Aviv, where you will note my new temporary address. We had to leave in a hurry, and the drive was difficult; our car blew a tire, but we're okay. Much, much has occurred since I wrote last, but I am too tired now to explain, and also too depressed. How can I be away from you for so long? I must get some sleep. Anderson has been secretive, as have some of the students he brought with him from Chicago. Who could have foreseen what we have discovered? I have not begun to tell you the half of it! For the first time in my life, my darling, I am truly afraid. Perhaps we have stumbled across something that was better left buried. But we have opened the door, and it is ajar. More tomorrow.

All my love,
Philip

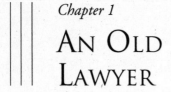

Chapter 1

AN OLD
LAWYER

JANUARY 1995

IT BEGAN AS A MYSTERY.

And I was the least qualified person on earth to get involved in it, or to solve it.

I am not the sort of person you'd expect to go in search of an adventure. I think my wife and children and friends would describe me as pretty conservative. I suppose I've always been that way.

I was raised by a mother who was left alone to fend for herself and her only child—me—a scrawny boy who liked reading books more than playing football. After the age of about five, I never saw my father again. In those days, in the mid-1950s, it wasn't easy for a woman to make it on her own, especially with a child to raise. She had to live with the stigma of being deserted, in a world in which independent women were looked upon with cold curiosity, if not outright disdain. She never dated or thought about remarriage, I suppose, which would have been possible in her situation with the proper legal advice.

She just got a job and went to work outside the home. She never complained.

As for me, as I was just beginning school, it was even more critical for me to feel exactly the same as any other little boy, carrying my Howdy Doody lunch box and wearing a Hopalong Cassidy string tie to school. But in those days, I can honestly say that I did not feel like every other small boy. I felt different, and cheated somehow of my just inheritance by a father who had mysteriously and permanently disappeared to parts unknown, for reasons my mother and I never ascertained. I can remember thinking it was perhaps my fault, something I had done. What would it take to make you leave your child? There was the case last year of the young mother in South Carolina who supposedly murdered her two young boys. Can we begin to understand her motive? When you cross the line, out of the circle of normal human emotion, there are no explanations. But that doesn't lessen the blow; her boys were still dead and my mother and I were still deserted.

My mother worked as a secretary in Chicago, in the Loop, and as the years passed, I became more and more focused on my studies, especially history and past cultures. Even at an early age, I was fascinated by individuals such as Alexander the Great, Charlemagne, and Genghis Khan. These individuals stood out in my imagination with an intensity and clarity beyond the printed words on the page. In my mind's eye, I could visualize each of them as he passed his way across the stage of history. Even today, I can recall the vivid legend of the great Khan, surrounded by his enemies and left to die on the hillside. But the great Khan confounded his foes, drinking his own blood and eating human flesh for sustenance. Such were the stories that filled my hours as a child, probably not less frightening than other bedtime stories of witches offering poisoned apples, or capturing children in the woods to cook them later for dinner.

But as I grew older, I began to see these same giants of history much more in the true context of their times. They were not so much the prime movers of their eras, but only one element in a much larger story. Still, I never lost my childlike fascination for the study of the heroic in history, for an understanding of the extent to which the individual—any individual—can shape his destiny, and to what degree we are shaped by events beyond our control, by forces that flow through our lives like deep currents in a stream. Later on in life, I turned this interest into a career as an academic, a teacher, finally settling down as a tenured professor in a small liberal arts college in the backwoods of Pennsylvania.

It was a natural choice for me: doing research, reading, writing the occasional academic paper, and having time to spend with my wife and children. Most men don't get the chance to be home during the day, to enjoy something as ordinary as seeing the mail delivered. I was one of the few lucky ones. I suppose one could say I lived a quiet life, and I think that would be fairly accurate. Perhaps even an old-fashioned life. I plead guilty to liking classical music and opera, not the sort of music displayed on the front racks of CD counters. That's why I think I was the last person you'd expect to get involved with all of this. Today, as I write these words—how did events move so quickly?—I still find it hard to believe how innocently it all began. Or, actually, how deliberately it started.

The past few winters have been especially cold in Pennsylvania, with much more snow on the ground than people could remember for a long time. But the air is brisk and clean, and there is a special beauty to the campus life of a small rural college in the Northeast. The rhythms are calm and regular as the current year's crop of freshman faces replaces those of the graduating class. In fact, it is exactly this placid kind of life that I liked the most; so when something happened to upset the neat orderliness of the college schedule, it stood out as special. Then again, the certified letter that I received that Monday morning would've stood out as special in anyone's life.

It was from an attorney in Washington who identified himself as representing a third party in whose last will and testament I had been named as the sole beneficiary. It seems I had inherited something of value from a deceased relative, who remained unnamed in the attorney's letter, and the will was about to be read; the attorney requested that I be present at the reading. To guide me in the right direction and persuade me to make the trip to Washington, the attorney included a round-trip air ticket. All I needed to do was call the airline and confirm the prepaid reservation. If I had any questions—and I had at least a dozen—the attorney further suggested I give him a call that day.

Sarah, my wife, was skeptical.

"I don't know, John—it sounds like a scheme of some sort," she said as she held the letter in her hand. "Then again," she said, "the airline ticket looks real enough. Why don't you call the airline first to see if it's genuine, then call this lawyer—try collect, see if he'll accept the charges. Then you can make up your mind."

Sarah and I have been married for eleven years. About four years ago, she and a partner opened a small bookstore off campus that specializes in mysteries. They call the store Private Ice. In general, Sarah is much quicker about business matters than I am, and the store has done quite well.

I watched Sarah head toward the top of the basement staircase to call the kids to dinner and knew that I loved her more than ever.

"Now, or after dinner?" I asked.

"What?"

"Should I call now, or later? He's probably not in the office at this hour. Maybe we're millionaires."

"Do you have any wealthy relatives you never heard of?"

"How do I know if I never heard of them?"

"It's probably not money, probably an old painting or dusty furniture. People are always leaving the craziest things. You never know what some people think is valuable."

"Maybe a Picasso," I said.

"Well," Sarah said, in the midst of looking at the boys' hands to see if they were clean—they weren't—"maybe we'll be able to sell it, whatever it is."

I looked at the letter again.

"Of course," I said, in my logical, professorial way, "if I never heard of him, or her, it could be anything, or nothing at all. . . ."

"John, why don't you call? I don't think I can live with the suspense through dinner."

I did call. The airline confirmed that the tickets were real enough. Unfortunately, however, the operator said that there was no answer at the number I gave her in Washington, and no, she couldn't leave a message on the machine. So, I wound up calling direct, asking the attorney to call me back.

We have two boys, Joshua and Oliver, eight and six. Aside from Sarah, they are the most important people in my life. In one way, I don't feel worthy of them, as though I'd been given a gift of immeasurable value that I could not possibly have deserved.

Dinner at our house is usually a noisy affair.

When the phone rang ten minutes later, Joshua picked it up. As the older child, he's appointed himself the official voice of the family whenever the phone rings. Racing to the phone on the wall, he nearly tripped on a toy truck he or his brother had parked under the kitchen table.

It was the lawyer, returning my call.

His name was James Frederick Stanton, and he assured me that his communication was indeed genuine. Aside from what he'd told me in his letter, however, he was not prepared to divulge any information before the reading of the will, though he informed me that he would reimburse me for local hotel expenses if it became necessary to stay overnight in Washington.

"Would you like me to make a reservation, just in case?"

"No, not necessary," I said, "but isn't there anything else you can tell me? Not even the name of the relative?"

"The will specifies that you be physically present for the

reading, Mr. McGowan. And this is a special case, in many ways. I am looking forward to seeing you. Will tomorrow be satisfactory?"

"Tomorrow?" I asked incredulously. "You want me in Washington tomorrow?"

"If convenient," Stanton said.

"I don't think so. I'll have to work it around my classes. It's just not possible to pick up and fly to Washington," I said, stating what was, I hoped, the obvious.

"I understand," the voice at the other end of the line said reassuringly.

"How about Wednesday?" I asked.

"Fine," Stanton said. "Why not call me here once you have your time of arrival. Let me give you the directions to my office—it's only a short drive from Dulles."

"Okay," I said, "but just one question, if you don't mind: How did you find me?"

"Wednesday," Stanton repeated. "I'll answer all of your questions on Wednesday."

Sarah looked at me with that quizzical yet searching look in her eye.

"What makes you so lucky?" she asked, and tossed her head back the way she does when there is a hair in her face. Sarah has bright red hair—wonderful, thick, lustrous red hair—that to my eye adds an accent of extra beauty to her appeal.

"Is Daddy lucky?" Joshua asked, twirling his fork in his spaghetti with two hands as though he were drilling for oil in the middle of his plate.

"Yes," Sarah said, "Daddy is very lucky."

—

I HAD BEEN TO WASHINGTON last about three years before when I was completing a chapter in my book on the strategies of World War II. The Library of Congress has a superb collection of material for the historian. I'd hoped someday to return to the subject of war and its consequences, but this time from a completely different perspective.

The taxi ride was brief. Stanton's directions had been perfect. His office was located on a quiet street in an older brownstone. I had the feeling that he had been at this location for a long time. As I rang the outer bell, I could see the interior foyer through the glass panel next to the door. With one eye peering through the glass, I could see an old man approach the door to open it.

"Mr. McGowan?" I heard him say.

"Yes," I said.

"Please, do come in."

The old man silently led me to a small room off the main hall. He walked slowly, and I followed behind. Not until he spoke again, when we were seated in his office, did I realize it was Stanton. Though he was perhaps eighty years old, or more, he possessed a much younger man's voice, the same voice I'd first heard on the phone a few days before.

"Welcome to Washington, Mr. McGowan," he said, catching his breath. "It takes more and more of an effort to get going these days," he added, as he extracted a long, dark brown cigar from the humidor that rested on his neat desk. "I'm not what you would call very active."

His hand shook slightly as he nestled the cigar between two fingers.

"First of the day," he said, "is always the best. I was waiting for your arrival before lighting up. They are much sweeter these days, since I'm not allowed to smoke. Like a boy in a candy shop—imagine not being allowed to eat the candy!"

I could smell the unlit cigar; it reminded me of something I could not quite visualize.

"Did you have a pleasant trip?"

"Fine," I said.

"Fine," he repeated, and then, after a moment, as an after-thought, "I'm sorry—would you like a cigar?"

"I don't smoke, but thanks anyway."

"Ah, too bad," he said, slicing the tip of the cigar with a special tool he removed from his vest pocket, then lighting it with great ceremony with a wooden match, burning the end evenly as he took the first puffs.

"We live in fearful times, Mr. McGowan. The doctors have taken all the pleasure out of life. No butter, no fat, no smoking. All the traditional pleasures that created civilization in the first place. What is the world coming to, I ask you? We're all healthy, we will die in our sleep when we reach a hundred, but won't remember ever having any fun. For my part, I'll take a dish of high-fat, high-cholesterol, high-taste chocolate ice cream anytime over no-fat, no-taste yogurt. I'm a prisoner of my generation, you might say."

His smoke filled the room in aromatic clouds. I watched in silence as he took long, deep puffs.

"There will be no one else here today, Mr. McGowan. You are the only one."

"Mr. Stanton," I said, unable to contain myself any longer

in the face of his calm, unhurried manner, "perhaps you'd like to fill in a few of the blanks."

"What would you like to know first?"

He took a long drag on his cigar and politely exhaled off to the side. I had the distinct impression he'd practiced this behavior often before.

"Well—"

"Be prepared for a shock, Mr. McGowan."

I waited.

"The name of the man whose will we are concerned with is William McGowan—your father," he said.

I said nothing. He was right: I was shocked.

"Would you like a drink?" he asked.

Even though it was not yet noon, I accepted Stanton's offer. He poured us both a drink in very ornate glasses, out of an odd-shaped bottle that looked like a very rare Scotch.

"Single-malt," he said. "Thirty years. Only special occasions."

I normally don't drink. I once got drunk during an undergraduate party in college and couldn't remember what I said or did the whole night. I hated that, not remembering, not being in control. But now, what surprised me, almost as much as what he said, was that the alcohol seemed to have little or no effect on me.

"I like it neat," he said. "I hope you do, too."

For the next ten minutes, Stanton went on to read a very short will and to relate a story that kept me bolted to my chair. It was my father's story, unknown to me since childhood. According to Stanton, my mother, who had died some years before, was aware of parts of the story, but not all of it. Why she had never confided in me he couldn't say. How the details had become known to her he also couldn't say.

He did relate that in the mid-fifties, when I was a small boy, my parents were living in Chicago. My father was driving a taxi at the time, which was something I had never known. It appears that my father was attending classes at night toward a graduate degree in archaeology at the University of Chicago. According to Stanton, at some time during that period, my father was approached by a professor who was organizing an expedition to the Holy Land for the purpose of excavating some recently discovered ruins. My father was thrilled at the chance to be part of this select group and, along with the professor and a number of other students, set off for Israel.

Stanton related these events factually and calmly.

He said that my father had been working in Israel when, one day, he was suddenly asked by the professor—who had by now become his mentor—to return to the United States. My father did return and soon after located Stanton in Washington.

He told Stanton that he wanted to hire him in order to make a will. Stanton thought this was rather odd, since my father was a relatively young man. Even more odd, Stanton said, was what my father asked next. He removed a thick envelope from his briefcase, handed it to the lawyer, and explained that it contained a number of personal letters. My father wanted Stanton to keep them in a safe place and upon my father's death, or in January of 1995, whichever came first, to deliver them to his son, who, of course, was at that time only a small boy.

Stanton said that my father paid him ten thousand dollars in cash, which, my father stated, he had obtained from a wealthy relative. This was equal at the time to Stanton's entire income for the year. The sum was to be used to defray any expenses during the next forty years.

At first, Stanton wanted to decline this client, regardless of the money offered. He doubted that the young student had a rich relative and was not sure he wanted to get involved in something that would last so many years. But there was something about Bill McGowan as he sat in the lawyer's office that made Stanton change his mind. Instinctively, he knew that McGowan was honest, or at least that his motives were benign. Perhaps he was fabricating a story to explain the possession of so much cash, but Stanton felt this was an innocent untruth, designed to make a believer of the attorney.

"I liked him," Stanton said. "Have you ever met someone you immediately and instinctively just liked? And as a result, I wanted to help him. It was that simple. I've never met anyone like your father ever again. He had an aura about him. It's impossible to explain, even meaningless, unless you've seen it firsthand for yourself. Of course, I'm sure you loved your father, though it's probably hard to remember him. You were only a child, correct?"

Stanton then drew up the will, with me—not my mother—as beneficiary. I was left the letters as my bequest. And since it was now January 1995, Stanton had contacted me to read me the will and to deliver the letters.

When the old lawyer finished relating this story and reading the will, I asked if I might have another drink. He gave me one. This time, I seemed to taste the Scotch much more.

The story he told was absolutely incredible, it seemed to me, and I'm sure Stanton could see the disbelief all over my face.

"I assure you, Mr. McGowan," he said in response to my unexpressed incredulity, "that everything I've just told you is the absolute truth."

"But it's hard to believe."

"Which part?" he asked.

"All of it. For example: What happened to my father? Why would he disappear? Where did he get so much money? Why did he pick you, here in Washington, when he was from Chicago? Why did he instruct you to wait all these years before contacting me? And why me? And how did you know where to find me?"

"The answer to all of your questions, and to many others which I am sure you have as yet not had a chance to formulate, is the same: I do not know. That is, to all except the last," Stanton said with a smile on his lips as he looked at the burning tip of his cigar.

"You see," he continued, "I have, shall we say, kept tabs on your whereabouts. Sort of kept up on your mailing address."

"For forty years?"

"For forty years."

I watched him. He was happy with himself, as though having just completed a taunting crossword puzzle, broken a difficult code, or made contact with an alien civilization.

"I am a patient man," he said. "Perhaps your father sensed that about me. And I was well paid for very little work, and in advance for my services. What more can an attorney want? Don't be so hard to convince, Mr. McGowan. It was really a lot less work than you imagine, and I've had some highly unusual cases over the years, though none quite as odd as this one."

Stanton and I continued in this manner for some time. I studied the will itself, which was very simple. In it, my father stated that I was his heir, to whom he left the letters which he had placed for safekeeping in the possession of James Frederick Stanton, a Washington attorney, whose address he gave as the same address I had now visited these many decades later.

"What if I had died?" I asked.

"What?" Stanton said in surprise, perhaps not hearing the question.

"I mean, suppose I had died before January 1995, let's say in Vietnam?"

"Were you in Vietnam?"

"No."

"All right, then."

"But suppose—let's say in a car accident. Anything could've happened."

"Usually, you're right, anything that can happen will happen. But not in this case. Perhaps you were lucky. Are you lucky, Mr. McGowan?"

"Lucky?"

"It's a very underrated quality in life. I believe it exists, much the same as intelligence or a strong pitching arm. You either have it or you do not."

I believed him. I recalled once reading that a particular general had been highly recommended to Napoleon. "Yes, but is he lucky?" the wily Corsican wanted to know.

The old attorney had me remain in his office while he went upstairs to collect, as he put it, my "inheritance." Upon his return, he carried with him a cigar box, around which was wrapped a thick red rubber band, and I could see from the expression on his face that there might be some concern he'd perhaps not yet shared with me.

"Mr. McGowan," he began, as he sat down in his chair behind his desk with some relief, being somewhat out of breath, "I do want you to understand that, as my client, your father was owed my loyalty and my confidence. But now that I have discharged my obligations to him, I feel a bit relieved. What I am trying to say, Mr. McGowan, is that I do not believe your father was entirely honest with me. In fact, I believe he withheld most of what occurred in the Holy Land. The questions that you now ask are very similar to the ones I myself asked so many years ago, when your father and I sat here in this very office, and have asked myself oftentimes in the succeeding years."

Stanton spoke very deliberately as he placed the cigar box squarely in the middle of his neat and orderly desk. The surface of the desk, in fact, was bare except for the cigar box. Though I didn't dwell on it at the time, it struck me as odd that a lawyer's desk would be so bereft of all the papers one would expect to see in such a place. But Stanton's desk had no depositions, no reports, no memos: just a cigar box with a thick red rubber band around it.

"I have always suspected that your father was involved in some sort of dangerous activity, perhaps government-related.

Where else would he legally obtain so much money? Did your mother ever mention anything at all, anything suspicious? Or have you ever had any thoughts along these lines?"

The old lawyer kept the box in front of him with his palms placed at either end.

"Never," I said. "How could I?"

"You see, in a way I am completing what may very well prove to be the last professional act of my life, Mr. McGowan. I may appear fit, but I assure you the facts are to the contrary. I do not have what you would call a thriving practice."

As he finished this last remark, he began coughing, a deep, rasping cough that continued for what seemed an abnormally long time. I began to get concerned. As I was about to speak, he slowly raised his hand to ward off any assistance. So I just sat there and watched, feeling confused, uncertain, while at the same time experiencing for the first time the effects of the two drinks. Then, for some strange reason, I thought of my mother and wondered how much she had known about all of this.

When Stanton had once again regained his composure, he turned toward the window and took a few very deep breaths before speaking.

"Time goes by so quickly," he said as if to no one at all, gazing out the window onto the cold Washington winter. "I can remember distinctly when your father came to see me. I never saw him again after that day." There was a note of regret that went beyond nostalgia in Stanton's voice, as though he missed an old friend.

"You said you were to contact me upon his death or in January 1995, whichever came first. How were you supposed to learn of his death, when and if he died? Did he leave you an address? Did he ever contact you after that day?"

"He never did, Mr. McGowan. As a matter of fact, I have no way of knowing if he is alive today," he added, faintly smiling at me. "Interesting, isn't it?"

Stanton gently pushed the cigar box toward the edge of the desk and closer to me.

"This now belongs to you," he said.

I looked down at his offering without moving toward it, and then, looking up at Stanton, I also turned to the window at my left.

"Yes," I said, "time does go by quickly. But that's not a new idea at all, is it?"

"A new idea? *A new idea?*" he asked with genuine surprise. "Young Mr. McGowan, there are no new ideas, just new people learning the old ones for the first time. The past, the present, the future—sometimes I think they're all the same, just one brew. Like a single-malt." He looked at his glass.

It had been a long time since anyone had referred to me as young, but it somehow seemed in character coming from this person seated opposite me.

"You know, I cannot tell you how many different theories I have had over these many years concerning the contents of these letters. When you review the material, you will notice that there are three letters in all. Two of them are addressed to Barbara Allison in Evanston, Illinois, from her husband, Philip. The third, in a different handwriting, is addressed to you, John McGowan."

Stanton paused and turned toward the window again.

"The two letters addressed to Mrs. Allison have been opened," he continued, "but not by me. They were given to me in that condition by your father. The third letter, addressed to you, is sealed. After your father left, I placed them in this very cigar box. Cuban, not legal anymore, though I suspect that will shortly change."

There was a stillness in the room which I hadn't noticed before. It was the thick stillness of a funeral parlor's reception area—neat and comfortable and very hard. Stanton was now speaking slowly, as if carefully measuring each word before pronouncing it. The room was filled with his cigar smoke. Shafts of light beamed through the high window, through the smoke, and onto the desk. I watched the smoke swirl into the tracks of light and then disappear upward.

"Yes," he said, "many theories."

I looked at the box again, wondering what to do. Stanton was not yet finished. He was a man who had to fill the silence in a room. My sense was that he'd waited a long time to fill this particular silence.

"There is one other thing," he said. "I suppose it is in the way of a confession." His voice seemed to take on additional resonance.

"About one month after your father gave these to me, I tried my best to find him. He had given me no instructions about a future meeting, but then again he had not prohibited me from searching him out either. He had been vague about his future plans, hinting that he was to return to the Holy Land. But curiosity had gotten the best of me—as it very well might take hold of you, I suspect. I found the phone number for a Mrs. Allison in Evanston—it was listed in her husband's name—and almost called her, but changed my mind. It was really none of my business and quite unethical for me to pursue it. But as I peered into the future, it seemed to me that I had been used by your father in some way that was unfair. At least, that was the excuse I used to . . ."

Stanton stopped speaking, looking down at his hands. After a pause, he wrapped his fingers around the cigar again and turned to me. In a voice filled with a confession that seemingly had gnawed at him for forty years, he said, "I read the letter addressed to you. I am sorry; I broke my word to your father. After reading it, I resealed it. No one else has seen it. I give you my word."

I wasn't sure what to say, or what to feel, about what he had said. Then he said the strangest thing.

"Do you believe in God, Mr. McGowan?" he said.

I don't know how much time passed as we both sat there in silence. For the first time, I realized how old Stanton was. I suppose I hadn't taken the time to think about it before. I looked around the room, the same room apparently where my father had been, and I wondered what he and my father had both looked like then. I had a few old photographs of my father, but they had never meant much to me. I couldn't get beyond the image on the paper to know the man who was shown there. Years ago, when I was a teenager, I think, I had tried to get inside those old pictures, to fathom the man, to get him to speak to me. But I'd failed. Old pictures were just that—old pictures and nothing more.

I saw Stanton's professional degrees framed neatly on the wall, surrounded by photos of Stanton and what were probably a wife and a child at the zoo, another in front of a large country house with autumn leaves littering the front lawn, and a large picture of a much younger Stanton and a girl—his daughter?—standing on home plate. Both were wearing baseball uniforms. Stanton had a broad smile on his face and, as always, held a long cigar in one hand.

I thought about Sarah and our sons and how impossible it would be for me to leave them, under any circumstances—how absolutely, positively impossible it would be.

And then, very old feelings of abandonment surfaced into my consciousness, like a powerful undertow that pulled me under against my will: a current that took hold of me and pulled me down into the deep well of memory and loss, the detritus of my boyhood. Everything I now owned and possessed meant nothing, lost as I was in the current . . . lost beyond the ability to surface.

It had been years since I had felt the fear of abandonment, of loss, of waking up in the middle of the night to see a shadow on the wall and know—really know!—beyond reason that I would not live to greet the dawn. All because my father had left us; all because I was a little boy, alone in the world, with only his mother to care for him. What had I done to deserve this fate? Why had he left me?

It would be fair to say that deep down in my developing personality, as I grew into adolescence and young manhood, I learned to hate the memory of my father. I hated anything that reminded me or my mother of the man who had left us. I hated anything that reflected his former existence, even as simple an act as completing a form with "Name of Father" facing me on the page to remind me of this fact which could never leave my life. The hatred lasted in its intensity until, sometime in my teens, my memory of him moved beyond the active emotion of hate to the frozen state of mere indifference, until my father was an irrelevant relic of my past, akin to my genetic makeup, present with me always but never part of my conscious life. Now, it all came home, like a bad dream—suddenly, like a pain I remembered.

I was aware that Stanton had asked me a question, something which surprised me.

"What?" I finally said. "Do I believe what?"

"In God."

"In God?" I repeated, in a drumlike monotone, almost without meaning.

"Why don't you take a few moments and read the letter your father wrote to you?" he suggested. "I think you will want to do that before you consider your next move."

Stanton opened the box, removing the red rubber band, which snapped and broke as he pulled it off. The open lid revealed three white envelopes. Stanton removed one of the envelopes and, leaning forward, placed it directly in front of me. He treated it with a certain formality—gently resting it on the edge of the desk as though it were an object of great value.

"Feel free to have another drink," he said, as he got up to leave the room. "I will return when you have finished."

I began to read.

Chicago
March 4, 1955

Dear Son,

This is my third attempt at starting this letter in
two days of anguish. I have thought and rethought
every possible way of beginning, but over and over
fall back on the same two words: I'm sorry.

I'm sorry for what I am about to do, both to you
and your mother. I'm sorry for the numberless
times I won't be there when you need me, in a thousand different situations I can only now imagine, as
you grow up and become a man. And I'm sorry for
not being the husband your mother expects.

Please believe me. Please believe that I do what I
am about to do not because I don't love you or your
mother but precisely because I do love you. What I
must do I must do alone, so I have devised this way
of dealing with it, the only way I can imagine that
makes sense to me. If I believe in what I am doing, I
have no choice. So when you read this, please understand.

About a year ago, just after my twenty-fifth birthday and when your mother and I had been married
for about five years, I was contacted by a professor I
once had for a course in college. His name was
Clement Anderson. At the time, I was driving a taxi
in Chicago, doing a little postgraduate work but
very uncertain what I was going to do with the rest

of my life. I grew up in the midst of the worst economic depression this country had seen in a long time—I hope you never see one like it in your time—but had been fortunate enough to win a scholarship to attend a top school.

Dr. Anderson was a professor of archaeology, and he said he remembered me from the course and my interest in the field. We met for lunch on campus, and Anderson explained why he had contacted me. It seems that he and a colleague were planning an expedition to the Holy Land for the purpose of excavating a recently discovered site and were now assembling a number of students who would work the dig, for which they would be paid and which would possibly further their postgraduate education. Anderson wanted to know if I'd be interested in joining them.

Honestly speaking, I was more than interested: I was elated by the prospect and I told him so. But I also told him that I was married and had a small child and didn't think it would be fair to leave them for what he was saying could be upwards of two years. At first, Anderson accepted this without much comment, telling me that if I cared to reconsider, the offer would stand for a couple of weeks, since they had not as yet selected all the members of the team. He suggested I further discuss it with my wife and think about it.

Well, son, that was, I thought, the end of that.

Your mother and I did discuss it; she wanted me to go, in fact. But I couldn't see myself leaving both of you for such an extended period. Anyhow, who said driving a taxi is all that bad?

I didn't really think about any of this again until a couple of weeks later, when I heard from Anderson once more. He said there were still a few vacancies and was wondering if I'd changed my mind. I told him I hadn't, but he suggested we meet anyway to discuss what he said were some new developments. That afternoon, when I met again with this man—this time in an office in the Loop—my life was changed forever.

I found the office whose address Anderson had given me, and in it I found Anderson and another man. Anderson said his name was Joseph Bertucci. He described this second man as a consultant to the project and an expert on ancient civilizations. For fifteen minutes or so, Anderson briefed me on the objective of the expedition—this was all old stuff to me—and the wonderful possibilities that would be available later on to those who participated in its findings, which, he assured me, would be historic.

Bertucci said nothing at first, or occasionally merely smiled or nodded his head in agreement with Anderson. You see, son, they were selling me something—something which was as yet not clear to me, but which every cell in my body told me had strings attached to it.

"You have a great future ahead of you, Bill," Anderson said. "There's no telling what we'll discover. This is really the first time anyone will be taking a close look at this area, I mean in such detail. What with our foundation grants, the university's backing, and Professor Allison's stewardship of this project, it could mean a wonderful future for you. Money will be no problem. Probably at least a teaching assistantship when you return. Wouldn't you agree, Mr. Bertucci?" Bertucci nodded in agreement.

Anderson rehashed every argument he could think of as to why this would be a terrific move for me. To be truthful, son, I'm really not very adventurous to start with, and you could also add that I can be quite stubborn. In fact, the more someone tries to sell me something—once I sense he's a huckster—the more I resist. And, dammit, they were trying to sell me on something that had nothing to do with archaeology!

Finally, in what appeared to be a desperate last attempt, Anderson walked over to the office door and snapped the lock shut. He then turned back toward me. For the moment, I thought he was going to hit me.

"Look, kid," he said. "This is a very complicated picture, and we don't want you to get confused. There are other layers here, do you get my meaning? Mr. Bertucci, I think we can confide in Bill here.

What do you think—should we welcome him to our team?"

"I like him," Bertucci finally said. "He's got an honest face, an American face. True and loyal. Am I right, Mr. McGowan?"

Anderson took a seat off to the side. I wasn't at all sure what was going to happen next. I was seated on a chair, Bertucci was sitting on the edge of the desk looking down, his face almost directly in front of mine. Bertucci and I were about the same age—he was much younger than Anderson—but it was clear he was in charge, there was no doubt about it. He tried to act a lot older, perhaps because he'd come very far very fast, or perhaps because we were contemporaries and he had to prove he was way ahead of me.

He was a short man, but very smartly dressed. He smoked like it was going out of style. I felt this man had something to prove.

"This is a great country," he said. "Probably the greatest country the world has ever seen. And that took some doing! Whatever people want, there is more of it in this country than anywhere else. And we've never lost a war, and don't intend to lose one now. You remember that, Mr. McGowan. Remember it well, because this country is at a crossroads. On the one side, the right side, we continue down the road of our great traditions of freedom and democracy, those traditions men have fought and died for since the founding of this great republic. On this side, we see good, clean houses, trees and gardens and little kids with red hair and freckles playing in the street. We can see their mothers cooking dinner through the kitchen window, pretty women, but also very strong, very patriotic women. This is America, Mr. McGowan, on the right side. But on the other side, the left road, we face a twisting, treacherous, threatening, and hazardous path. Bleak buildings, cold and gray, thin soup, sad faces, no kids. No freedom to live, just freedom to die."

Bertucci said these final words in a hoarse whisper, as though they were too terrible to utter in a normal voice. He looked me straight in the eye.

"Two roads, Mr. McGowan, two choices that face us each and every day as Americans. And if we make the wrong choice, there's no turning back. We might as well put an H-bomb under the streets of Washington and light the fuse. It's that simple a choice, Mr. McGowan. But in making that choice . . ." He leaned back a bit. "Thank God, we do have some help—a few helping hands that are not willing to let this country go by the boards. To do whatever is necessary, Mr. McGowan. Not what is possible, but necessary. Make no mistake, these are desperate times, and desperate times call for courageous men."

Bertucci lit another cigarette and offered me one.

"Bill," he said, "would you like to step forward

and help your country in this desperate hour? Are you that kind of American?" I turned to Anderson for help, but he remained impassive. Bertucci carried with him the air of command.

"What do you want?" was all I could think of saying.

Bertucci smiled, jumped off the desk, and walked around it to the other side. He turned now to face me again.

"What I am about to tell you must remain confidential," he said. "It must never leave this room. Are we agreed, Mr. McGowan?" I said I understood.

Bertucci explained that he was indeed a consultant, but was attached to a branch of the government, which itself was connected to our foreign bureau. He never put it in so many words—and that added to the mystery and authority of his position—which branch or which bureau he was referring to. His specialty was to develop long-range capabilities in those areas of the world where the government had vital interests and where those interests were threatened, now or in the future. He made it clear that his authority to plan and execute plans was authorized at the highest level and he only consulted on those projects which had top priority.

He was now working on one such project, in the Middle East. It involved the creation of a private communications network linking certain cities in the area with a base in the United States, so that in the event of hostilities, communications would remain unbroken. This was a top-secret program that was extremely complex. As part of it, the archaeological expedition, though authentic in itself, was the framework in which they operated. It was important that I understood this. The communications links would be created inside the digs selected by the team. It was that simple. My job would be to act as a liaison between Anderson and another man in the Middle East and the team leader in Washington, who was Bertucci. From time to time, as contingencies dictated, I would be required to report back to Bertucci on progress. That was it. The result of my work, I was told, would be of profound benefit to my country.

And I would be paid; money was not an issue, Bertucci stressed a number of times. If I chose to continue my studies afterward, I would be granted a full scholarship, plus a salary, plus housing accommodations. On the other hand, if I chose to continue my service to my country, I would qualify for a position with Bertucci's bureau. A man could move up very fast, he assured me, if he was the right sort of man. Given my experience in the Middle East, I would be getting off on the right foot—he tapped his foot under the desk when he said this. "Not the left foot," he said. "Any way you look at it, Mr. McGowan, you'll have the world on a string."

This world is a big place, son. When you read this, I'm sure the world will have changed considerably, at least on the surface. It would be impossible to predict changes in the future. But this is what I know now, in 1955. Even though Bertucci appeared to my taste somewhat starched and bureaucratic, and more than a little cloak-and-daggerish, his offer was very appealing, especially to someone like me whose immediate prospects were circumscribed at the time by the windows and doors of a Checker cab. Anyhow, this is the greatest country in the world and, with the Lord's blessing, will remain so for a very long time to come. Who knows, maybe I was supposed to accept his offer. My mother always said I led a charmed life.

Suffice it to say, I took the plunge that afternoon, even though I was sure I was getting only part of the picture.

That was about a year ago.

Much has happened in these past few months. For one thing, your father has gotten a lot older. It seems that Bertucci and company were indeed creating a communications network linking various cities in the Middle East to each other and via other links to a base in the United States. But what Bertucci did not tell me—well, he did not tell me a great deal, first about what they suspected they might find on this expedition, and second what they did find.

That's what I want to tell you about, son. Think of this as our personal time capsule—a voice out of the past to the future, one generation to the next. Or think of it as a discovery you've made that will change the course of your life. No, I don't think I am exaggerating, because it will do exactly that.

After I arrived in Israel, I was introduced to an Israeli national named Ari—that's just a nickname. Ari was my counterpart with the local Israeli authorities and, I was told, an archaeology fan as well. All of this may have been true, but it omitted the most crucial detail about Ari—that he was also an agent of the Mossad, the Israeli intelligence service. Soon after, when we crossed over into Jordan—which in itself is a complicated story, since these two countries are still in an official state of war—I met other individuals who were likewise introduced to me as government officials, or archaeology buffs, or professionals of one sort or another who had been conscripted for our project.

For the next six months, I crisscrossed the region from one location to another. I was a messenger, mostly with messages in coded form, or broken into parts. I had thought this kind of thing happened only in the movies—up until then. Our group was far-flung, into Turkey and Iran, but also much farther out. I'm sure you can read between the lines. I hope your world is a better world, son, but as I write this, anyone and everyone is under suspicion. Bertucci was right: This is a war; yet somehow in the midst of the shelling, we're forgetting what we're fighting about. If God is watching, he must wonder why he set us all in motion in the first place.

Most of the time, I worked with a small group of Americans, sometimes at the digs, but usually in the cities. I was actually enjoying myself. In some sense, I felt at home in my element. Then something unexpected happened.

I was in Tel Aviv for a couple of weeks. Ari and I had developed a pretty close friendship during this time. Then one afternoon, out of nowhere, he confided in me the complete picture of our mission. What's more, he told me that as far as he was concerned, future wars with Israel's Arab neighbors were almost inevitable, since these countries persisted in their desire to drive the Jews into the sea. The Arabs refused to recognize the fact that the Jews inherited this land from time immemorial and, even in the face of defeat by the Romans and subsequent conquerors over the centuries, continue to look to Israel as their homeland. Someday, Ari predicted, the Jews would recapture all of their lost land, particularly the old city of Jerusalem, their most sacred and beloved home, site of their ancient Temple.

Ari related all of this very matter-of-factly, not so

much as opinions, but almost as a news report of things to come that were as certain as tomorrow's sunrise. We had taken some time off and were enjoying a day at the beach, taking in the Mediterranean sun. Ari reclined on his blanket and stretched his large frame. His skin was deep-tanned, over an already naturally dark complexion, yet I could discern a long scar that traced all the way from his collarbone to just over his navel. It was thin and pale and snaked along his midsection like a river through a brown plain.

Ari smoked incessantly, even there on the hot sand under the midday sun. He was addicted to Luckies. He was a good man and a good friend. I never asked him where he got his scar. I had learned to accept people as they are in this land; few Israelis did not have one kind of scar or another. Ari's was just more visible than most.

"There is a story I heard that I want to relate to you, Bill. I want to tell you this because I have come to like you and I believe it is important for you to know. I don't know whether you will believe it or not. It will remain our secret—yes?"

Some birds flew overhead. I nodded.

"You see," he said, "this project is only partially about this secret communications network. That is real enough, for we need these lines. This is in itself important. But we are on a much more important quest, my friend. We are in search of God."

"Of God?"

"Yes. . . ."

I listened intently, not knowing what to think.

"A few years ago, about the time of the discovery of the Dead Sea Scrolls, an old Bedouin approached us with yet another tale, one that concerned the location of lost relics that date to the destruction of the Jerusalem Temple. The Bedouin claimed that he knew the location of these relics and indeed had seen them. He claimed that they predicted the future and foretold the final coming of the Messiah at the third millennium."

I could hear some children laughing in the distance. Ari was very serious as he spoke.

"I can tell you this," he said, "for you must know it. The Bedouin claimed that these relics prophesied the end of the world: where and when and how."

The children's laughter abated as they dashed off into the water.

"Quite a story, is it not, my American friend?"

"And you believed him?"

"Oh, yes," Ari said, "for he is my father."

Ari lit another cigarette and looked out over the blue expanse of the sea. Strange as it may sound, I could see reflected in his eyes all the hopes and fears of this land, one so old and so young at the same time.

"You see," he continued, "my mother is Jewish, and so I was born on a kibbutz, not far from here.

But there are also other inhabitants here." He gestured with this muscular arm stretched out over the horizon. "People who have been here for very long. This is also their home. Before the state of Israel was established, even now, there are many instances of friendship. You see, my mother and an old Bedouin—he was not so old then—started one of those friendships. An interesting story—yes?" he asked, as a smile broke out across his face.

"Yes," I said.

"Also, I have been to the site."

"Which site?"

"The site where my father first saw the Temple block."

Ari told me that a large stone block had been discovered in Shiloh many miles from Jerusalem. This stone block was determined to be from an outer wall of Herod's Temple. The only remaining part of the Temple is just one wall, which the Jews are forbidden to visit, since it stands in the Jordanian sector of the city. But what is amazing, of course, is its location: How did the block get there? And why?

Ari said he had been to the site a number of times. At first, it was considered a curiosity, of really no great importance. But then, as more and more of the immediate area was excavated, they discovered other relics: parts of swords and shields, both Roman and Jewish, as well as two large caches of Roman coins. And at about this time, two Americans became interested in this dig, Allison and Anderson and someone called Kurzon. Immediately, according to Ari, anything and anyone associated with the excavations in Shiloh took on a higher significance, and before long the entire project was shrouded in official secrecy. When the Americans became involved, information needed to be filtered carefully through many hands before it was released.

Ari's father, the old Bedouin, had made an additional discovery, one that he introduced to Ari on their last visit to the site. Here Ari paused in his narrative as if to collect his thoughts.

"There is a reason for everything," he said, and paused again. "Even you, Bill, there is a reason you are here."

I wasn't sure I understood what Ari meant.

His father, he said, had discovered a large urn, or a vase, perhaps as large as a small kiln, or oven. He described it to me as circular in construction with a removable lid. He found the urn buried some distance from the Temple block. He and his friends spent five days carefully extracting it from its ancient burial place and lifted it out into the daylight with great care. It was extremely heavy. When they opened the lid, they made an amazing discovery: three stone tablets standing upright in the container. That is when Ari's father decided to contact his son, who, he knew, would know what to do.

Ari said that the last time he saw the tablets was at

night, having arrived late. The plan was to visit the site at first light, but Ari's father could not contain himself and led Ari to the location at once. When they reached the spot, Ari's excitement grew. And when his father removed the lid, he could not believe his eyes. The tablets inside literally glowed in the dark. They produced their own light—a radiant, white light that rose up out of the large vase and filled the immediate area around which they stood, like a full moon in the night sky, Ari said, or a spotlight beamed to the heavens.

"It was the most beautiful sight I ever saw," he said simply.

Eventually, as he, his father, and their associates stood transfixed in the presence of the light, Ari reached down into the urn and touched one of the stones. It was warm to his touch, but not hot. There, in the middle of the night, ages after they had been placed in their secret closet, Ari and the men lifted the stone tablets out of the urn and placed them on the ground in front of them. Each stone radiated bright light into the surrounding darkness. Ari realized that he and the men could be seen by anyone in the immediate area. As he looked down at the tablets, however, he instantly understood that they contained a significance that was beyond his limited understanding—for each had writing chiseled into the hard granite surface, from top to bottom, a different language for each.

"You see, I realized we stood in the presence of something very extraordinary. I have known fear in my life, Bill, but this was a different fear. It was the fear of the ultimate."

"A major find—" I began, and he cut me off. I, too, was suddenly afraid.

"No, my friend, something much more significant . . . something vital and alive . . . a message. You see, at the bottom of each stone, carved by some ancient hand into the surface, there appeared a word totally out of place or context, not in the same language as the others, this I could tell . . . even the letters were different."

"What was the word?" I asked.

"MCGOWAN," Ari said and gently tapped the ash of his cigarette onto the sand.

When I reached this part of my father's letter, I placed it down on Stanton's desk and walked over to his office window. The gray January of Washington was framed in the glass. I could see life as it was in 1995, yet somehow was drawn back to the beach in Tel Aviv four decades in the past.

I could smell Stanton's cigar smoke and had no idea how long he had been standing there.

Suddenly, I felt cold, as cold as stone.

"Finished already?" he asked.

The old lawyer had quietly reentered the room while I was reading, and I hadn't noticed.

"Almost. You've read this letter?" I said.

"Yes," he said. "In fact, I read it again this morning for the first time in forty years."

"What do you make of it?"

"What do you mean?"

"I mean . . . what do you think?"

"I think you'd better finish it before I answer."

Stanton sat down in a chair by the window. I could see him watching me out of the corner of his eye. As I picked up my father's letter again and resumed reading it, I found myself standing by the desk—had I stood up when Stanton reentered the room?—and glanced over at Stanton and beyond him to the streets of Washington, which I saw as a reality and anchor to which I could return.

"That's not possible!"

"Perhaps not," Ari said.

"You mean my name is on those stone tablets?"

"I mean exactly that. It is your name: McGow-an."

"It's not logical."

"No, it is not logical at all."

Ari told me that each stone tablet was about three feet square and arched at the top edge, almost like a cathedral window. The night he first saw them, he decided to contact his superior officer, because he was at a loss as to what to do next. Ari confided in me that up to that point, he had not believed in God, but after that night, well . . . he was "definitely unsure," he said with a smile. Over the next few days, his superior officer and others took charge of the Stones. The languages were determined to be Aramaic, Latin, and Hebrew. The Stones were photographed—no flash was necessary—and a full transcription of their texts was made.

But Ari's father never saw them again, nor did he ever receive or request payment.

It appeared that the text of each was identical, the only difference being the language. And at the bottom of each, in English, was my name: McGowan.

"What do the Stones say, Ari?"

"Let's walk along the edge of the water. It will be good to walk." Ari was right; it was better to walk.

Ari said that the story told on the Stones was in three parts. The first part related in graphic detail the destruction of the Jerusalem Temple. It told a tale of death and horror visited on the Jews by the Romans. It told of their sorrow and the unbearable anguish it brought to the survivors, who suffered twice—once for the loss of their Temple and their country, and once for living, since each day they were forced to relive their torment.

But the second part was different in tone and content. It told a story of hope and the final coming of the Messiah in two thousand years, at the beginning of the third millennium. It described the Messiah in general terms, and as it described this individual, it began the last segment of its narrative: the Signs of the Messiah and how he would appear, bringing peace to the world, but also bringing an end to the world. This last segment was the briefest and contained specific information on these Signs and certain powers inherent in the Stones.

The transcription that was made was very clear, Ari said, and translated precisely the same in each of the three languages. Two groups, one in Israel and one in California, did separate translations. No, the translations were accurate, there was no doubt about that part, at least.

"Was there any doubt at all?"

"There is now," he said.

We stopped by the edge of the water and looked out over the calm beauty of the Mediterranean. A lone bird soared high in the distance.

"The Stones have disappeared, my friend."

With that, Ari began walking away from me. He tossed his cigarette in the sea and before long was running as fast as he could down the stretch of sandy beach. I tried to keep up, but fell farther and farther behind. Though he was a big man, he moved his bulk with considerable style.

Ari said he was afraid when he found the Stones, and this confused me: Here was a man who was clearly not afraid of anything. If he was afraid, though, I was afraid. Yet, I did realize one thing for certain—I had to find out everything I could about what Ari had told me, even if it took longer than I imagined. Or the rest of my life. I was in the middle of something and I had no idea how I'd gotten there. Worse still, I had no idea how I was to get out.

Son, believe me, if I could have imagined anything at all, it was not what actually did happen. But I saw myself getting drawn into a very old story, and realized that I was destined to play a part in it. How could I give up what was so precious to me? How could I keep what was even more valuable? That is the reason why I disappeared from your life, from your mother's life, and from everything I knew and loved. It was for the Messiah Stones.

Stanton could see I had stopped reading.

"Obviously," he said, "there is a portion of your father's letter that is missing. How long a portion, we'll never know, nor the contents. But I'll tell you this—I think he was about to describe something we would have a hard time understanding anyway. Something very unusual happened to your father out there, and we're left with only outlines and shadows of the real substance. Who knows, perhaps he just ended it there himself. Let's not look for reasons where there aren't any. Life is complicated enough, Mr. McGowan."

"Is this the way you received it?"

"Yes."

"So my father made trips back and forth?"

"Yes."

"And finally returned to Israel for keeps. Why?"

"Maybe he saw something?"

"What?"

"That is the question, isn't it?"

I remained standing, looking out the window. "You know," I said, "I'm basically a rational person, a historian by training. I'm probably what you would call a conservative. I'm also a husband, a father, and sometimes a coach of a soccer team for the kids. Little else. I don't remember the last time I was in church. This is not what I expected, Mr. Stanton."

"It isn't? What did you expect?"

"Something else."

"I envy you, young Mr. McGowan."

Then I asked him the one question that had been echoing in my brain for the last twenty minutes—an echo I could not control.

"Do *you* believe in God?" I asked.

"That's what I asked you," Stanton said.

"No, I do not."

"That is what I suspected," the old lawyer said.

Chapter 2

THE WAY BACK

STANTON HAD LITTLE MORE to say to me after the reading of the will and after I had also read my father's letter and one of Philip Allison's letters to his wife, Barbara. He confirmed again that he'd met my father only that one time. My father told him that he'd gotten the lawyer's name out of the telephone book. As to why my father had chosen a Washington attorney, or why my father had been in Washington, or where he'd gotten so much cash, Stanton simply couldn't add anything. For his part, my father—when asked by Stanton why he'd chosen him—said he was looking for the best attorney and the best were in Washington, weren't they?

"What's funny," Stanton said, "is that I did it. However he knew I would do it . . . well, he just knew."

Stanton repeated that he had tried his best to track my father down, but only once, and not very diligently. After a while, there would be long periods of time when he didn't think about my father, or about the letters. As the years passed, and his practice thrived, the entire incident receded into the background, only to reopen time and again like a perennial flower that came up every year.

"It was never completely out of the room, so to speak. Your father has remained with me all these years. He was a special person, John."

This was the first time the old lawyer had called me John. I watched him as he sat quietly in the corner of the room, smoking his cigar.

"You know," he said, "there is one small thing you can do for me. You have probably guessed what it is."

"Yes," I said, not knowing at all what it might be.

"I'd like to know what happens, with you, with the Stones. You are young, John. I'm almost ninety years old, and failing fast. This," he said, holding up the cigar almost as a trophy, "this is my only pleasure. My wife died fifteen years ago, and our daughter is also dead. Nicole was the light of my life. She was our only child. In a way, I had only one more thing to do myself, and now that too is done."

The room took on that strange stillness again.

"John, do you know what is life's cruelest tragedy? To live beyond your years. I do not think I belong here any longer, and I am curious to know what lies beyond. It is the only mystery remaining for me, except for what lies in that cigar box, the mystery your father saw."

"Would you like copies of these?"

"No," he said. "They were not meant for me. I am just a messenger. They were left for you. And I don't know how much, in truth, I really believe in all of this. So much of it is mixed up in my mind with other events. Maybe you have to live a life devoted to only one truth; maybe that's what your father discovered. You know, I hardly remember your father. Except that you remind me so much of him. It's been so many years, but I think you look like him. He and I had a contract. I think I've lived up to my part of the deal. Yes, I think so."

I felt a sadness for this man I hardly knew.

"Will you be all right—I mean later, after I've left?"

"As all right as . . . yes, I will be fine."

"I'll send you copies."

Stanton didn't answer me. His eyes were closing as he spoke.

"You don't mind showing yourself to the door, do you, John?" he said as he placed his cigar in the ashtray in the small table next to his chair. "Have a pleasant journey," he said, as his eyes closed. He was asleep in an instant.

I walked over to him and crushed the cigar out before leaving. I was worried about him.

I DIDN'T HAVE A PLEASANT JOURNEY. I could think of nothing else on the flight back but my father's letter and Allison's letter, and each of the individuals so carefully sketched for me, people who were shadows out of the past, forty years back in the distance beyond my memory or knowledge.

I could not help thinking about all of them, even more than the astounding story of the Stones and their eventual disappearance. What also troubled me was the missing portion of my father's letter. I didn't think Stanton had lied to me. I believed he had delivered to me everything he was given, just as he received it. Which only raised additional questions in my mind as I read and reread my father's letter on the plane. The other two letters from Allison to his wife, Barbara, were apparently undelivered by my father. I had not yet read Allison's second letter to his wife. What was Churchill's famous description of Russia—a riddle wrapped in a mystery inside an enigma? Three letters in all that were like brief film reviews of some mammoth all-star Hollywood production of the past that included a cast of thousands, yet which to my eyes was only visible through the limited keyhole of the reviewer, and so I was shown just a piece of the truth broken off at the edges.

Then it struck me: Suppose it was true? The dig, my father, the Stone tablets, Ari, Allison, and Anderson, the prophecies of the Messiah. How could it be possible?

I hadn't lied when I told Stanton that I did not believe in God, yet I gave him what I have to describe in all candor as the simple answer, perhaps for dramatic effect. The complete answer was much more complex. Yet it was true that I did not believe in a stereotypical deity who sits on high and creates the world in a few days, judges his creations, and rules the world, perhaps by proxy. Everything I ever learned about history and the intricate matrix of forces and people that shape our lives told me that there was no such being. I recalled the old joke that was current about the time of the design of the first computer. The inventor of the computer sits down at it one day and asks it if there is a God. Some minutes pass, the whir of artificial intelligence buzzes, and these words then appear on the screen: "There is now!" A joke. But there was a double twist to this joke: Was the computer the new god, or was it the inventor who had made it the new god?

I have a confession to make: Though I don't believe, I have

been intrigued by the idea of God for a long time, and especially by the enormous appeal of this concept to human beings over thousands of years. I can't put my finger on the exact quote, but didn't Einstein say something to the effect that God doesn't shoot dice with the universe? That things happen in an orderly way—no, that things have been *ordered* in an orderly way, with an intelligence behind the scenes. Perhaps Einstein's idea of God is what I am trying to express: a mind that is separate from our own and that exists beyond our view.

Oh, what was I doing!

Something so philosophical loses any meaning at all, and instead becomes some vague notion of Good and Evil, like a theory of behavior, dependent on our individual interpretations. But my father's letter to me and the history of the Stones were not theory, not philosophy, but concrete, actual events that gripped me.

I closed my eyes and tried to sleep on the flight from Dulles back to Pennsylvania. I had another drink, a double. I had now had more alcohol in a day than I usually had in a month or more. But the drink helped, and I slept.

I had a dream.

In my dream, it was snowing, a steady blanket of flakes that dressed the earth in sheets of white. I could see tall mountains on the horizon and their snow-capped peaks. All at once, in the magic of the dream, I stood on top of one of those peaks, no longer only an observer in the distance—on a flat mountain-top, like a landing strip for an airplane. I was alone and very small, tiny almost, as I watched from a vantage point on high. I walked to the edge of the peak and stood on the tip, looking down into an endless, vast carpet of lush forest where there was no snow, only green. I looked up and saw the sun, bright and round and large in the sky, like a torch.

Then the snow began to fall more and more heavily, until it covered everything in its path, including me and the mountain on which I stood. The last image I had, before the snow completely covered me, was the light of the sun that burned through the snow, refusing to go out.

As I opened my eyes and left the world of the dream, the plane entered a cloud bank of cotton candy. I fell asleep again and did not awake until we landed with a surprise thud.

In the taxi ride home, I thought of all the ways I could share my fantastic day with Sarah. I wondered also if I should consult with some sort of specialist—a priest? a minister? I had some vague idea in my mind that I needed a guide to help me. Perhaps I'd had too much to drink, which I had, and it was affecting my thoughts. I was on slippery ground here, and this was a new sensation for me. All of these thoughts, plus others, swirled in my mind like dust caught in a sudden breeze. For a moment, I found myself unable to catch my breath.

When I finally arrived home, I entered an empty and quiet house. Funny—I had been so preoccupied with my own thoughts that I'd forgotten that it was evening. Sarah would be at the bookstore working, and the boys would be with her. She would have picked them up after school. So I had at least another hour before they arrived.

Something my father had said in his letter kept returning to me. It was his fear, the same fear Ari had felt upon seeing the Stones. Please understand: I am not the conspiratorial type.

That's more in Sarah's line; her bookstore is replete with novels of one conspiracy or another. But then again, I'd never been faced with anything like this before in my life. I'd made history and historical themes my life's work, and it was interesting work. But I was not a detective, let alone a detective unearthing clues to a mystery that was two thousand years old.

I did believe, and still believe, that through the study of history we are given important insights into our existence as human beings, as the masters of the planet. If we do not learn from history, we repeat it, with all the war dead along the side of the road for proof. I believe it is the responsibility of historians to find the threads that bind people together, for isn't that the secret to humanity, our common connection? But the older I got, the more threads I saw, and therein grew the paradox. It's as though everything and everyone is special, as though one period really has no relationship to any other, as though except for basic human needs—such as food, sex, love, power, ambition, and all the others that drive our human soap opera—there are no eternal connections, no universal threads linking Imperial Rome, Imperial Russia, or the American push to the Pacific. We repeat all the mistakes over and over, rehashing the same historical plot, learning nothing. In all, I've come to exhale a huge sigh of frustration at the impossibility of ever learning anything worthwhile.

Yet, I search for answers, having no definitive understanding even of the questions. I feel like the primitive man deep inside a dark cave, who because of where he is sitting, can only see shadows on the wall, which to him are the reality; he has no concept of life outside the cave, the true reality.

Have I been studying shadows dancing on the wall? Can I ever begin to understand what it's like outside the cave?

Well, I did have one ace up my sleeve for answers, and that was my wife, Sarah. Sarah is a redhead. I have a theory about redheads, which makes no sense at all, I admit, but which I've come to believe nevertheless. I think their intuition is more acute, more in tune with the universe, than that of ordinary people. Every time I've met a redhead, he or she has had this special power. In Sarah's case, it's strengthened by her ability to separate the wheat from the chaff. She can get to the core of an issue.

When she opened her bookstore, I knew from the start that it would be a success. I like to tell her that she has four jobs and I have only one: She runs the store, runs our house, raises two boys—that counts for one—and keeps me out of trouble. I recognize the fact that I am a very lucky man.

I desperately needed to speak with her.

I took the letters out of the box. Two were addressed to Barbara Allison in Evanston, Illinois. They had no stamp on them and had obviously never been mailed. This troubled me: Why had my father not delivered these letters? I wasn't sure I'd ever find out the reasons.

I don't know how long I held the letters in my hand, turning them over and over. I had already reread my father's twice when I heard the familiar chatter of the boys outside as they ran toward the front door. Sarah was right behind them.

"Wow," Joshua said to Oliver, "you're slow!"

Oliver looked up at his mother for help.

"He's fast for his age," she said, "and maybe a little faster than you were at the same age, Josh. So be careful—little brothers have a way of growing up very quickly. Hi!" She turned toward me.

All three charged into the house, threw off their coats, and headed immediately for the kitchen.

"So," Sarah said as she disappeared behind the boys, "are we rich?"

"Let's talk," I said.

The boys were happy with the jars of peanut butter and grape jelly that were placed in front of them. They liked to make their own sandwiches, and, left alone, they did a pretty good job of it. Sarah and I retreated to the living room.

For the next hour or so, I told her everything that had happened that day and gave her time to read my father's letter and the Allison letter I'd read. The boys were now upstairs in their rooms, possibly doing their homework, but more likely playing Nintendo or watching television. The silence upstairs gave them away.

Sarah hadn't said much during this time. She is generally a quick study, but as she read the letters—especially my father's—I could see that she was taking her time.

"People don't write letters anymore," she said, by way of thinking out loud. She played with her hair as she looked at the letters, then began to speak quietly.

"If we are to believe your father—or, at least, this Ari, whoever he is, or was—then the name McGowan was carved into stone tablets about two thousand years ago, by people who spoke no English, probably centuries before the name even existed, then buried these stones in an urn, not far from a block that is thought to be a relic from the Second Temple of the Jews, which was destroyed by the Romans at about this time. Have I got this right so far?"

I nodded in agreement.

"Furthermore," she continued, "these three tablets glowed in the dark, were self-illuminating, kind of charged with their own energy source. Of course, these would have to be long-lasting batteries, that go on and on and on. But that's not all, John. These Stones predicted the arrival of a Messiah and the end of the world. And you've got one more of these letters from—what was his name—Philip? Let's call it 'Philip's Letter to the Americans' to keep to the biblical theme. How am I doing so far?"

"You don't believe it?" I said.

"I didn't say that. I'm only trying to draw a conclusion from this. It isn't easy, John—you've handed me one hell of a crazy story!"

"What conclusion?"

Sarah paused.

"Well," she said, "I see two possible conclusions. Either this lawyer in Washington, for reasons unknown, is out of his head or is pulling your leg, having concocted one terrible hoax, or these letters are genuine and your father, for reasons unknown, was taken in by Ari, or Allison or Anderson, or—"

"So you don't believe any of this?" I said with exasperation.

"Do you?"

"I'm not sure, Sarah—but a hoax? Who'd go to all this trouble?"

"Look, John, let's assume for the moment that . . . no, let's take everything at face value, that all of these people actually believe what they're telling us. I'll admit that it's possible for people to bury objects for thousands of years, that it's possible for some people to believe in God and a Messiah, or even the end of the world, and even that through some mysterious, natural radioactive process granite tablets can glow in the dark like holy lanterns. But John, my dear, dear, gullible husband, how and why in God's name—no humor intended—would the name *McGowan* be a part of this? Are you some unknown prophet come down to earth?"

"Get real?" I asked innocently, with probably a sick expression on my face.

"Absolutely!"

I couldn't agree with Sarah, but then again Sarah hadn't seen Stanton, nor had she been abandoned as a child. Everything she said was true. I was no prophet. I was an ordinary man.

"I'm going upstairs to check on the boys. It's too quiet up there," she said.

As Sarah went upstairs, I sat down in a state of complete dejection. I suppose I had known in advance what her reaction would be, though I had hoped against hope she would find some shred of truth in the story. Then I wondered: *Why* did I want her to believe? Was it because it would strengthen my own belief?

It grew dark around me. I switched on a light.

Then I decided to read the third letter.

Jerusalem
November 16, 1954

Dear Barbara,

We are working hard on Site 4, which as I told you is in Shiloh. Our hope is that we will uncover a villa dating back to the Herodian period. So far, we have had little luck.

But something has happened.

We heard a rumor about a secret burial ground adjacent to our dig. Actually, it is not so much a rumor, but a story that has been handed down by some Bedouins who make camp near here. One of the Bedouins seems to be something of an oral historian. He speaks Hebrew and is friendly with the Israelis in the area. I have seen and heard him repeat story after story in his oral tradition. He chants them, like songs, standing in the middle of a circle surrounded by his audience. There is something uncanny about him.

Two of his stories have to do with the Jews and their Temple in Jerusalem. In both of them, he relates that there developed a special group of priests whose sole responsibility it was to defend the word of God. In the first tale he tells, the word of the Lord was inscribed in the Tablets of the Law, or the Ten Commandments, which were given to Moses on Mount Sinai. These first Tablets were smashed by Moses when, upon descending from the mountain, he found his people worshiping a golden calf. Later, Jehovah created a second set of Tablets to replace the first.

But—and here's where the story diverges from the traditional text which has been handed down to us—both the smashed set and the new set were housed in the Ark, guarded by this elite group of priests. Eventually, they would be found in the sanctuary in Jerusalem. Now, much of this narrative has been known to biblical scholars, though there is conjecture about some details. However, the Bedouin chant goes on to tell of yet another set of stone tablets which was beloved and sanctified beyond all else by the Jews and protected by the priests. These were the Tablets of the Messiah, or the Messiah Stones, which were also given to Moses by Jehovah when the Jews were wandering in the desert. These Stones—there were three of them—were guarded "most privately" and known only to a handful of priests. But in a long passage that's both lyrical and frightening, the Bedouin recounts that "there are no secrets under heaven to those who search for truth."

This chant was sung by the Bedouin in his ancient language and has been transcribed by a member of our team. Yesterday, I was shown a translation. Here is the section, as I have seen it, that the Bedouin calls the Signs of the Messiah:

He will know the world and its ways—having often lived among us.

He will be scorned and ridiculed.

He will know the power of miracles.

He will appear like the sun in the morning over a dry and thirsty land.

He will be seen at the Wall.

He will live among us from the beginning of days to the end of days.

He will speak to each of us at once, worldwide.

He will return the Light to the world at the third millennium.

He will ingather all souls, living or dead, to return to Eden's Garden, the Garden of Life.

He will arrive for the last time when the Jews have returned to Zion, when Zion and its neighbors are at peace, and when the two great empires of East and West have reconciled.

He will return to us the power of dreams.

He will remove our knowledge of Good and Evil.

When we have returned to the Garden, the Lord will decide the fate of the world.

During the period of the Roman wars, the Jerusalem Temple was destroyed. Even though I could not understand a word of the Bedouin's chant, I could feel the terrible anguish, the bitter, bitter sorrow in his voice as he sang of the misery and defeat of these people and the destruction of their Temple. In his rendition, two groups of priests were able to escape from Jerusalem and carry with them the sacred sets of Stones—one to the south with the Tablets of the Law, and one to Shiloh with the Messiah Stones. Unfortunately, the first group was captured by the Romans. Their fate remains unknown. But the second group was successful and escaped to safety.

Barbara, I must tell you how absolutely enthralled I was listening to this man. His eyes shone with a luminous brilliance I have never seen. His hands clutched at the air as he chanted the words of the fate of the Jews. His arms swung out in large circles as he pointed to the stars above, explaining as he must the fate of the world. He cried for the Jews.

I believed his story—not just as a legend, but as historical fact. I know this will come as a shock to you, because I am a scientist and have kept my distance from the legends of this land that swirl through the air like so many dust storms. Yet, I have no better way to explain it—something spiritual overcame me, something I find it impossible to describe in words. I realized as I sat and watched the Bedouin, listening in the night, that I became as it

were a different man, a member of a new group.
The Bedouin, of course, is not Jewish at all, but he
was the voice of a people nevertheless. Then it
struck me how irrelevant the labels were, whether
Bedouin, or Jew, or Muslim, or Christian. This was
not a Bedouin crying for the Jews: This was a man
crying for men! That was the point. This was one of
God's creatures crying for the destruction of God's
home. He was reliving the pain of generations
which had not been assuaged by the passage of time,
that pain which, I saw in a rush of insight, is the
most profound of all—separation from the Eternal.

Can you understand what I am trying to say?

Please believe me, Barbara, when I say that I
haven't lost my senses. I know how you think about
these things, but for the first time in my life, I feel I
have actually captured all my senses!

I must share this with you, my love! How can I
not? How can I live with this knowledge and not
share it with the one person who means more to me
than life itself?

The Bedouin's chant sang of the power of the
Messiah Stones. His chant stated that the Jews had a
secret name for Jehovah, which the priests used in
the Temple on only the holiest days. This was a
name that entered their minds when they were in
the presence of the inner sanctum, but left them
when they went out. When used, this secret name
gave the speaker the power of miracles.

The Bedouin sang of the beauty that had once existed in the dry and thirsty land. And finally he sang of a message in the Stones, describing the end of days and the location of the Garden to which we will all return.

Perhaps, as is written somewhere, there is a special providence that shapes our ends. I don't know. I have confided in one of the Chicago students here, told him everything I've discovered in these past months. His name is Bill McGowan. I like him. His name . . . is he the son we never had? Bill and I have theorized that the priests attempted to re-create a temple of sorts in Shiloh, or perhaps waited for the day when the Messiah would arrive. We do not yet have enough evidence to confirm our theories.

But how can anyone believe what we have learned? I wish I were younger. I will be among the dead when the Messiah announces himself. Perhaps Bill will be there, perhaps not. Bill has a son; his name is John.

Yesterday we uncovered a granite object that is round and smooth and about the size of a basketball, worked to perfection by its maker into a perfect globe. Carved into it is one word. It says SARAH.

What do you make of this?

All my love,

Philip

My mother raised me without religion. We never went to church that I can recall. We were Protestants, most of our family being Methodists. But this wasn't something that I thought about much. My mother also never spoke about my father, and it was not until I was in college that I learned how much she'd been hurt by his leaving.

I was visiting my grandmother at the time. She had taken ill with cancer, a disease that would eventually kill her. She lived in New York City, not far from Columbia, where I was an undergraduate student. It was a rough neighborhood even then, with people sticking their hands out and asking for money. It's gotten a lot worse since. My grandmother, on my mother's side, had been widowed at an early age. She had three children, all girls, yet somehow found the resources to raise all three and return to school, where she became a nurse. When I visited her one afternoon, she was still working part-time at a local hospital. It was she who told me how heartbroken my mother had been when my father never returned.

I hated my father for that.

Now, as I read Allison's letter to his wife, I thought about my grandmother again for the first time in a long time. My grandmother, my father, my mother . . . in the last twenty-four hours I had given these ghosts of the past more thought and concentration than I had in many years. What was happening to me?

Upstairs, I found Sarah asleep in our bed, off in dreamland. She'd put the boys to sleep and turned in for the night. I hadn't realized how late it had gotten. I checked the clock by our bed; it was past eleven.

I tried not to wake her. She hardly moved when I got into bed beside her. I was tired, very tired. I fell asleep.

I had another dream.

In it, I stood on a cliff overlooking a valley. I was an old man, wrinkled with age. My hair was gone. But I was not sure it was me. I thought it was me, it looked like me, but still I wasn't sure. I watched this person gaze in silence over the valley. I was warm, happy to be standing on top of the cliff. Yet, I was afraid at the same time, standing as I was at the very edge of such a precarious height. Then I could see it happen: From every corner of the valley, in each spot where there had been a bush or a shrub, a small mound of earth appeared, green and round. The valley quickly became a vast surface of mounds, row upon row, each row moving in a unified rhythm to a high-pitched sound I could hear in the clouds.

In my dream, I tried to grab hold of myself, to not let go, to not fall down deep into the valley. I placed my arms around my waist, trying almost to attach myself to the rocky cliff. But it was useless. The shrill, piercing wail grew louder, the mounds swayed and multiplied, and as if pulled upward by an invisible force, I was lifted into the air and floated high above the valley.

Yet, I was not afraid.

I floated down, down, closer to the earth, as if buoyed in an invisible safety net. As I was inches above ground, I could see the entire landscape spread out before me. Facedown, I could see and touch the beauty of the valley. As never before, I could hold the beauty of the earth in my hand, and breathe deeply into my lungs. I knew that life was beautiful. The mounds opened, one after the other. Up rose my grandmother, my mother and father. From beneath, an intense light, as bright as the sun, rose with them.

And I awoke in a sweat.

IN THE MORNING, I called in early and canceled my classes for the day. I informed the department secretary I might be out tomorrow as well, since I had a bad cold and was running a fever. I'm not sure she believed me.

When Sarah was just getting up, I already had both boys dressed and ready for breakfast and school. They were having their juice and cereal when Sarah came into the kitchen.

I had made up my mind—I had to find out more.

"What's this?" she asked with a huge sigh of disbelief. "Is it my birthday? Is it Christmas? Good morning!"

The boys mumbled something through their cornflakes that sounded vaguely like a greeting. Coffee was already brewed, and Sarah sat down with a full cup in her hand. Black.

"I hope you don't expect a big tip," she said.

"Did you sleep well?"

"Like a log. What time did you come up, anyway? I was out. I didn't hear a sound. You could've walked off with the house!"

"We need to talk."

"So, are we rich?" she asked.

"Are we rich?" Joshua piped in.

"Rich!" Oliver echoed, probably not knowing the meaning of the word, but if his big brother said it, it was good enough for him.

I don't think I was ever so efficient. Sarah watched in amazement as I helped the boys put their overcoats on and waited with them at the door for the school bus to pass. Our house was near the bottom of the hill, and the boys would run out once we saw the bus pull up. When it did, they were gone in a flash.

I walked back into the kitchen and sat down next to Sarah. She hadn't budged from her seat.

"Before anything else, you have to read this. It's Allison's other letter. I read it last night."

I gave her the letter and took a cup of coffee for myself. She finished reading quickly.

"I still don't believe it. Someone's trying to put one over on us."

"I believe it," I said. "How could anyone have known your name? And even if someone did, what's the point? Who would make up a story like this?"

Then I told her about the two dreams I'd had.

"You're imagining things," she said.

"Yes, I am. I'm imagining all kinds of things, Sarah, and I need your help."

"What are you thinking?"

"Look, we've got to get to the bottom of this, or at least I have to. I've been thinking about this all morning. I called in sick. Even if there's a glimmer of hope that this is true, do you realize what this means?"

"My name on a globe? And these letters were supposedly written forty years ago? Come on, John, we have no proof."

"I want to find his wife. I want to find Allison and Anderson, if they're still alive. And I need you to help me, Sarah."

"Well, I am in the mystery business. Don't worry, it won't be too hard to track them down if they exist, or ever existed."

"Do you think so?"

"Trust me, John. I've got an idea or two. You're not the only one who's been thinking about this. It is intriguing, I'll admit that much."

"So you believe it?" I asked.

"I believe something is going on, like in the song, but I don't know what is, not yet anyway. Let me make a few calls. It's early, John. You know I can't think this early in the morning. And thanks for taking over the boys. In the meantime, if you're serious about this, I may have an assignment for you."

It was hard to tell what Sarah believed and didn't believe.

"You know, it just occurred to me that you may have drawn an incorrect conclusion from the evidence," she said.

"Stop speaking like a detective."

"I'm not," she said. "I'm just trying to be logical about the data. On the surface, at least, it's pretty illogical."

"What conclusion?"

"The name that was on the Stones—McGowan—your name, your father's name."

"Yes?"

"Well, it's also my name, isn't it?"

I looked at her in amazement. Of course, what she said was true, but it hadn't occurred to me that the reference might be to her.

"And now that we have a second clue, my Christian name on the stone ball, I'd say that the odds the references are to me are pretty good. Don't you think so?" she asked as she sipped her coffee.

"Perhaps it's to both of us."

"Perhaps."

I tried to think of other possibilities, but as always, Sarah was way ahead of me.

"Of course, it could mean us all, including the children. Maybe other McGowans, as well. Maybe there are other names on other globes for other people. We're not so special, are we, in the final analysis? Intriguing. Isn't that what I said?"

"Sarah, suppose it's true . . . I mean, suppose it's really true. What do you think will happen?"

"You mean do I think the Messiah will arrive and usher in the end of the world?"

"Yes."

"You're an educated person, John. Does such a scenario seem likely to you?"

"I wouldn't have thought so a few days ago. Now I'm not so sure."

"Then again, assuming for the moment that the Messiah is on his way, or her way, and assuming as well that the Stones speak the truth, why in God's name should *we* be singled out?"

I watched her as she seemed to erect a structure containing every doubt she could imagine.

"I mean," she continued, "it's already ridiculous on the face of it. Even if one believed in God, which in and of itself may be a stretch, why go to such lengths and play these name games all over the place as though it were some Saturday-night mystery dinner?"

I could sense a slight trace of anger or annoyance in her voice as she curled a wayward strand of bright red hair back into place over her ear.

"Don't get upset," I said.

"Upset? Who's upset?" she said with emphasis as she got off the stool to refill her coffee mug. "I'm probably drinking too much coffee."

"What's my assignment?" I asked.

Sarah was in control again.

"Okay, let's start by determining the theological validity of what's in these letters. Perhaps it's so much bunk, I mean from a theological viewpoint. Like science fiction, that sort of thing, that would be known only to a scientist, but in this case a theologian. Oh, I'm not being clear—but I think you get the point. Don't you?" she asked with a weak smile.

"I think so, but what good would that do? How would theologians know whether or not it was true? If it was all such a well-kept secret for two thousand years?"

"They wouldn't, but at least we'd have another opinion."

"Whose opinion?"

"Find an expert at school, a theology professor, a minister, a pastor, a guru—someone who can comment on what we know so far. We need an expert opinion, John. Religion is somewhat off the beaten path for us, isn't it?"

"You know," I said, "I have a feeling this is not about religion at all."

"I understand," Sarah said.

"And what will you be doing?" I asked.

"I'm going to find Barbara."

For the moment, I wasn't sure who Barbara was.

"If she's still alive, that is, on this side of heaven. Who knows what we're getting into!"

The phone rang. Neither of us moved at first, we'd been so caught up in our thoughts. Sarah picked it up after a few rings.

"Where's Joshua now that we need him?" she asked.

I could see Sarah listening intently to the voice on the other end of the line. She cupped her hand over the receiver and silently mouthed the name "Stanton" to me.

"Yes, hello," she said, and then was silent for what seemed an interminable period to me. All she did was listen, looking down at her cup of black coffee.

"Yes, thank you for calling, Mr. Stanton. I'll tell my husband," she finally said and hung up.

She took a sip of her coffee.

"Interesting development," she said, and then paused.

"Yes?" I asked, raising my voice in exasperation.

"That was Stanton. He wanted to remind you to send him copies of the letters. He said I could give you the message. You know what's odd, John? I had the feeling he didn't really care about the copies, or to speak with you at all. There was something else on his mind. It took him a while to get around to it. Odd," Sarah said, sipping her coffee.

"Okay," I said, "I give up," again with a touch of frustration in my voice. "What was on the old man's mind?"

"He wanted us to say a prayer for his wife and his daughter, at the right time . . . in the right place. He misses them very much."

"He what?"

"That's what he said. He wanted to ask you when you were in his office in Washington, but he didn't, he said. He said he forgot, but I don't believe that. He said he hasn't been practicing law for some years now."

"A prayer for his wife and daughter?"

"Yes."

"Why should we pray for them?"

"That's not all, John. He'd like us to say this prayer in Jerusalem . . . if we go to Jerusalem, he said."

I looked at Sarah in disbelief.

"Jerusalem, Israel," she said.

"I know where Jerusalem is, Sarah!"

"Now who's upset?"

"I am not upset!" I said, completely upset at Stanton, at Sarah, at everyone and everything.

"I wish I had met him, John. I liked the sound of his voice."

"Well, the next time we receive a mysterious certified letter from an unknown attorney in Washington who informs us that someone has died, you have my permission to run with the ball!"

I don't know why I was so annoyed, even angry, as I left the house that morning. Sarah was only trying to help both of us get to the bottom of it all. Yet, I was angry, angry at the pull these events out of the past had on me, as if I were being dragged back into things that had long since vanished into the dusty attic of time.

I drove to the campus, oddly untroubled by the possibility that, supposedly ill, I would be noticed by members of my department. What was troubling me was the conviction I had long held as a historian that what is past is past, over and done with. Make the argument, if you will, that the past was prologue, but it certainly was not a continuing event that somehow jumped in time into the future to determine events that had not yet happened. That was the great leap of civilization over superstition: our ability as thinking, modern people to separate factual events from inferences or mere beliefs. This conviction, that what's past is past, was now being challenged in a very subtle way.

I recalled a kind of parable one of my professors used to tell over and over again in an introductory history class. It concerned a caveman, our common ancestor, who left his cave and went out hunting one morning. As he was looking for food, he noticed in the distance another caveman at the foot of a mountain. Suddenly, there was an avalanche and the poor caveman at the foot of the mountain was crushed under the weight of the falling boulders. Our caveman, the observer, said aloud to himself: "Oh, too bad, look what's happened to Ug," and went on his merry way. Eons later, the professor would continue, there was another scene. In this one, a descendant of the original caveman also went out hunting, and also chanced to witness one of his fellows crushed under the weight of an avalanche. This time, however, the more modern caveman thought to himself: "Oh, too bad—I wonder what Ug did to deserve such a horrible death. The gods must be angry with him."

"Fact from inference, fact from inference," the professor would say. "Try not to jump to conclusions. Remember, you are only a poor observer of the natural world. Don't try to fathom what is in the minds of the gods!"

I've often thought of that lesson and used it many times myself in class when students tried to draw meaning out of events too quickly. But now, as I found the office I was looking for, I wasn't at all that certain. "What," I asked myself, "what had Ug done to deserve such a horrible death?"

Her name was Martha Schmitt and she was a professor of comparative religion. We had last spoken at a president's dinner about a year ago, but she stood out in my mind as someone who might be able to shed some light on what I had read in the letters. I had consulted on a book she had written some years before, dealing with the development of written history and how it was affected by a belief in the supernatural. (The book won a major literary award and was pretty controversial at the time, stating as it did as one of its conclusions that all decisions were emotional, later justified by the facts.) I had enjoyed working with her a great deal and, probably as much as anything else, felt myself drawn to her for that reason.

I recalled that she was referred to by her colleagues and the administration as Miss Schmitt. She had been a refugee who escaped from Germany during the 1930s, along with her father and other prominent academics. Her father had authored a standard text on chemistry. Both of them arrived in Pennsylvania and took up permanent residence near campus. Miss Schmitt had been there ever since.

As I sat in her office, I could see that the years had indeed caught up with her. Yet, there was still a sparkle in her eyes. She spoke with a clarity and precision not uncommon to those who learn English as a second language and must learn to use it with accuracy in an academic setting. She also retained a thick German accent.

She wore her hair in a neat bun. It had once been light brown, perhaps, but it was now all gray. A pair of fashionable designer glasses rested permanently around her neck, tied with a chic golden cord.

I had brought the letters with me and waited as she read them. When she reached the Signs of the Messiah, she made some notes on a pad. I wasn't sure what her reaction might be, but whatever it was, she was taking these letters very seriously.

"I am very interested in the Bedouin chant and what he called the Signs of the Messiah. It is a common tenet, in Western theology for the most part, that such a Messiah will come, or that he has been here and will come again. These are truisms, John. And the Signs, as they are called, are very much in that tradition, with some interesting variations."

"So you think this might be genuine?"

"Genuine? Oh, yes, it is genuine, but the question is much too naive. On what level are they genuine? For example, this point concerning the return to the Garden of Eden seems clear to me, as though it might even be a specific geographic location as described in the Judeo-Christian story of the original Garden of Eden. But it is hard for me to conceive of billions of people coexisting somehow in such a biblical Central Park. Could this have been written by a man, or was it divinely inspired, as the Bedouin chant indicates? The prediction regarding the Messiah's appearance over a dry and thirsty land also seems very specific, almost an address. I must admit, John, that I have never encountered anything quite like this before. In fact, this is new—there is nothing resembling this in the extant literature."

"Is it possible?" I asked, and at once realized how foolish my question was.

"Do you want me to say that anything's possible and leave it at that? Do you believe in UFOs in the desert, or visitors from other worlds who carve intricate geometric designs in the ancient sands of Peru? I can show you pictures of fantastic shapes, huge and very beautiful, in fact, that really only reveal their full beauty from a height above the earth. These earth sculptures of triangles and trapezoids, birds and whales and spiders, are miles long and centuries old. No one really knows what they mean. So, an ancient art form, or visitors from outer space who even today are giving us a message, using our planet as some sort of giant chalkboard?"

"Is it possible?" I repeated.

"Allow me to begin with a postulate that may appear very foreign to you, given your professional viewpoint as an historian."

"That's all right, Miss Schmitt. These letters have taken their toll on me. I'm not sure—"

"Very well then, John, consider this then: that there is a level of truth, vitally important to human beings, which lies beyond the explainable, demonstrable natural world. In fact, this truth is often more important and sustaining to human beings because it is an eternal truth, not changeable, never at the mercy of different historical theories—forgive me, John—or the whims of the scientist, or the observer of heavenly bodies. This truth, in a sense, is our spiritual food."

I wanted to say something, but she continued.

"These Messiah Stones, John, excite me. Do you have any idea what happened to them?"

"None at all."

"I've never encountered them before, but the world is a constantly surprising place, don't you think?"

"I didn't use to," I said.

"The closest thing I can compare them to is the Mormon belief in the existence of golden plates which were discovered and translated in the New World by a man called Joseph Smith. This was in the nineteenth century."

"Could those plates have existed?"

"Of course—anything is possible—there, I have said it! As you will recall"—which was a favorite phrase of hers, as well as mine, often used in the classroom to impart information by making it appear that the lecturer was merely refreshing the student's memory, when in fact he was raising something entirely new—"the plates tell the story of the Israelites who were divinely led from Jerusalem to America, where Jesus appeared to them and delivered his teachings."

"As a matter of fact, I do recall the story," I said. "I have a lot of respect for Mormons. Howard Hughes would only allow Mormons to be his bodyguards, isn't that right?"

"Maybe he knew something we don't."

"He was a very rich, eccentric man," I said.

"Yes, these Stones excite me a great deal. . . . Just imagine for a moment if it were true," she said, with what I can only describe as a mysterious quiet, as though she suddenly were seeing something played out in the past. She seemed to look beyond me, fixing her gaze on the door to her office at my back. For a moment, I felt like turning around to see if anyone was there, but didn't; it would've been rude.

"Don't we learn new things almost daily," she began again, "about ancient voyages and new discoveries of what were previously believed to be unexplored lands, and don't we see new theories about the universe pop up with frightening regularity? Let's assume the scientists are right, but who is to say that one of the Creator's days is not hundreds of billions of years? We are too arrogant, John, and we suffer for it!"

She adjusted her glasses and studied the letters again.

"Columbus did not discover America, John. The poor man was hundreds of years too late! I wouldn't be surprised if the first thing he saw was a McDonald's owned and operated by a Norwegian sailor!"

"Then why—"

"Listen to this," she said, and removed a well-worn black volume from among the many on the shelf above her desk.

"This is from the Mormon Bible, which is called *The Book of Mormon*. It is one of my favorites. Let me see here," she said, searching through the pages. "Ah, yes, here is a typical passage. Allow me to quote it to you: 'And then I will gather them in from the four quarters of the earth, and then I will fulfill the covenant which the Father had made unto all the people of the house of Israel.'"

"Yes, I know, but isn't there an enormous difference between Bible stories and historical facts? The history of living and breathing men and women who actually lived and shaped events is not the same as the poetic visions of prophets and priests, regardless of how beautiful they are."

"No, John, I'm not sure there is a difference. I quoted that one passage just now to make a point. I could have quoted others, from the Catholic or Protestant texts, or the Jewish, or others, including variations on this theme found in Eastern religions, which is this: that faith, the food I mentioned, bridges the span of time, that the need to believe is universal, and most important of all, that in faith we are still dealing with physical facts, as real as atoms and neutrons. We want completion in our lives, John."

"We have a need to know, is that it?"

"Very much so . . . a real need. It's part of our genes, built in. We really do not want to accept a haphazard world. It's too messy. We want neatness. We are emotional beings, John."

"All decisions are emotional . . ."

"Later justified by the facts," she said. "So you remember?"

"Yes, I do remember."

"We will be brought together and the covenant will be fulfilled. Can anything be clearer? So, you questioned whether or not it is possible. Is it possible?"

I was almost embarrassed by the childlike simplicity of my answer.

"Yes, Miss Schmitt."

She replaced the volume in the correct position on the shelf. "Well, now at least we know the right question. That is the beginning of true knowledge."

"I don't know anything at all."

"That, too, is a beginning, but in truth, John, you know a great deal. I wish I were younger. I would welcome the journey with you."

"What journey?"

"The journey to the answers."

"I don't know . . ."

"Of course, you will have to determine the validity of the Messiah Stones for yourself. No one can do that for you. But truth comes slowly, John, like a frog in water."

"A what?"

"A very old experiment—don't you know it? Place a frog in boiling water and the frog will immediately jump out. It will be too hot. But place the frog in temperate water and slowly increase the temperature to boiling, and the frog will not jump out. It will just sit there. Unfortunately, it will mean the death of the frog. Perhaps that was a poor analogy, John."

"I hope so."

"Death is frightening . . . and our days are so brief," she said.

As I sat in her office, listening to her, I became enthralled by the simplicity of her stories. We do live in a cynical world, but this woman had gained wisdom that, like her frog, jumped over it to land somewhere else. And yet, I sensed a deep loss in her, an emotional vacancy that I could not define. Perhaps it was the way she said our lives are brief, with a very definite undercurrent of regret in her voice.

"Would you like something to drink?" she asked. "I have a coffee machine here. It was a Christmas gift last year from an old friend. I could make us some coffee. I am very proud of my coffee. It is made with chicory, from New Orleans. Not bitter, don't worry!"

"Yes, thank you, that would be nice."

"Fine—it will just take a few minutes. I have the filters here somewhere. It is a beautiful day, isn't it? I have always liked the view from this window," she said.

What was she trying to tell me?

"Why don't you look out the window, John? Tell me what you see."

"Look out the window?"

"Yes, just tell me what you see."

She placed the coffee in the paper filter and carefully poured an exact amount of bottled water into the chamber.

"I won't make it too strong, if you are not used to it."

I thought of Sarah and a lot more, too.

The view from her window was of a wintry campus. The bare trees spread their thin branches out in haphazard fashion down toward the cold earth, but also upward toward the clear sky. The large quad in the center of the campus was empty, except for a few students hurrying between classes.

It was a cold Pennsylvania scene. For a moment, I had a strange thought: I was grateful it was there.

"What do you see?"

I described what I saw.

"But what you describe is not really there," she said.

She poured the coffee into two cups and placed them on two saucers. The set looked like fine china.

"Sugar or cream?"

"Black," I said.

"Good, that is the way I like it, too."

It was the best-tasting coffee I'd ever had.

"Tell me what you mean, Miss Schmitt. I'm curious."

"Our world, our universe, is a factory of facts, which runs like a perfect engine. But it could just as easily *not* have happened. Imagine, if you will, just the slightest alteration of one atom in the water molecule, or the slight dislocation of nitrogen in the air we breathe, or an imbalance in our DNA. All of this, John, is just a hairbreadth away from nonexistence. Even more significant, let us imagine a Big Bang that did not bang. It could just as easily *not* have happened. One day, we are told, it will all disappear. To what? Everything you see will not be there. Will it all revert to just nothing, John? Can you imagine *nothing*?" She sipped her coffee slowly, savoring the taste.

"A bleak thought, John. And for the last few centuries we have taken the measure of our world with a scientific ruler that calculates the chance collision of atoms in the dark, a bump in the night of particles of dust, in some corner of the attic in the universe. Is that all we are, John, just rather interesting assemblies of atoms chattering away in a corner of a vast universe? Is that all that separates us from the blackness out there? I think not; but more important, we need to believe. I know science has given us a lot that is good. But, in the final analysis, John, science explains nothing to us about eternal truths, it just leaves us with more facts, so many more facts. Do you see my point? It cannot explain the meaning of the trees we see out this marvelous window, or the presence of the students who pass between the buildings. We as human beings need to know the *why,* not just the *what,* because the what is only temporary, it changes, whereas the why . . . well, it is because there is chicory in the coffee, that is why!"

She was a beautiful person, that was all I could think. I had nothing to say.

"I agree certainly that we have basic instincts—I, too, have seen the movie. For food, for sex, for money, power . . . the list is well known, reanalyzed in each generation according to the latest style. But we also have another instinct, equal to if not higher than the others, and one that refuses to be silenced under the heavy, iron blanket of scientific facts. Yes, John, an iron blanket has descended on us!"

She enjoyed the moment, relishing the echo of Churchill's famous phrase.

"I call this instinct the instinct to return, to reconnect with our essence, to understand, to feel that we are made from the same substance as those trees out there, that we are one with the bosom of the universe. Do you understand me, John?"

"The way back," I said.

"Exactly! That is our path. We must stop preaching this speech about looking forward, as though progression into the future leads to happiness, or wisdom, or truth. I hope I am not becoming too maudlin in my old age, John, but your Messiah Stones have . . . have . . ."

She held her cup delicately in her hand and lifted it to her lips.

"They could make me feel young again, John. How did I grow old so quickly, I wonder. Can we not gather wisdom in our old age, or is it too late? Are we only interested in fancy new computers and trips to sunny resorts?"

"I don't know," I said, not knowing what else to say.

"We have lost the way to the palace of wisdom. We do not know the way back. Can your Messiah Stones guide us in the right direction?" she asked.

Miss Schmitt and I sat in silence for some time. It is a very, very difficult thing to do—to sit in silence. Our world is filled with sounds, and we've come to feel that we must fill any void we encounter with our voices, or the radio, or the TV; almost anything will do, as long as we're not burdened by deafening silence. But there is a special beauty, I was coming to see, a special peace in quiet that is beyond words or the trappings of this world. But, oh, it is so difficult not to speak!

"I tell the story in my classes about the farmer in the valley whose house becomes flooded. You know this one, John?"

"No, I don't think so."

"Oh, you should know it! It is worth telling. You see, there is a farmer living in a valley. The farmer is a God-fearing man. One day, heavy rains come and floods fill the valley. The water level rises dangerously around the farmer's house, so high that a boat sails by. The captain of the boat stands up and calls to the farmer, 'Come out! Jump, save yourself!' But the farmer refuses. 'No,' he says, 'the Lord will provide, the Lord will provide.' But the rain continues and the water rises ever higher, flooding the house, threatening the farmer and his family. But he sees another boat and again they call out to him, 'Come out! Jump, save yourself!' But the farmer refuses again, replying, 'No, the Lord will provide.' Well, you can imagine what happens next. The entire valley is flooded and the farmer and his family drown and die. Up in heaven, the farmer meets his maker. 'Where were you,' the farmer cries in anguish, 'where were you when I needed you?' The Lord looks at the farmer with great sadness in his eyes. 'Where was I?' he replies. 'What do you mean, where was I? I sent two boats to save you, didn't I?' "

As I left Martha Schmitt's office that afternoon and stepped out onto the wintry campus, I wondered about what she had said and how it differed from what I had believed all of my adult years. And I wondered about what the way back would be like. The quad was mostly bare of students as a cold wind swept across the open space. There stood the tree I had seen from her office window. It was an old, gnarled oak tree that had been a silent witness to decades of seasonal change. As if for the first time, I approached the tree in anticipation and actually touched its rough skin. The tree was alive; it was made of the primal stuff of life; we were both made in the bosom of the universe. In touching the oak, I was touching myself. How could I explain the sensation of joy, of pure exhilaration, of oneness with this silent tree? Was this the joy of life? The words of the poet echoed in my mind like a rhyme dimly remembered from childhood:

Footfalls echo in the memory
Down the passage which we did not take
Towards the door we never opened
Into the rose-garden. My words echo
Thus, in your mind.

Chapter 3

DOWN
THE PASSAGE

SARAH FOUND BARBARA ALLISON living in a nursing home in a suburb of Chicago.

"How did you do it?"

"I'll have to admit it took more than a few calls," she said. "I don't look forward to our phone bill. But I am constantly amazed by how much information people will give you over the phone without your ever leaving the comfort of your own house. It's scary."

"Okay, I'm duly impressed, as usual, Ms. Holmes. Pray tell, how was it accomplished?"

I'm not nearly as big a mystery fan as Sarah is, or as I should be, married to a woman who co-owns a bookstore specializing in mysteries. Over the last few years, since Sarah and her partner bought the store—her partner is a divorced mother of three whose ex-husband is the athletic director of the college—my wife has had the rare opportunity to combine her love for mysteries with the desire to run a successful business. When the location became available, she and her friend jumped at the chance to buy it. Most of their customers are faculty and students. I've often wondered how they have time to read all those mysteries, when they should be studying calculus or French grammar instead, or, as in my case, researching new material for a paper.

"I assumed," she began, "that Dr. Allison was affiliated with a university, probably Chicago. But as it turned out, it was not Chicago, but Columbia, in New York. I also assumed that his work might have been underwritten by a grant of some sort— which turned out to be correct. A computer check of grants and studies of the 1950s in archaeology, cross-referenced with Middle East Judeo-Christian studies, revealed that a number of them had been piloted by a Dr. Philip Allison of Columbia. Allison was a graduate of Columbia. Allison worked closely with an associate, Dr. Karl Kurzon, out of Chicago. It was these two who set off for Jerusalem and environs in the mid-1950s."

"How did you find his wife?"

"I tracked down the people in charge of the schools' alumni associations and told them I was Barbara Allison, and that I had not been receiving any alumni correspondence for a while. I said I was thinking of making a small bequest. Could they check the address where they'd been sending the material? The lady in the office that paid off was a temp, a student I think, but very nice. She read out the computer address to where everything had been going for some time, a nursing home in Evanston. Schools are always looking for money. You could be dead and still on their list for years. Anyhow, she wondered if I'd moved. No, I said, but I'll be certain to check the mail more carefully in the future—perhaps I was getting forgetful in my

old age. It was a good excuse—she felt sorry for me. She understood, she said; she did volunteer work at a senior citizens' residence twice a month."

Sarah and I were in bed. The boys were asleep.

"There may be a murder or two still unsolved that the police
could use help on," I said. "I am impressed."

"Well, don't be. I'm still not a total believer in this caper,
and yet . . ."

I wondered what she was thinking.

"Barbara Allison turned out to be quite a woman. I'm still
not sure of what to make of our conversation."

"You spoke with her?"

"Sure did. I had to coordinate a time with the nurse to be
certain she was in her room. It turned out to be right after her
lunch. That was no problem. The real problem was how to
approach the subject."

"Which—?"

"This whole thing, John, which is pretty foolish. And the
last thing I wanted to do is confuse some little old lady in a
nursing home who may be long past her best days."

I noticed it began to rain. I could hear the patter of drops on
the roof. In the country, the rain is always louder at night.

"As it turned out, Barbara Allison was as clear as a bell. She
could recall in detail her husband's expeditions back to the
1930s! They had met on one such expedition into the Brazilian
rain forest. They fell in love and got married."

"Was she one of his students?"

"Hardly! She was a published author in her own right. Her
maiden name was Barbara Alexander, and she'd written a

number of fairly successful and well-received books on primitive societies. One of them was translated into sixteen languages!"

"How long did you speak with her?"

"Almost an hour. As I said, I dread the phone bill. But, hey, we're on a case, right? Anyhow, she's a pretty unusual woman."

"Well—"

"I don't mean just because she was an author, or a 'woman's woman' before her time, or anything trite like that. That's not what I mean."

It began to rain harder. I could hear the night wind pelt the rain against the side of our house. Upstairs in our bedroom, our nightstand lamp must have shone like a tiny beacon in the darkness of our secluded country house.

I told Sarah about my session with Martha Schmitt, but she brought the conversation back to Barbara Allison.

"Did you tell her about the letters?" I asked.

Sarah looked at me with that serious, impassive expression on her face. She was sitting up in bed, two fluffy pillows behind her back. Her long red hair flowed over the white cotton of the pillowcases. I could see that she was thinking on many tracks simultaneously as she spoke to me.

"I didn't have to," she said. "She already knew about them."

"She what? But they were never mailed. My father gave them to Stanton. We have them."

"Yes," she said.

"Then how—?"

"There's a part of this story that I only began to appreciate halfway through our phone call," Sarah said. "It's as though we've been given a preview of what is to come, only a small sampling of the main attraction, which hasn't yet started."

"I'm not sure—"

"Barbara Allison met your father, John. She met him in the 1950s, before he returned for the last time to the Holy Land."

"How do you know that?"

"Because she told me."

Sarah pulled the blanket up higher. Her hair flowed over the pillow like delicate red feathers displayed against an artist's white canvas. She was beautiful in the night.

"I've done nothing else today but think about this, John. It was all I could do to put the boys to bed tonight. It might sound half crazy, but I felt an immediate attachment to Barbara, closer than I've felt toward a stranger in a long time."

"What sort of preview?"

"I had the impression that she almost expected my call. It was not much of a surprise to her. It was like Stanton, just waiting out there. Do you understand? She only sounded a little relieved that it had finally happened. You know what?"

"I'm afraid to guess."

"She knew my name would be Sarah."

"Because of the carving on the globe?"

"Yes."

"And she knows about the Messiah Stones?"

"Yes."

"And the Signs?"

"Yes."

"Does she know where the Stones are?"

"I'm not sure."

I heard the rain again.

"I told her we'd be coming out to see her, John."

"You're kidding!"

"No, I'm not."

"When?"

"Tomorrow."

"Tomorrow?"

"This is a caper, John. Whoever or whatever's behind it, it's gotten my attention. Don't be afraid, my love."

"Of what?"

"Of finding out who done it, of course," she said and closed her eyes, retreating under the blanket.

I shut the light and was asleep myself in minutes. Whatever I dreamed that night—if I did dream—I don't remember, except that I awoke at the crack of dawn and could not get back to sleep. I noticed the rain had stopped. I heard Sarah in the bathroom taking a shower. I wasn't surprised: She was on the case.

We were able to arrange for an overnight baby-sitter and took the first flight we could manage to Chicago. I had called in sick again, and our department secretary still sounded suspicious of my lingering cold. Sarah had spoken to her partner and had gotten some part-time sales help to fill in at the bookstore.

On the flight to Chicago, curiously enough, we hardly spoke at all. We sat next to each other at the rear of the plane and flipped through the in-flight magazines. Sarah had never been to Chicago, and I hadn't been there for years.

We took the train out to Evanston.

Barbara Allison was a permanent resident in a nursing home located in a quiet, secluded area not far from the railroad station. Our taxi driver knew the place. When we arrived, however, we had to wait to see her—she was receiving some therapy and wasn't available to see us for about half an hour.

We waited in a comfortable lounge well stocked with the latest issues of all the popular magazines. Large bay windows allowed sheets of light to enter, filling the room with brightness. The walls were covered with colorful paintings of autumn barns, country roads, a display of pumpkins on a lawn. Sarah guessed it was the work of the residents.

As we waited, I saw an elderly woman being assisted as she hobbled along with a cane, and a curious thought struck me. She was doing her best to walk, resting most of her weight on her cane. She was dressed in a housecoat—a thin, cottony, all-purpose garment decorated with blue petals. It seemed the wrong size, too loose and too short. She wore soft slippers that squeaked as she shuffled across the slick, polished floor in the hall. It was hard to tell exactly how old she was—eighty, ninety, more. She was bent over, her upper body bent forward as she faced down, looking at the floor as she shuffled along. Her hair was very thin and sparse, and all white. I could see her scalp, since she was partially bald. It was pink. She had an attendant at her side, a large woman who held her by the arm and patiently waited for her to take the next step down the passage toward her destination.

I watched them carefully and wondered if my mother had been like this. She too had been in a nursing home, in Florida, with her sister. I had been there only once, but remembered it well. Why hadn't I visited more often? As I watched the pair slowly progress out of sight, it struck me that over the last couple of days, I too was being guided, just as this old woman was being helped by the attendant. And my guides shared a distinct appearance: They were old as well, like Stanton, like Martha Schmitt, and now like Barbara Allison.

I was lost in these thoughts; I didn't want to be there.

"What are you thinking?" Sarah asked, shattering my reverie.

"Nothing," I said. It was a lame answer. I was thinking about so many things.

"Me, too," she said.

"Does this make any sense?"

"Let's withhold judgment," Sarah said.

We were at last escorted up to a room on the second floor, toward the front. I felt as though we were entering a time capsule, transported back into the chambers of the past. Last summer, we'd taken the boys to Plymouth Plantation, where actors play the parts of colonists in period dress, living and working on a reconstructed plantation. Joshua especially loved it. He played the part of a TV announcer in front of each new location for the video camera we had brought along. Now we were visitors again, weren't we?

I began to feel cold, although it was quite warm in this building. I shivered for an instant, reacting the way we do when, old wives tell us, someone has walked over our grave. Sarah could see this, and smiled at me.

"I know," she said, as we walked behind the young candy striper leading us to the room. Sometimes Sarah and I could almost read each other's thoughts. I wondered if she was also cold.

We were led into a room. The young girl showed us to a sofa. An old woman was seated in a comfortable wing chair in front of us. She appeared asleep, or at least her eyes were closed. Unlike the earlier resident we'd seen, this woman was dressed in a blue suit, with a red rose pinned to her lapel. I could smell her perfume, which was fresh, not overpowering. Her hands lay folded in her lap. Her nails were manicured. She had the hands of a much younger woman. They were soft and delicate.

As the young girl left the room and closed the door behind her, her thick, rubber-soled shoes squeaked, waking the old woman.

"Oh," she said, startled. "I must have been asleep! You must be Sarah and John."

"Yes," Sarah said. "We spoke yesterday. How nice to see you."

"I'm happy to see you! Would you like something to drink? Have you had lunch? I can have something brought in—it's no trouble, we can just call," she said with renewed energy, and genuine hospitality.

"That's awfully nice of you, but we ate on the flight," Sarah said.

"Did you have a good flight?"

"Yes," I said.

"I miss flying," Barbara said. "It's one of the few things I do miss. Getting around, anywhere really."

"Would *you* like to have something?" Sarah asked.

"Oh, no, I've had lunch. I won't eat again until five-thirty.

Every night, it's five-thirty. Can you imagine what it's like to eat every night at five-thirty? Not five, or six, but always five-thirty?"

"No," Sarah said.

"Well, I really don't like to complain. I'm a lucky woman, really. The body may be a bit rusty, maybe no oil or gas, but the engine up here still hums. I don't know what I'd do if I lost that," she said. "Probably shoot myself."

Sarah turned toward me.

"Oh, just kidding," Barbara said. "It's part of getting older, kind of coffin humor."

"We're so happy to see you," Sarah said.

"Yes," I said.

"Where would you like to begin?" Barbara asked. "Please call me Barbara. You must have a thousand questions."

"Yes," we both said at the same time.

"Fine," Barbara said.

After a few beats, Sarah jumped in with both feet.

"Tell us about your husband," she said.

"Yes, that would be a good place to begin, Sarah. I've always liked the name Sarah. It's so solid. But let's begin at the beginning, as Alice said, or someone in that book."

Sarah and I were now characters in our own real-life version of *Alice in Wonderland* as we sat in Barbara's room.

"As I told you over the phone, I was a researcher when I was younger. My area of interest was primitive societies. The more primitive the better. I had developed this interest early on as a child. I had a brother who was born with limited intelligence. It is now fashionable to say 'challenged'? Well, whatever it is called, the result is the same. He could do very little for himself as he grew older. He was a boy in an adult's body. My mother would give him rags, and his chore was to clean the house. This repetitive exercise pretty much kept him occupied for years. We really didn't know much better then. Watching him develop this way, I became fascinated with human personalities, but in their early, primitive stages. Is this okay? Is this what you want to know?"

Sarah and I nodded.

"Yes," I said.

"You see, I don't get a chance to visit much these days. It gets stored up. No one to tell it to. I led a busy life; do you understand? I'm so happy you're here! I think I've expected you for some time now."

"Could you explain that?" Sarah asked.

"I'll try, but I'm not sure I can explain it to your complete satisfaction. Would you like a sucking candy?" Barbara asked.

"No, thanks," I said.

"Yes," Sarah said, taking one. "Thank you very much."

"Would you hand me one as well, dear?" Barbara asked, pointing to the colorful tin resting next to the lamp.

Sarah gave her a candy.

"Green," Barbara said, sucking the candy with relish. "I like green." After a pause, she refolded her hands in her lap and spoke again.

"There is a legend that is told in one of the ancient mystical tracts. The legend is a sort of commentary on a famous biblical passage, which I'm sure you recognize: 'And God said, let there be light.' According to this legend, concerning this light which

God made, it was the first light, the primal light, if you will. It is the light from which all other light comes, a kind of Prometheus torch. But it is also the light in our eyes, the spark of our being. It is the light which God showed to Adam, the first man, in the Garden of Eden, the light which illuminated the Garden and allowed Adam to see the world from one end of it to the other. What I mean to say is that Adam could literally see the world, spatially from one end to the other, but also see it in his mind as well, from the beginning of time to the end of days. Do you understand?"

"We understand," Sarah said, placing her hand on mine and preventing me from speaking, which I had not intended to do at all.

"This was the light that the Eternal showed to King David and to Moses when Moses stood on the hill and was shown the promised land, which he was not allowed to enter.

"It was also the light which God gave to Moses as he stood on the summit at Sinai to receive the Commandments. In this story, Moses, having seen the face of Jehovah, is forced ever after to wear a veil over his own face to protect his fellow Israelites from the blinding radiance of God's light.

"This was that same light," Barbara said, stressing each of those five simple words in turn like the beats of a melody that rang in her ear, a tune familiar to all.

"In 1954, Philip discovered a set of these Stones, or Tablets, in the middle of a dig in the Holy Land, in Shiloh. He referred to them as the Messiah Stones for the simple reason that they concerned the coming of the Messiah and God's eventual judgment of the world. Philip and his colleagues were somehow mixed up with the government—everybody was a spy in those days. Seems silly now, doesn't it? Philip had heard rumors for years; I think he suspected what was out there. But it was your father, John, who first told me what had happened. You see, Philip was prevented from reporting the news of his discovery. Your father said that the authorities had put a lid on it. They believed the find would set off a chain reaction in the public that would be difficult to control. I don't know, maybe they were right. I don't know. The times were different. Philip, though, was determined to let me know at least, so he sent your father to me with the message and some letters."

She smiled at this point.

"I let your father keep the letters after I read them. They were as much his as mine, in a way. He wanted to pass them on to his son. He knew he wouldn't live to see the Messiah, but you would, and your wife, whose name would be Sarah. It was left to you to tell the story, you see.

"I never saw Philip again, or your father. But I have been waiting."

"For us?" I asked.

"According to your father, John, my husband postulated that the Messiah Stones were given to Moses at the same time he received the Ten Commandments on Sinai. And it was onto these tablets, the Messiah Stones, that Jehovah entrusted the primal light, the light of the world. Philip also thought that the Stones were deposited in the Temple of Jerusalem and kept secure there for generations. Not until the Roman conquest of Judea, about two thousand years ago, were they moved to Shiloh, where the Ark of the Covenant itself had once been housed. That's why the Temple priests brought it there, to Shi-loh, and buried the Stones, because it was a way of connecting with their own past, sort of getting back to the beginning. Even then, I suppose, people were people, searching for their roots. There they were buried for later generations . . . for you and your wife, John, but also for me and Philip and everyone else, for when they were needed. I think I told you, Sarah, a leap of faith is required."

"But why us?" Sarah asked.

"Oh, it's not just you!" Barbara said with emphasis.

"But 'McGowan' was on the Stones, and Sarah's name was on the other rock, the globe," I said.

"Yes," Barbara said. "But do you remember one of the Signs of the Messiah? That he will speak to *each* of us worldwide, simultaneously? Apparently this is the way it is being accom-plished."

"You mean we're not the only ones who have been—" I wasn't sure of the right word.

"Contacted? Chosen?" Barbara suggested.

"Yes," I said.

"John, when I met your father he was a young man. I'm not sure why my husband selected him to see me. There may have been others better suited. As it turned out, your father had a family he was forced to leave. It was not an easy decision for him, I'm sure."

"Why?" I said. "Why did he do it?"

Barbara unfolded her hands and pointed at us.

"For you," she said. "And probably for his God. I'm not sure we can ever really know. He only played a small part. Like a relay race, you see. The baton is now with you two, but you're so much closer to the finish line. I couldn't take part in the race. The baton was handed to me, but I didn't take it. It's hard to explain, but I suppose I just didn't believe at the time. Philip knew this about me. Maybe that's why he never came back. Maybe he knew I would never leave. I don't know. But I did know I wouldn't be forgotten, that someone else would call. A McGowan, or a Sarah. Someday. Was I right?"

I could see that Sarah wanted to change the subject. Both of us noticed tears in Barbara's eyes.

"Yes, Barbara, you were. Can you tell us about him, about John's father?" Sarah asked.

"Not too much. When he came to visit me, I had half expected him. I hadn't seen Philip in almost a year, and his last letters were filled with strange comments about these latest expeditions. He called on the telephone once or twice, but whenever he asked me to come out there, I just changed the subject. Perhaps that's why he sent your father to me, as a way of keeping connected, yet perhaps also a way of saying goodbye."

"What happened to him—your husband?" I asked.

"I don't really know. I could tell you what they told me, but the bottom line is the same: I don't really know."

Barbara said these last words almost in a daze, as if recalling a memory only partially understood, yet at the same time trying to grasp all of it, like a name she could not quite vocalize.

"Barbara?" Sarah asked.

"Yes?" the older woman answered.

"Tell us whatever you can remember. We need to know. Please try."

Barbara folded her hands again, almost in slow motion. In her brown eyes, I could also see reflections of Stanton and Martha Schmitt, perhaps even reflections of myself and Sarah in the years ahead. This was a new window which was being opened for me.

"He was about twenty-five, your father. But when I met him, he seemed much older. He gave me the letters to read, from Philip. He told me what he knew. I think your father and my husband were creating a kind of insurance, like a chain letter, to make sure the message got through, when the time was right. The year would be 2000."

"What message?"

"That the Messiah is coming again. Please, my dear, open that drawer," she asked Sarah and pointed to a small table next to her bed. Sarah walked over and opened the drawer. She removed what looked like a photo album and gave it to Barbara, placing it in her lap.

"You are beginning to understand," Barbara said. "Women seem to understand first, you know. It is our legacy," she said, smiling at Sarah. "But not necessarily a blessing."

"Our legacy?" Sarah asked.

"You'll laugh," Barbara said.

"No, I promise I won't," Sarah said.

"Even now, it's hard for me to believe. It's my nature, doubtful and stubborn, I suppose. But I've learned so much in these years. What I mean, about our legacy, is one of the things I've learned. I believe Eve was born a restless spirit, because God knew the world needed restless spirits, because if we were all placid, no progress would've been made. Eve was always searching. She was the curious one. So now we all search, but are also confused and doubtful."

I could see the album in Barbara's lap as she gently rested her hands on its white borders. It was square in shape and covered most of her lap. She placed her palms down flat on its cover, spreading her fingers out wide almost in some silent benediction, as though she were caressing a long-cherished family heirloom.

She said, "This is the album your father brought with him, which he left with me. He said it was for me, but also for others who would come later. I have cherished it always."

"This has been a great burden for you, hasn't it, Barbara?" Sarah asked.

"Oh, yes and no," Barbara said. "To know finally, to be aware, is very precious. I would never give that up. It is now with me each day of my life. You know, there are only a few years left until he comes again, the third millennium. But I lost a husband, as you lost a father, John. Every gain has a loss, I suppose. I don't know. All I know is, people live and die, and that's what we all have in common. All of us want the same things. Aren't we always a child at heart, in that we're never fully grown and capable? Don't we all doubt? Don't we all need encouragement?"

I looked at Sarah. This was more than a caper, much more. I needed to know her thoughts.

"But you're right, Sarah," Barbara continued, "it has been bittersweet. I've been alone too long, I suppose. Memory plays tricks. Who knows what really happened? You know what I thought of just yesterday? Do you recall the movie *Citizen*

Kane? Philip and I saw it three times. Well, there's a scene in it when one of the characters, I forget his name, he's an old man, he's being interviewed about Kane, what he can remember of the old days. As it transpires, he can recall a great deal, the minutest detail. Then he says something extraordinary, about what people remember, what shapes their lives. He tells us he took a ferry as a young man, to work one day, I suppose, and he sees a beautiful young girl seated opposite him on the ferry. She's wearing a white dress and carrying a white parasol. They never speak. Not one word. She gets off, he gets off, and he never sees her again. And that was the only time he ever sees her, mind you, just that once. But he tells us, now in his old age, that a day hasn't gone by since that he hasn't thought about her, this young girl he saw only once on a ferry, years and years ago.

"Can you understand? How can you evaluate what a person remembers? This is how I've thought about the young man who was your father, and my husband, both of whom I never saw again. Can you imagine how difficult it was for me? Please take this, it was meant for you, for both of you," she said, extending the album to us. "It's as much yours as mine, maybe more."

Sarah and I quickly stood up and accepted the album, both of us holding it by the edges as we took a few steps back and sat down again on the sofa. Barbara, too, sat back and seemed to relax in her chair.

"I'm sure you'll want to look at it now," she said, sighing deeply. "Please, I'll just close my eyes for a bit, if you don't mind. If you want anything, coffee, or something, I'm not really a Jewish mother. . . ." Her eyes closed and she dozed off.

Sarah stood up and placed a pillow between Barbara's head and the side of the chair.

"Should we leave the room?" I found myself asking almost in a whisper.

"Let's stay; I'm more comfortable here."

We sat side by side and rested the album between us on our laps. We turned the cover to open it. Sarah held my hand. I could feel how cold she was.

The first page of the album showed a drawing of what looked like the interior of a slave ship. It was a cutaway view from above, looking down into the bowels of the vessel, where the slaves were kept for the transoceanic journey. I had seen depictions like this before. The slaves were lined up in rows, chained head to foot to maximize the use of space. They were human cargo. In these drawings, which illustrated the slave trade from Africa to the New World, the slaves were placed, as was typically described, like sardines.

But this drawing, though similar, was different in one extraordinary respect: Though the view was from above—looking down from some distance on high from outside the ship—the face of each slave was distinct and particular, a portrait in miniature like a microphotograph, revealing eyes, ears, nose, features. Sarah and I could make out these faces as though we were seeing real people, each an individual thumbprint of a person on a virgin sheet of white paper. We had never seen anything like this before, nor had anyone else. It didn't seem possible. The drawing—if it was a drawing—filled the page from edge to edge. No words, no captions.

We turned the page.

And saw a second drawing.

This one depicted a woman, a slave in her early twenties, standing on an auction block. She was naked to the waist. Bright sunlight reflected tears in her eyes. A young boy of about five stood right next to her. She held his hand. Sarah and I could see how tightly she held it, as we held each other's hand, fearing events beyond her control. This, too, was more than a drawing—it was an expression of human emotion we could feel as though we were there with her.

The mother's face and the boy's showed that same intense quality of living detail. We could see the fine texture of skin, feel its softness, experience the sweat beneath their brows as they stood on the auction block under a hot noon sun.

We turned the page in the album.

There appeared a third drawing, of the same woman and boy. This time they were joined by a man who with one hand brutally jerked the boy away from his mother, and with his other hand whipped the woman with his riding crop as she desperately implored and pleaded to be sold with her son.

Sarah and I could understand—could feel—the tale that was unfolding before us as though we were personal witnesses to the scene. This was some new medium, hard to describe, hard to resist. It existed on the page, yet the page itself seemed to take hold of us, to speak to us. Silently, Sarah turned the page and we read these words:

A Story of the Return

These five words were hand-drawn on the page, in an archaic script, yet the letters were sharp and distinct. They stood out from the page in three dimensions, with depth. Like the slaves' eyes, each letter radiated its own light, yet was part of a whole. Sarah gently ran her finger across the page, barely touching the words. I watched her do this. Barbara was asleep in her chair.

On the next page, and for a number of sheets following, Sarah and I read the story that lived on those pages, "A Story of the Return," which had lived with Barbara all these years, and now lived with us. The words were in a handwriting that I could recognize, but could not quite place.

Then I knew why as the narrative began:

Dear Son,

You have found Dr. Allison's wife, as I knew you would. Nothing has ever been more certain to me. You have also found this album, which I created for you, and for Sarah, who must be your wife. It is a beautiful name, Sarah, and I am sure she is a beautiful woman. Someday I hope we will meet. I look forward to knowing her and you, son.

What you are about to read is a story that has been given to me, but in a way that I must explain. If you can think of it as a vision, that will probably suffice, but that is not the entire explanation. What is a vision, anyway? Do people still believe in visions? By "given" to me I mean it has been made part of my consciousness, like my name or my address, yet even more: It is like my knowledge of the world, which tells me that if I pick up a stone and toss it upward, it will fall back to earth. This is a physical fact I know. So, too, is the story you are about to read: It, too, is a physical fact that I know, that can never be altered, nor erased from my being. It is a story that was given to me one night in Jerusalem as I slept out under the stars, just before my return home. It transformed my life and gave it the direction it has taken for the rest of my days.

So, I hope it does the same for you, my son, as it becomes part of your life. How the pictures were drawn, why they radiate the way they do . . . I think you'll come to appreciate. I am not an artist, but I'm sure my hand was guided.

Be well.

No signature. No name.

Sarah and I read the paragraphs penned in front of us like children absorbed in a favorite tale. Each word resonated, forming a picture we could see which drew us deeper down the passage of time toward our inevitable destination.

We began to read the text.

He will know the world and its ways—having lived among us often. He will be scorned and ridiculed. He will live among us in every period of our lives, from the beginning of days to the end of time.

These are the words of the Signs of the Messiah, handed down generation after generation, even unto these times. He is always with us.

And so it was as he saw the woman and her children auctioned off as slaves, for he too was a slave, awaiting his turn to be sold. The journey in the ship had been beyond description as he lay chained in a row with other captured men and women, and boys and girls. Some he knew, some he didn't. The constant moans filled the belly of the ship as it heaved from side to side through the ocean. No tears, no more—only moans of deep pain and fear, which filled the darkness. He slept in his own waste and ate in his own waste. Worse than hogs, for these were human beings with minds and awareness, with hopes and knowledge of good and evil, sparked with the light of the Creator.

He had known this fear before, in other lives. He had known this aching thirst for water before, in other lives; but this was as if for the first time; it was always as if for the first time. The moans. How was it possible for the quintessence of creation to be transformed into such a mass of aching hearts?

This was a return to the world he had long feared—to be so humiliated, to be so scorned, taught him valuable lessons. He must remember them when the time came, of how he felt to be chained or stretched on this hard board. He must remember how he thirsted for water. He must remember that he was fed like an animal, kept alive to be sold—chained and watered and fed merely for profit. He would remember. Oh, God, how he would remember!

Could there be anything worse than this frightening voyage over the dark ocean? He closed his eyes and journeyed through time to the top of his mountain.

Days and days later, he was removed from the inner cavity of the slave ship and marched up to the deck. Many of his fellow slaves had died. What would be done with their bodies? How many were children?

He was standing waiting to be sold at auction. He was behind a young mother with five children at her side. Had they been captured with him in Africa? Or had they been added to this group for some other reason, brought from a plantation in nearby Maryland? He was not sure. He was too weak. No one would say.

He was a witness to all that took place.

Two of the woman's children were sold to one master, two to another. Each in turn was prodded and fondled on the auction block by their prospective buyers. Two boys, two girls. Their mouths were opened and their teeth counted. The buyers jerked the hands to test their strength. Limbs were squeezed.

These girls and boys were brothers and sisters, born of the same mother, who had to stand and witness their departure. She would never see them again; she knew in her heart that she would never see them again. Oh, he could feel in his own heart the bottomless agony she endured, though she was silent and could not speak. Oh, he would allow her to speak when her turn came . . . heaven itself would hold its breath! She would be the first to speak, as he was her witness.

Then her turn came, and she was sold to a man who wore a high black hat and who held a riding crop in one hand. His boots were black. He wore a wide, thick leather belt around his waist, snapped tight with a silver buckle. His beard was gray. His hands were thick. His nails were rough-edged and dirty. Oh, he would remember this man when his time came!

But the woman clung to her last child, the little boy, who would not let go. She screamed now, and pleaded for the one that remained . . . begged for this one child . . . just this one last child! But the man refused and kicked her away, separating the boy from his mother, pushing at one, pushing at the other, tearing the two apart without mercy.

He was a witness.

He saw the mother, barely more than a girl herself, half naked as she lay on the ground. He could see the tears in her eyes, the tears down her cheeks, hot, salty tears that fell one after another onto the earth. And, oh, again that moan, of loss, of pain, of endless suffering. He saw her crawl away from the man, beaten into the ground, no longer the mother of her children, she was now something that lived with the dust beneath the stones. Yet, yet she spoke! He would remember her words to the end of time: "Oh, Lord Jesus, how long, how long shall I suffer this way?"

He was not the carpenter now; that was before. He was a slave like her, a witness to her suffering. But until the end of days, he would remember her tears. He would remember, and he would make each of us remember. He said, in his heart, that this should not pass unpunished.

Once, he had been a woman. He understood women's suffering and could not bear to think of it. But he was not that strong now.

His days were bitter and unending, with no rest. He worked and lived on a tobacco plantation. He saw infants tied to their mothers' backs as the women worked in the fields. These children began their lives in the fields and died in the fields. Here they were nursed. He spent his life among them. Each day he spent from day clear to first dark, his overseer never far away. Once, he fell behind and felt the whip on his back. That was an especially hard day.

At day's end, he would return to his cabin, tired beyond despair, his arms like heavy weights he couldn't lift. Now he had to grind the corn and prepare his dinner, as well as the gruel he would eat in the field tomorrow to sustain his strength, to work another day.

He had a family.

This was his lot as a slave on a tobacco plantation in the year of our Lord 1849.

He had been a slave before and knew their suffering.

He had returned for yet another time to be among us, to be a witness to our lives.

And so, that hot day on the auction block, he altered one of the foundations of the world. He could see beyond time, beyond the limits of the universe, beyond the farthest reaches of the imagination, to declare this change: that upon that day in the future, that day we all long for, we will all return to the Garden for final judgment, all of us, living or dead, except for three: he who murders, he who rapes—he had lived this terror in another life—and he who buys or sells another human being. For these three alone, now including the last, there will be no return. Their souls will be ground to dust and they will suffer the severest of penalties, which is separation from the Eternal for eternity.

These things were made known to me in Jerusalem as I slept one night under the stars. They were
given to me to relate to you, my son, and to Sarah. I
was made to understand, to feel, the suffering of the
woman on the auction block, and of the witness to
her suffering, and also of the man who beat her, for
he too will suffer in the days to come. It was given to
me to understand the metamorphosis of the Messiah, the beings he has been, always among us, always in each of us. The truth of his existence is
complex, for he is like a seed planted in each generation that grows to maturity in our lives. He is the
knowledge of the divine in our hearts to whom we
must return. He does not have one name, or one
color, or one being, though he is one. He is all
names and all beings. He is the Light in our eyes.
And he will come again in your time.

I don't believe for a moment that I am the only
one of my generation who has been given this insight. When I saw the Messiah Stones shine in their
brilliance, I knew I wasn't unique. More people
must know what I know. Don't you see?

His final days were spent in the fields. He was
sick, hot with fever. His stool was streaked with
blood. He had a large boil on the side of his neck.
His head throbbed and a loud, shrill sound like
screams in the future distance filled his mind. He
could almost hear the cries of women and children,
off in the distance of time and space, but he could

not make out any words of the strange language. Only, there was such a piercing whistle, like a train down through the tunnel of time, it broke his heart!

Which life was he living? Which time was this? Whose plantation was this? In such moments of sorrow, different incarnations often became mixed and confused for him. He must summon his energy to remember the place and the names, and especially the faces. It was with the faces that he mostly connected the tribulations. Oh, there were so many faces! Who would have thought there would be so many faces? So many, when there were only two in the Garden? It seemed so long ago . . . the Garden . . . the Light that shone from one end of the world to another, from the start of time to the end of days, the last sunset when darkness again ruled . . . unending, silence . . . this was another journey among us. See the Garden, the trees, the pain!

"How long," the mother asked, "shall I suffer this way?"

"Not long," he answered to no one but himself. "Not long."

There was an old woman in the field next to him who applied a cool, soft cloth to the boil on his neck. She saw the thick red stain on his trousers. "She, too, is a slave," he thought. "She, too, has a master. I must remember this."

"Peace," she said, humming an old song he could recall from his childhood. She rocked her body back and forth and held him in her arms, on the ground. His legs were draped over hers. Was this his mother?

"Oh," he said, "the beauty of the Garden!" The woman sang her song and watched him die. She cried all that day and night, with no relief.

Sarah and I read these last words and found our lips moving—we had been reading out loud.

The album still lay open, spread between our laps. I still held Sarah's hand, but it was no longer cold. I turned to her and could see huge wells of tears in both eyes. She took her hand from mine and slowly closed the album.

"This is ours now," she said. "It's in our hearts forever, I know it."

"Yes."

"John," she said, "we have to go to Jerusalem. We no longer have a choice."

"I know," I said.

"We have to find the Stones."

"Do you think they're in Jerusalem?"

"No, yes—I don't know!" She wiped her eyes with a tissue. "I would like to have known your father, though. He was quite a man."

"Yes," I said. "We are rich, aren't we?" Sarah smiled that amazing smile of hers.

"So you believe now?"

"No, yes—I don't know anymore! All I know is we have to

take this wherever it leads us, and all roads point to Jerusalem. I don't know if the Stones are there, but . . ."

"Then why do you want to go there? What about our lives, our children?"

"Don't worry, nothing bad will happen. Maybe we'll just wait. It's only a few years now, isn't it?"

"Sarah . . . ?"

Barbara awoke. Our voices must have awakened her. She lifted her head, and the pillow fell to her side and onto the floor. Her cheeks were flushed.

"I'm sorry," she said, opening her eyes.

"Do you feel better now?" Sarah asked, picking the pillow up and placing it on the sofa.

"Oh, yes," Barbara said. "I'll do this a few times a day. Can't help it, really. Have you read the album?"

We told her we had.

"This may sound crazy," Barbara said, "but I think I was that woman—the one your father describes who was sold on the auction block. I didn't use to believe in reincarnation, not at first, but I've read and reread that album so many times, I think I was that slave woman. I can remember it, apart from reading it. It's a reality for me. I know that sounds crazy, but it's what I feel. You know, we're here more than once, just like him."

"Would you like to keep it?" Sarah asked.

"Oh, but it's yours, it was meant for you," Barbara said. "We have all been that woman, at one time or another. Sometimes it's my turn, sometimes it's yours. I'm not saying I can prove any of this. In a way, it's like a primitive belief—we know it because we know it. My ideas have certainly changed over the years. Philip died thinking I didn't believe—'too educated,' he used to say. And he was right. But now . . . now, we're close to the end, aren't we, Sarah?"

"How long?" Sarah asked.

"Oh, I think it'll be the year 2000, give or take. Who knows if we've been counting correctly, anyhow? We've changed calendars so many times. But soon, I think. Then he'll come again, or to be more accurate, he'll make himself known to us. He is here, of course, you can see that now, can't you?"

"Barbara," I said, "where do you think the Messiah Stones are?"

"The Stones? There's so much evil in the world, so much. I think the Stones protect us somehow. Maybe they act like a marker placed at the scene of the crime. I think they were once in Poland. It would be logical. Now, maybe in Jerusalem . . . waiting. I've only seen part of the story, and it's late for me."

We remained with Barbara for the rest of the afternoon. Then we returned home, leaving the album on the sofa next to her chair.

It was hers.

Chapter 4

MIRACLE AT
THE MAYFLOWER

SARAH HAD CHANGED. She seemed even quieter now, more contemplative, always thinking. She stared out the window of the plane on the flight home, barely speaking to me. She wasn't angry at all, just somewhere else. When I could get her attention, she turned toward me, but was in a daze.

I think I've always been in love with Sarah. To my eyes, she's always reminded me of a painting by Toulouse-Lautrec he called *The Girl with the Red Hair*. It's a painting in profile of a beautiful young girl, who actually doesn't resemble Sarah—in physical appearance, I mean—but has that same strong quality about her. It is a beauty that goes deep beneath the surface to the very soul of the person. But it is also a strength, an honesty. Here is a person who is unafraid of the dark, but if she sees it, she enters it.

Sarah has always been that special person to me, probably from the day we first met. Now we were on a journey together that would take us to places yet unknown. Did I begin by saying this was a mystery? If I did, I was only partly correct: it was life itself that was the mystery, and I didn't know if I was supposed to be afraid, or to embrace it with anticipation.

I'd agreed to leave for Jerusalem, but I have to admit I still had my doubts. It was true that the album had named us, and I couldn't explain the way it looked, but we were now contemplating a pretty big step, something I never would have even considered without Sarah. We'd traveled to so many places together since we'd taken that first trip eleven years earlier on our honeymoon to Paris. But this was entirely different.

Barbara had moved us deeply that afternoon. Before we left, she fell asleep again in our presence, but Sarah and I did not immediately get up to go. It would have been rude to just leave.

We studied the album once more. The drawings had not lost any of their incredible vividness and luster. The people remained sharp and real in miniature, the tears on the faces of the slaves almost reflected the light in Barbara's room. Sarah touched each page with tenderness, yet also with a tentativeness. These were not ordinary sheets of paper.

"I have an idea," she said. "Something I've been thinking about."

"About Jerusalem?"

"No, about Bertucci."

"Who?" I had forgotten.

"The government man who met your father with Dr. Anderson. If he's still alive, we should talk to him. Maybe he'll put us a few steps closer to the Stones. In a way, though, I'm not so sure what we can find out on our own, John. Maybe we just have to wait—be at the right place at the right time, and wait."

Some minutes passed. An attendant gently opened the door and stuck her head in to take a look. She saw that Barbara was sleeping and quietly withdrew.

I looked at this old woman carefully. She had lived a long life, a unique life in many respects. She had been given a view of what lies beyond the horizon of our breathing lives. I was beginning to understand what she said: that there are many people alive today who are given the same view. To think that life ends—forever—when we die is as foolish as thinking that a seed dies when it's placed in the ground, or that a bird dies when it disappears over the hill.

Sarah and I were now among those who could understand what our ancestors had always known, and what we'd forgotten in our yearning to invent spinning jennies and computer chips: that life is a passage, not an end. The great discoveries were not penicillin, or flight, or even space exploration. These did not alter *who* we were as human beings. The great discoveries were about the truth of our being, the reason for our existence. "There has to be a reason!" Joshua always said as I read bedtime stories to him at night, and he was right. We had lost sight of the reason we were here.

Barbara helped us understand that.

All my adult life, I had avoided such topics as the search for the root of Good and Evil, judgments that a historian can never make with impunity. We had a recent president who once categorized our adversaries as an evil empire. At the time,

I had joined in the laughter at this remark, but now I knew I had been wrong. They had been evil, and all he was doing was stating that fact. It was a simple truth, just as Sarah and I were uncovering another simple truth—what Martha Schmitt referred to as the "food" of life. This was the sustenance that sustained our hope after centuries of war and destruction. Our quest for the Eternal was so instinctive that to deny it was as foolish as a fish denying its need for water, or a bird its dependence on air for flight. I could now see the validity of this truth, although I was still being pulled, like the slave child, in divergent directions.

Was Sarah also being pulled? Was Barbara correct when she said that women see certain things first, that it is their legacy? These were questions that refused to go away.

When Barbara awoke, she talked about her work with primitive people during the 1930s. This had been an exciting time for her, she said. She asked us if we had children. We told her. She said she envied us and regretted never having any children. She loved children, but when Philip never came back, she couldn't see herself marrying again.

"We were married ten years," she said. "I gave up my freedom, to a large extent. We tried to have a baby, but it never happened. Oh, they gave us reasons, but who cares? I had my work. We all lose something in living. Does that sound regretful? That's why primitive societies always fascinated me. They are so close to nature, they see birth and death each day. It's part of the natural order of things. They understand loss."

"Is it nature, or something else?" Sarah asked.

"Ah, Sarah, you're beginning to catch on!" Barbara said with animation.

"Something above nature," Sarah said.

"Yes," Barbara said with a sudden burst of energy. "Primitives are closer to the source of life; there is less distance between them and God's light. We're too smart for our own good, aren't we? We have theories, but little understanding. We forget how much longer their wisdom has survived than our relatively recent—what should I call it?—trivia? We're too smart by half. We've buried our primitive sides, and now we're paying for it."

I still wanted to ask her so many questions I didn't know where to begin. For starters, why did she think the Messiah Stones might be in Poland?

"Yes, I think they could be, John," she said. I sat amazed. I had not verbalized the question—I had only thought it.

"But look around," Barbara continued, "and I think you'll see a change. There's something in the air, and people can sense it. Something is coming—it always does when we've hit bottom. Our needs are deeper because our lives are emptier. We're less sure of ourselves. I can see it even here—it's on television every day. We've lost so much. It's time to regain the sense of who we really are."

I was trying to unravel too many threads at once. I was used to a more logical sequence of events. But what an amazing person Barbara was! As I looked at her, I was only sorry about one thing: that I hadn't known her when she was younger. I was sorry to leave her.

We did leave, though, and, like pilgrims of old, took the flight back to Pennsylvania.

THAT NIGHT, BACK HOME, Sarah and I put the boys to bed and sat down at the kitchen table with the letters in front of us. It was time to unravel a few of the threads.

First, we reread all the letters. We shared our memories of the extraordinary drawings and my father's letter to us in the album. We analyzed our encounters with Stanton and Barbara. We reviewed what I could remember of what Martha Schmitt had said. We went over all of it again and again, and came to a single simple conclusion: For some reason, Sarah and I had been chosen—perhaps along with others—to bear witness to the arrival of the Messiah in the year 2000.

We believed it—didn't we?

But where were the Stones?

Were we supposed to find the Stones?

Sarah had been silent for a while. She doodled with a pencil on a pad, played with a wayward strand of hair, then looked up at me.

"Why didn't the dog bark?" she asked. "Why didn't he bark?"

"What dog?" I said.

"It's a classic line from a Sherlock Holmes story. You see, Holmes deduced that at a critical juncture in this particular story, a dog should have barked, but didn't. There was no barking. It should've happened, but didn't, and that was the point, that was the clue. Its absence is what interested Holmes!"

"What's absent here?" I asked.

"Well, let's assume for the sake of the argument that Dr. Allison, Dr. Anderson, Ari, and your father are telling the truth—of what they discovered in the fifties, its tremendous spiritual power, its fantastic meaning for mankind. Don't you see, John?"

"See what?"

"They didn't bark! Why keep it a secret? Why not shout it from the rooftops? And then, look what they do instead, or what your father does: They go to all the trouble of writing letters, leaving clues, creating a mystery out of something that should've been much simpler. You see what I mean. It's too complicated by half, to use Barbara's phrase. The simple solution would've been to proclaim it to the world, hold a news conference, write a book, write five books like Moses did, show everyone those fantastic drawings . . . just shout it out: 'The Messiah has been here, is here, is coming again!' "

Sarah held the letters in her hand as proof of her thesis.

"But, no," she said. "We're not given this simplicity. Instead, we're given complexity, a maze, a mystery. Why didn't the dog bark, John?"

"Because it was too early," I said.

"Exactly! Your father and the archaeologists stumbled onto the greatest discovery of all time—but too soon! It was a true time capsule whose time had not yet come. They were forty-five years too early! Who would have believed them? Just try going around telling people that the Messiah is coming, that the world is coming to an end . . . see what happens to you, John! Look at the early Christians. They probably also believed that the Kingdom of God was at hand. Look what happened to them."

"But they had proof."

"Who had proof?"

"The Christians . . . my father, the archaeologists . . . the drawings, the Stones themselves! Those couldn't be explained away."

"But the Stones disappeared," Sarah said.

"But they saw them, didn't they?"

"They certainly did—especially one man who had the power to do something about it."

"Who?"

"Bertucci."

Sarah swept a lock of her red hair in place behind her ear.

"Bertucci must've known what the team found. Maybe they were on some sort of clandestine mission. Maybe it was the CIA, who knows? Crazier things have happened. But try to remember what the times were like, John, in the mid-fifties. People were afraid of their own shadows. Communists, flying saucers, men from Mars, H-bombs. Remember the movies with the giant ants, the killer blobs, the creatures from the black lagoons? Those weren't science fiction fantasies for children, John. Those were reflections of real fears people had. Now, really for the first time, their entire world could instantly explode into a giant mushroom cloud with the simple press of a button. Can you imagine the fear and panic that would've spread if it was announced, and confirmed, that something as real and powerful as the Messiah Stones had been discovered?

Look what the government did to suppress the UFO crashes in the desert in Arizona in the late forties."

"Wasn't it in the New Mexico desert?"

"They were everywhere!" Sarah exclaimed. "People were seeing them in their sleep!"

"So you think Bertucci—the government—concealed what they found in the Holy Land and is still hiding the truth?"

"I don't know, but in one respect it doesn't matter at all, does it? If what we've found out is accurate, then we'll know soon enough. Anyhow, *we* found out! We have your father to thank for that."

So, it was my father again! How could someone who was absolutely out of my life for so long suddenly reappear with such a presence? I was being led along by the hand, like a child.

"He wanted us to find out for ourselves, didn't he?" she asked.

"Okay," I said, "let's accept for the moment that Bertucci, as a representative of the government—by the way, whose government? Ours? The Israelis'?"

"Maybe both, maybe others. Does it really matter?"

"The mother of all conspiracies—is that what you're suggesting, Sarah?"

"There's another famous quote that comes to mind, courtesy of that famous detective."

"Holmes?"

"Sherlock himself, dear John, who said that when you eliminate all the solutions that prove impossible, what you're left with, however improbable, must be the truth."

"So what are you saying?"

"I'm saying someone didn't want the world to learn about the Messiah Stones—probably still doesn't—and it has to be someone or some group, with enough influence to make it stick. And I'll go further: I think they have the proof."

"Go on."

"Men—and women—can resist anything, except temptation, as the saying goes. Remember Pandora, John? We're human—we have to look inside the box. Someone knows the Stones exist and can prove it."

"Bertucci?"

"I think we're close, John."

"How close?"

Her idea was simple. Sarah believed that the Messiah Stones existed—somewhere. She believed what the letters told us, and, probably most of all, she believed Barbara. She could not deny the luminous images in the album that we had held in our hands. But she also believed that there were others who knew about the Stones. What she proposed was for us to contact different government offices and simply inquire about the discovery that had been made in Israel in the mid-1950s and that was being kept in safekeeping in their files. We were going to beat the bushes and see if a snake crawled out.

"Somewhere, someone will react," she said.

"What if they don't?" I asked. "It's been forty years, Sarah. Even if there is a record somewhere, even if the Stones exist somewhere, why would anyone remember? Besides, they could all be dead."

"Like Stanton? Like Barbara? We have to start somewhere,

don't we? Maybe we're being helped along the way, John. You're not the only one having dreams—no, don't ask, I don't remember the details, just the feeling. Anyway, it'll be easier to make the calls from here than from Jerusalem."

"So, we're going, aren't we?" I asked hesitantly.

Sarah's doodles filled a whole page—smiling faces, frowning faces, balloons, stars, crosses. She was actually a talented artist.

"In another age," she said, looking down at her handiwork, "we would pray and say we are in the Lord's hands. Who knows—perhaps we are."

"Sarah, I have only one other question."

"Just one?"

"Why Poland?"

We had quizzed Barbara, but she had refused to explain this cryptic remark of hers. She said the answer would come to us, as all the other pieces had. In time. It had come to her in a dream, and dreams were very personal, weren't they?

Were they? Or were they something else instead, a kind of dialogue between our spiritual selves and the Creator? Was this something else we had lost in the psychoanalytic smoke of the last hundred years?

I needed a breather, and got one.

It was Saturday morning, and all government offices in Washington and environs were closed until Monday. We had a couple of days to think and to refine our plan of action. One of the things that had bothered me over the last few days was the speed at which events were happening. As I said, I was much more comfortable with a regular, orderly sequence of days, probably because I was an academic and followed a regulated, predictable schedule. In my own life—my desk, my office, my checkbook—I was pretty haphazard about things. But when it came to classes, I was a stickler for punctuality. Each day a paper was late, I deducted one more grade. It didn't make me too popular, but it definitely got the papers in on time.

Also, over the weekend, Sarah and I had a number of chores with the boys we couldn't get out of. In fact, we looked forward to doing them; it would take our minds off things even for a few hours and put a little enjoyable, mindless trivia back in our schedule.

Then at breakfast Saturday morning—the boys were still asleep—Sarah wondered what the impact of a Messiah would have on Joshua and Oliver. Would their lives as boys end? What would happen to them? It was a frightening thought, so we stopped talking about it.

But I had made quite a journey in the last few days, I realized. My visit to Stanton's office seemed so long ago. I was no longer a rational, pragmatic, academic thinker whose vision extended only as far as the tip of his nose. I was instead a modern prophet, a seer, an apocalyptic explorer whose waking moments were now filled with conversations about magical drawings, radiant Messiah Stones, and a slave in Maryland who was not really a slave at all.

All of this was happening to me, to us, not because of anything we did, but because some force outside of us was directing traffic and we were simply on the road. I closed my eyes and sipped the black coffee Sarah had made. I could not absorb what was happening in all its totality. Would I ever?

In a way, I was laughing at myself, because I knew I was no prophet. If I had an overabundance of anything, it wasn't vision, but pride—pride, that is, mixed with a heavy sprinkling of doubt that I admitted to myself only in private moments.

I was elected to drop the boys off at a birthday party down the road. Sarah said she had some research to do at the college library.

"Just a long shot. You take care of the boys, John."

I liked taking care of the boys, but usually found that I didn't have enough time for them. Today, as usual for a January day in our neck of the woods—literally woods, since our contemporary was stuck away on three acres off a county road—the ground was covered with old snow awaiting new snow.

It took me about fifteen minutes to help the boys into their coats, boots, hats, and mittens, and then, at the last minute, Oliver remembered that the birthday present Sarah had bought for his friend was upstairs in the hall closet. Finally, on time, as it turned out, present and boys in hand, I dropped them all off. When I returned home, I decided to try to take my mind off things and relax. Long ago, in high school, a favorite teacher of mine told me to go to the movies before a big test, to get my mind off things, and it usually worked.

So I popped a movie into the VCR. It was *E.T.* The boys had been watching it, for the hundredth time probably, and the tape picked up in the middle.

The house was unusually quiet. Relaxed and alone, I fell asleep in front of the television.

I had a dream.

If you had asked me a few days before, I would've said I didn't dream, or didn't usually remember my dreams. But now, so much had changed. Dreaming had become just another channel of consciousness for me.

In my dream, I was an old man at the end of my life. I could see myself sitting on a rock at the entrance to a cave. I was very short and wore the simple clothing of a peasant, perhaps a farmer. I could see sandals on my feet. I had a thin, sparse beard with a few gray hairs and wore one of the large cone-shaped hats that keep the sun and rain out of people's faces in the fields of China and Vietnam.

I was out of breath, having hiked up to the top of the hill where I now sat. I could see that it was dusk and there was no one else about. I was weak, very weak, as I raised myself up and walked toward the mouth of the cave. I took small steps and walked slightly bent forward. The years had not been kind to me.

At the entrance to the cave, I found an old oil lamp resting on a hook on the wall. It was lit, giving off a faint light in the surrounding darkness. I gently lifted it off the wall and held it at arm's length in front of me as I journeyed deeper into the blackness.

I could see that I—the old man—was afraid. He trembled as he walked. Was it cold? Was he ill? It was cooler inside the cave, and wet. He heard the sounds of an animal in the distance, the quick flutter of wings, and saw a flash of eyes dart across his path as something like a bat scurried into the safety of a nearby hole.

But he continued on his journey. I was relieved and yet anxious that he continued. This was no idle nighttime excursion into an unknown corner of a mountain.

I could feel what the old man was feeling as readily as I could feel the beat of my own heart. I was indeed the old man, not just in a dream but in life, perhaps a former life. This came to me as I saw him advance deeper into the cave, and I knew it was true.

Then, tired and trembling—it was difficult to catch his breath—the old man stepped out into a vast open chamber deep in the bosom of the mountain. He held the lantern higher to see better, and as he did I could see a smile emerge on his face. There were other lanterns there, hanging on the wall, unlit. He was in a round room of sorts, with no hint of life. There was nothing at all there—nothing, that is, except for one monk seated on a large rock against a side of the cave wall.

The old man smiled as he saw the monk, who was also an old man, even older than I was in my dream. He sat on his chair of stone and gazed into the empty silence of the cave room. He seemed to be waiting. For me?

I lit all the lamps, one after another, in the circle around the monk. The room glowed in brightness as I stepped toward the monk and sat on the cold ground in front of him, looking up. For some time we sat in silence; for I knew that it was in silence that we would begin to speak. And I knew how difficult it was to be silent, especially when there was something that needed to be said. I would show the monk I could be silent. I would pass this first test.

I would not speak first. My presence alone was a statement. I would wait. He would know when to begin. He had been in this situation before. He was more experienced. Then, when he finally did speak, I was surprised by the sound of his voice. It was warm and deep, not old and decayed, like mine.

He said, "It is a long journey up this mountain."

"Yes," I could hardly answer.

"I hope you will find what you seek. Many seek, these days."

"I seek you, master."

"We are old men. What do you want in life that you have not yet found?"

"I do not seek life, master. I seek death, final death: I do not want to be born again. I want this life to be the last. I do not want to return. Teach me how, master, so I will have final peace."

As I said these words, the monk made me face one side of the cave wall. I could see the blackness of deep space, the flickering of countless stars in the universe, and a huge, spinning wheel with glittering spokes as it rotated past us in its travels through time. The vision faded from the wall and into the night.

"You will be dead soon," the monk said. "It is too late to teach you these things. You cannot learn in the blink of an eye what takes a lifetime to teach. True wisdom is not words, but feeling."

"I must learn, master," I said. "I am weary of this world. I am weary of returning, of finding pain again. Teach me—I will listen with my last strength."

"You have come a long way up this mountain, my friend. It is not an easy journey. You have a kind face."

"Thank you, master."

The monk gazed down at me. I looked deeply into his eyes. I could see myself, as though in a mirror, in my old age. I did not like what I saw.

"I will tell you what you have to do," he said. "It is a test, the most difficult of all, for in it you must lose the burden of your humanity. But if you pass this test, your soul will be removed from the wheel of time and you will not return to this world. You will be safe, outside of time and pain. But first, you must pass this final test. Few pass."

"I will pass it," I said. My breathing became shallow and quick. I felt a deep chill inside my bones.

"You must try very hard," the monk said. "You must try beyond your endurance. The world is not easy. We carry it like a huge weight on our back up the face of the mountain. It teaches bitter lessons we must learn. And even when we think we have learned, there are still yet other lessons awaiting us. It is not easy to step off the wheel."

"What must I do, master?" I asked, growing weaker.

"You must not cry out. Whatever happens, you must remain silent. It is only through silence that you will pass this most difficult test."

"I will," I said.

I could see the dim glow of the oil lamps get dimmer in my view and flicker in the distance. The cold, hard floor of the cave beckoned to me. I lay down and rested on my back. I looked up at the roof of the cave and closed my eyes. My breathing quickened. The monk's voice passed into the silence of the distant walls and disappeared in the shrill buzz of my mind.

Suddenly, I was conscious and vibrant with energy. The flickering lamps had gone out and I found myself deep inside a pitch-black enclosure, surrounded on all sides by complete darkness. I spread my arms out, pushing with my elbows against the vast emptiness, as far as I could. I could feel wet walls surrounding me. They were warm and pressed against me. My palms moved up and down these walls, trying to grasp onto something, but unable to do so. The walls pressed closer to me, enveloping my entire body, surrounding me in a bath of wet, warm ether. I could feel the smooth, comforting force— the walls of being, of time, of home—the walls encasing me, encircling my entire body, pressing closer and closer on all sides—as my arms were forced back against my stomach.

The walls, wet and warm. The darkness, complete.

All at once, I could feel another force, this one outside the walls. It was rhythmic and powerful, a pulse with a life of its own. It controlled the walls. It pulsed, and beat and squeezed the walls, which in turn pulsed, and beat and squeezed me. My arms were now pressed tightly against my sides. I was unable to reach out toward the wet and warm walls. Now again—a pulse, a push—that rhythmic squeezing which grew more frequent and more intense, more powerful as the force tried to expel me into the world beyond the walls and the ether—into the darkness and the fear of a universe beyond the safety and comfort of my walls.

Then, with a final intensity, greater than before, I was squeezed forward as though into a narrow cavity—back in my mind toward the mouth of the cave, but not the cave— compressed and squeezed into a narrow passage too small for my arms and shoulders. I was now merely an object inside this hot and wet world, pushed forward and down through a narrow passage. How long would I be pushed? How long? The pain was in my arms, my back, my shoulders. My head itself seemed to collapse . . . out of shape until it could not be squeezed anymore.

I could not endure this journey, this pain . . . and all at once, at the extreme edge of my endurance, a huge rhythmic pulse squeezed every part of me—and head forward, I was expelled through the hot, wet mouth of the cave into a bright light—I had never seen a light so bright—as enormous hands grasped my head and guided my final passage into the world of birth and being.

I was born again, held upside down by my feet, cold and dazed, greased with the blood of my cruel passage, displayed like a trophy for all to see, in a strange room among strangers. My warm, comforting world was gone, and now I was naked to the ravaging of nature.

I was a girl.

I was born into a noble house. I was a princess.

As I grew into childhood, I was given all the advantages of nobility and privilege. I enjoyed the special life only wealth could bring: tutors, fine food, thick wooden furniture that was constantly polished by servants, wonderful clothes of many colors, and so many toys! I held big dolls in my small hands and slept with them in my bed. My pillows were soft and made of the finest goose feathers.

I was special, and so was my world, except for one problem: I was born mute. No words could pass my lips. Not one sound, not one cry, had been formed by my voice since my birth. My tutors had been unable to teach me to speak. Specialists of all kinds had been brought to our castle, even from faraway lands, but none had been able to propose a cure for this silent disease.

I could not speak.

Yet, I was a beautiful little girl, and happy. I was a princess. My parents were devoted to me.

As I grew older into young womanhood, I remained silent. I spent most of my days on our royal estate, riding horses or reading in the gardens. One day, as I was out riding, I crossed the path of a young man from a neighboring estate, someone I had not seen since childhood. I liked him. We began to spend our days together, until we discovered we were in love. He asked me to marry him, and, with my parents' permission, we were wed, for he, too, was of royal blood.

Our wedding was the event of the season in our kingdom. There was much joy in all the homes—for a princess had been wed. And I loved my new husband greatly.

With the passage of time, we had a child together, a baby girl. She, too, was beautiful and a princess. I loved her more than life itself and devoted all my time to her well-being and education. She was perfect in form, beautiful in spirit, and she was kind.

I did not think I would ever love another human being as much as I loved my daughter.

We spent our days together in complete happiness. One day, when she was a young girl, we went out riding together on a new trail, far from our estate. She was an excellent rider. We rode for hours, deep into unfamiliar woods. All of a sudden, out of nowhere, a freshly cut tree fell and blocked our path. We halted; the horses reared in fear. Before we realized what was happening, two men jumped out of the bushes and pulled us down off our mounts. The horses reared. My daughter screamed. I fought with all my strength against these men, but could not defeat them. They were more powerful, and very wicked.

One of the men punched me hard across the face and knocked me to the ground. The other twisted my daughter's arms behind her back and tied her wrists together with a length of rope he removed from around his waist. He pulled her, screaming and kicking, into the woods. The man who had punched me followed them.

I tried to stand, to get up, to help my daughter. I stumbled and tripped. I could see my daughter's eyes, wide with fear. She turned her face toward me as her attackers continued to drag her across the thorny ground. She cried and begged and pleaded. I could not look. My entire body seemed to convulse in a spasm of fear. I could feel the explosive pounding in my chest, the trickle of blood down my nose where I had been punched, the pain in my throat that I could bear no longer. This was my daughter, the light of my life, the soul of my existence. I loved her beyond my own life. Her eyes were wide with fear, like those of an animal caught in a trap.

"No!" I screamed. "No!" I screamed again with all the force of my lungs. "No!" I screamed a third time, and the sound of my scream echoed through the forest like explosions beneath the earth.

"*NO!*"

My body trembled as I saw my daughter for the last time—
and woke up at the monk's feet, in a ball, sobbing.

"It is the most difficult test," the monk said, "because it is
the test to overcome our humanity, our love for another. We
must overcome this last barrier if we are to step off the wheel.
You have failed this test, my friend."

I looked up at his face, at the flickering lamps on the cave
wall behind him, and I knew I would have to ride the wheel
again, spinning into a new orbit, accepting a new life, bearing
the pain of love, and finally of loss. Death would win again.

"Oh," I said in my dream, "how hard it is to be silent!"

IN THE DISTANCE, coming closer, was the sound of the VCR
automatically rewinding at the end of the movie. I was at home
in my favorite chair; the movie was over. No boy; no bicycle.

When you live your entire life a certain way, whatever way
that is, with definite beliefs, and then your cosmos is shattered
like a plate-glass window through which someone has heaved a
rock . . . you take a few deep breaths before you can continue.
That's what I did. I must've looked foolish, sitting there and
breathing like that, when Sarah walked in.

She had a genuine look of concern on her face.

"Are you all right?"

"No," I said, "but I will be. Just give me a few minutes."

I told Sarah my dream.

"What does it mean?"

"Good question," she said. "Let's have something to eat."

Sarah made us tuna sandwiches, but I wasn't really very
hungry. My dream had been too real, haunting me now as I

tried to regain my balance. I remembered that one of the Signs of the Messiah was that we would be given the power of dreams again, which was fine by me, if only I could comprehend what my dreams were telling me!

"Maybe we'll find out later," Sarah said. "Maybe it's not so much a meaning to be discovered as a meaning to be lived."

"It was real," I said. "Much too real."

"John, do you remember what Barbara said? Didn't she say something about primitive people? What we give up when we grow up? We lose our innocence, the kind we're born with. Maybe we're supposed to get it back. Call it gut, call it faith, call it what you will, but I think that's what's happening, John. We're making progress: we're going backward!"

"What's happening to us?"

"One thing at a time. Maybe the big answers will fall into place if we can fit the small ones in first. I found one small one this afternoon, in the library."

Our college library has microfiche copies of the English editions of Jerusalem newspapers dating back to the fifties. In one of them, Sarah found a report of an archaeological find in Shiloh that promised to be of major significance. Drs. Anderson and Kurzon were quoted in the article, along with a vague description of certain "stone relics" which were unearthed. The article went on at length to discuss the period of the Second Temple in Jerusalem. In fact, the rest of the piece was a retelling of the historical narrative of how the Jews were conquered by the Roman general Titus, how the Temple was destroyed, how the Romans took the Jews off as slaves.

"I spent a good few hours reading these old newspapers,"

Sarah said. "So much has changed in the Middle East in forty years, and yet so much has stayed the same. Some of the biggest stories were about terrorist attacks, just like the one that happened last year on the bus. But it was odd."

"What was odd?" I asked.

"The way the article was written about the archaeological find in Shiloh. The news was the discovery, but it was lost in the article."

"What are you getting at?"

"Well, it's almost as though someone had rewritten the news, or replaced it with filler. It just didn't feel right."

"Sarah, now I think you're starting to dream. Let's not create mysteries where there aren't any. We've got enough to deal with."

"Where there aren't any? Take a look at this, John. Notice who the author of this article is?"

Sarah had circled the name of the author under the headline and handed me the photocopy. The headline read:

Biblical Relics Found in Shiloh
Americans Make Recent Discovery

The writer was a "Special Correspondent," Joseph Bertucci.

"Bertucci?" I said.

"You guessed it. I think Bertucci was having a really good time," Sarah said.

"But why would he use his real name?"

"Why not? No one cared, no one was looking. It's not as though people expected something to be found in Shiloh.

Maybe Bertucci was a frustrated journalist. He buried the story on page seven, John. Probably got wind that they were going to print something, and had this substituted for it."

"Why not kill the whole thing?"

"Maybe it was too late, but if he made it innocuous enough, no one would notice. Pretty cute! You know what, John? I think we should locate Mr. Bertucci. He's an old friend of your father's, isn't he?" Sarah said with a chuckle.

"Sarah, all this happened forty years ago! This guy is probably dead, or retired somewhere. We'll never find him. Remember who he worked for—they don't just give out phone numbers!"

"No, he's not dead, and he's not retired. As a matter of fact, he's still working for the government, and it is the CIA."

"He what?" I said in exasperation.

"Joseph Bertucci is alive and well and living in Virginia."

"How do you know?"

"Because I spoke with him, that's how I know."

"Wait a minute, Sarah. You'd better back up a few hundred miles and take me through this very slowly. Remember, I'm only a Ph.D.; you're the mystery buff!"

"Look," Sarah said, "we've got to assume our government was involved—is involved—in a major cover-up, even if it did happen forty years ago. Someone realized how devastating these Stones were and decided to put the whole thing under lock and key. Okay, let's assume CIA. Why not? It's as good a place to start as any. Anyhow, they'd have jurisdiction. It happened outside the U.S. And something else pushed me in that direction. Our government, like any government, is a bureaucracy, and a bureaucracy refuses to die—if a file exists, it keeps existing, somewhere. All we have to do is find the right drawer. So I called the CIA and said I wanted to speak to Joseph Bertucci. I said it was a personal emergency. In a way, it is, isn't it?"

"It's Saturday!"

"I know. They said they were closed. I gave them my name and number at the library."

"So?"

"So he called me back."

"I don't believe it!" I said.

"I did have a little bit of help," Sarah said. "God helps those who help themselves. He sent out a boat and I got in."

"You were ready to get in," I said.

"You can almost say I was waiting for it to arrive."

For some reason, I was a lot calmer now.

"Let's not get too mystical about this, John, but I have the distinct impression that we're being helped along the way. Don't you?"

"All I know for sure is that you're one hell of a detective, and if we ever get to the bottom of this, it'll be because of you!"

"Because of me? Well, you might just as easily say it's because of you, or even Bill McGowan," she said. "Maybe he's at my shoulder pointing me in the right direction. What do you think?"

I looked at her and didn't know what to say.

Bertucci had agreed to see us on Monday, but not in his office. He specified a restaurant in downtown Washington and gave Sarah directions to get there from Dulles Airport.

I was going back to Washington, this time with Sarah.

For the rest of the day, and the next, Sarah and I lost ourselves in the wonderful, mind-numbing minutiae of our boys and family. If you had asked me, I would have confided that I was a very lucky man indeed.

I had no dreams that I can recall on Saturday or Sunday night.

When I called in sick again on Monday morning, our department secretary was plainly disapproving. For a moment, I felt like telling her the truth, that we were tracking down ancient Stones which prophesied the coming of the Messiah and the end of the world. We only had a few years left, and I was tempted to suggest that if she had any unused sick days or vacation time accumulated, she should take them now.

But my more reasonable side took hold of me—she was actually a nice person, but convinced it was her duty to be up-to-date on everyone's life—and I decided to concoct a more believable story, knowing she'd never accept the truth anyway.

I gave her the first excuse that came to mind. If I had consciously tried to pick it, it would never have been this one.

"It's my father, Ruth. I didn't want to say anything earlier in the week."

I let her imagination fill in the rest. Her tone of voice changed immediately, now that she had a chance to express her sympathy.

"Oh, I'm so sorry, Professor. I didn't know."

"I'd appreciate it if you'd keep this confidential, until the tests come back. I may have to take a trip out to see him."

"Oh?" she asked, after a pause.

"New Mexico," I said, and she appeared satisfied.

I arranged for my classes to be covered by a colleague and, in a few instances, rescheduled. Ruth was very helpful, now that she was privy to what she believed were the facts.

Sarah had been able to arrange for a baby-sitter. We decided to drive down to Washington to meet with Bertucci.

THE HIGHWAY WAS long and flat. It had been quite a few months since Sarah and I had taken a drive of any kind without the boys. We shared the driving and made one stop along the way. We had left early and were eager to get there.

"You know," Sarah said, turning off the radio and allowing me in on her thoughts as we cruised along, "there's a catch-22 in religion most people have trouble with. It's pretty basic."

"I was hoping you might be thinking about something else."

"In order to believe," she said, without missing a beat, "you have to believe. It says somewhere that in order to please God, you have to believe he exists. Pretty basic, I think."

"If you believe."

"But even if you don't believe. What I mean is, we believe in each other, don't we? We give each other the basic respect that is due—we acknowledge each other's existence. Doesn't it seem reasonable that God would expect the same fundamental courtesy—belief—before extending himself in any way toward us? It's hateful to be ignored."

"But we know each other. We don't know God."

"There's the catch, John, because unless we allow ourselves to know him, he won't reveal himself to us. Simple, huh?"

"Who makes the first move?"

"Depends on who needs it more."

"Needs what?" I asked.

"Salvation."

"This is getting too deep for me," I said.

Sarah turned the radio on. We listened to a mindless call-in program about politics. After a while, she turned it off again. Within five minutes, it was impossible to recall anything we'd heard.

Sarah said, "One of the problems I've always had is why he made the search for him so difficult. It should be evident, clear, plain as day—certainly if it's as fundamental as all that. But the exact opposite seems to be the case: The better educated we become, the more we read and learn, the stronger our skepticism. Now, this . . . a Messiah? Do you actually believe, John?"

"Yes, of course. Why do you keep asking me?" Actually, she hadn't kept asking. I wore my frustrations and doubts on my sleeve like stains I couldn't remove.

She said, "I'll tell you what I really think. I believe we're in the middle of one of the greatest discoveries any person can have. I don't yet know how we got here, or even how we'll get to where we're going the rest of the way, but I believe, John, I believe with all my heart, that we *are* being spoken to . . . by someone, or some force, by some special presence. It's like a hymn echoing in a cathedral, but the church is so crowded we can't see above the heads of the parishioners around us. The voice lifts up to the roof, and we can't quite place its origin. We just hear it and know it's there."

Sarah's comments drifted off as she curled her hands in front of her, trying to give a physical expression to the hymn as it drifted up to the cathedral ceiling.

". . . a power beyond us . . ."

"Is it God?" I asked.

"God, or a Messiah . . . beyond us, yet in us," she said, and then she did something I had never seen her do in all the time I'd known her: She cried, softly, like a child, but with a smile on her face.

"Tears of joy," she said, "but also of fear. I'm afraid. I don't know, John, maybe we'll be happier when we find whatever it is . . . but I don't know. . . ."

"Yes," I said. "I understand."

I turned the radio back on. The call-in talk show continued for the remainder of the drive like the din of mindless raindrops on a tin roof. But it filled the silence between us. The host assured his audience that he was in a daily pursuit of the truth. When he was not pursuing the truth, he was selling subscriptions to his newsletter, plugging his books, or offering his listeners everything from garlic pills to iced tea. Most of the callers were in search of . . . the truth? Getting themselves heard? Something else?

We arrived about noon and found the restaurant Bertucci had chosen. We parked in a municipal parking lot and walked the two blocks back to the restaurant.

It was another bright, cold, clear day in Washington. This was my second trip to this city in the past week. I thought of Stanton. Should we call him? What would we tell him? I decided against it.

In a way, I was retracing my father's steps, back in time,

back to him. All along, he entered my thoughts at the oddest moments, as I wavered back and forth in my feelings toward him.

When we entered the restaurant, we asked the maître d' for Mr. Clinton's table, the name Bertucci had asked Sarah to use.

"Yes," the maître d' said with some assurance. "Mr. Clinton called and said there'd been a slight change of plans. He hoped you'd understand. He won't be coming."

"He won't be coming?" I asked with exasperation. "We drove all the way—"

"Well, no," the man said, confused and at a loss; then, as if he'd thought of an acceptable consolation, he said, "But would you like a table anyway?"

Sarah looked at the maître d' for a moment without speaking. I could see that she was thinking. "Did he say anything else?" she asked.

"Just that he hoped you'd understand."

"No, thank you," she said to him. "Let's go, John."

We left a somewhat confused maître d' and walked outside.

"What next?" I asked.

"We wait."

"Wait? Where, here in the street?"

"I think our friend Bertucci is playing with us, John. Maybe this is some kind of cat-and-mouse Washington game. I don't know."

"We're not spies," I said.

"I know that, John. I'll vouch for you and you'll vouch for me, won't you?"

"You think he'll show up?"

"I think he's here."

We must have waited fifteen minutes. It was cooler than I thought, maybe because we weren't moving.

Then, walking up to us as if he'd just met a couple of old friends, a man said, "Sarah! John! What a small world!"

It was Bertucci. He asked us to accompany him, and, like tourists, we obeyed. Turning the corner, we entered a hotel and walked through the ornate lobby to a restaurant off the hall.

I was glad to be inside and sitting.

Bertucci must've been in his sixties, but appeared younger and more vigorous. He sported a healthy tan and had a full head of jet-black hair, with only slight traces of gray neatly etched along the sides. He said nothing until the waiter arrived to take our order.

He removed a gold cigarette case from his jacket and extracted a cigarette.

"Politically incorrect," he said, "but emotionally satisfying."

He offered Sarah and then me a cigarette. I couldn't believe my eyes: For the first time in five years or more, Sarah was smoking.

"Thanks," she said.

I declined Bertucci's offer.

"This is my favorite hotel," he said. "The Mayflower was used for Calvin Coolidge's inauguration ball. Did you know that? We're due for a reevaluation of his presidency. Didn't say much, but quite a classy guy. JFK used to bring his girlfriends here, too. Another classy president, but highly overrated. I suppose you can say it's been a favorite watering hole for both parties. I first crossed its portals in 1953, John, when I met your father. Or thereabouts. Some things get fuzzy. Had no trouble recognizing you, though, did I, John? You even walk like him. I was about his age, mid-twenties. Been out of Georgetown a couple of years by then. They tried to tell me I was too young. But I was filled with piss and vinegar in those days. Pardon my French."

The waiter arrived with our drinks. Bertucci ordered a Chivas on the rocks. Sarah had a glass of white wine. I had a Diet Pepsi with a twist of lemon.

"Cheers!" Bertucci said.

"We appreciate your seeing us," Sarah said. "We weren't sure you'd come."

"Oh, I was looking forward to it. Sorry for the false start. I wanted to make sure you were alone. Not that anyone cares anymore. It's just that I consider our meeting personal almost, kind of closing a chapter on unfinished business. I'm glad you found me. It's been a long time since anyone cared about all of this."

"Can you talk to us?" Sarah asked.

"The Company doesn't really know much about . . . this. Just a few of us, who kind of took a special, personal interest over the years. Most of the original people are dead. It was kept within a very small circle, a few of us in the Company and a few others, here and there. You were right, Sarah—there's a file that exists. I have one. Must exist in a few other places too, I'd bet. It's hard to destroy anything these days. Create a file and you create a virus."

Suddenly, this robust individual, healthy and tan, began to

cough in a prolonged fit from deep within his chest. His face became red, and I could see thin blue veins appear like wounds around the corner of his eyes. He tried to control himself, placing his handkerchief over his mouth to mute his rasping, hacking cough.

"Too much good living," he finally said, taking a sip of water.

"Anything we can do?" Sarah asked.

"Yes," he said, "you can get me a new pair of lungs."

When the food arrived, Bertucci had regained most of his composure.

"Please," he said, indicating the dishes. "Begin. I don't think I have much of an appetite today. Actually, I don't eat much. You won't believe this, but I've lost . . . what, forty pounds? I may look like a dapper middle-aged executive, but it's all packaging. The insides are as rotten as bad cheese, and the stink is getting worse by the day. But, hey, we'll go out in style, won't we? So, you see, boys and girls—John and Sarah McGowan—if there ever was a reason for me not to talk about this, the reason is fast becoming history. You're his son, is that right?"

I nodded.

"Well, then, it's practically in the family then. It's a pleasure to meet you."

Bertucci was a short man, with fine features. His fingernails shone with clear polish. He wore a classic blue suit, and his tie looked expensive, perfectly knotted at his throat. I wondered how high his position was. Here was a man who had survived and succeeded. But the price of his success was beyond me. He paused before speaking again.

"So much to remember," he said, "and so little time to do it in. What took you so long?"

Sarah put her cigarette out. She had taken only a few puffs. I was in love with her all over again.

"We got here as fast as we could," she said.

"I'm a grandfather now," he said. "Two boys and a girl. They're in San Diego with our daughter. She's divorced. Who knows whose fault it was? She's our only child. They tried for a reconciliation, but it didn't work. The kids are the ones who suffer in the end. Don't ask me why they're in San Diego. She's a computer specialist of some sort. Says it's better there. My wife and I will see them next Christmas, unless we can get out sooner. Of course, we would need an invitation from them. Can you believe that?"

Sarah extended her hand and placed it on Bertucci's. He didn't move his.

"My wife thinks I'm on a diet, which I am, in a way. Call it a forced diet. Hell, call it whatever you want."

Bertucci ordered another Chivas on the rocks. This time I joined him. I had suddenly become a Scotch drinker.

"We were full of piss and vinegar, as I said, and we had all the answers. And they were always the same answers, whatever the questions. I can't believe people these days. There's nothing to hold on to anymore."

Bertucci drank to forget, or to remember, or both. He looked down into the caramel-colored liquid in his glass.

"What do you want to know?" he asked, looking up.

"What you remember."

"Have you found the Stones?"

"Not yet," Sarah said.

"What I remember? What I remember could fill a book. Right here in this hotel, more than forty years ago, we met with your father. We were recruiting. Your father was just one of many. We were no more than kids. God! We needed couriers, operatives, contact points between Washington and the outer circumference of the circle. I had a big map in my office, with a big circle and Washington in the middle. I was a kid on the loose in the world of all the grown-ups. This was my first assignment."

"Who was his contact in Jerusalem?" I asked.

"Dr. Kurzon. Kurzon was only a part-time archaeologist, if you can call him one at all. Most of the time he worked for us. Try to picture the tenor of the times, John and Sarah. This was a real war—not a cold war, I always hated that phrase; the only thing cold about it were the bodies killed in action—but a real war against a worldwide conspiracy that extended from Moscow to the Mediterranean to Maryland. We were on the verge of a world conflagration. Children scurried under their classroom desks, remember? Commies had secret cell meetings around the block from Macy's and Bloomingdale's. A Commie could be anyone. Sure, today we look back and make judgments, but you have to remember the times. So we planted our own seeds, here and there, under any cover that made sense. In fact, we still do. Even then we knew the Mideast was a key region, as it has been for thousands of years. It was like building a chain, link by link. Your father was just one of the many links, or so we thought."

"What do you mean?" Sarah asked.

"The Messiah Stones," Bertucci said. "Isn't that why you've come?"

She didn't answer him, not directly.

"What was he going to bring you?" she said.

"We had a deep-cover operative in Teheran who worked in the Soviet embassy. It was his product that was transmitted through Kurzon and your father. The expedition was basically a cover. Real enough, but a cover."

Bertucci lit another cigarette.

"My first assignment," he said, taking another drink, "as it turned out, was the most important of my career. For one, we lost your father after he returned to Israel. Don't misunderstand—we knew where he was, he just refused to come home. So we let him stay. For another, Kurzon made a great discovery, along with Allison. They found the block in Shiloh, then they found the Stones. It was almost by mistake. They weren't looking for anything so spectacular, and here they find the key to the kingdom! Kurzon went insane, tried to use the Stones, make miracles. You want to know what I remember?"

Bertucci held his whiskey glass in his hand and lifted it up to the light. He slowly turned the glass until the cubes began to float in a circle. He watched this slow, revolving pattern and seemed to come to a decision. Quickly, he finished his drink off and put the glass down.

"The Stones!" he said. "It was all about the Stones. Even I didn't understand at first how momentous the discovery was.

The Stones took on their own existence. The Company, Kurzon, the Israelis, Allison, even your father—everyone became focused on the Stones. First they tried to explain that huge block they found in Shiloh. But there was no explanation for it. You know what it was like? I'll tell you what it was like: It was like emptying the Red Sea and staring down at the damn footprints of the Children of Israel and the chariot tracks of the Egyptian soldiers right there in the middle of the sea—that's what it was like! You knew somehow you were in the same room as God! And then when they found the Stones themselves, and that strange ball—my God, there was some kind of uproar around these parts, I can tell you that! You see, no one knew what to make of this. What do you do with the find of the century, or even the millennium? Plus, those damn Stones glowed, they actually radiated as if they were plugged into some remote-control generator! I was, I guess, ordinary in my beliefs. Catholic, Italian by heritage, first-generation American. Made Georgetown on a scholarship. You know what my father was? A garbage man. That's right. The day he died I graduated from college. So don't tell me about discrimination!"

Bertucci seemed to be off somewhere. He paused, coming close to us.

"Do you remember the Signs of the Messiah?"

"Which one?" Sarah asked.

"The Messiah will know the power of miracles," Bertucci said. "That's what Kurzon was after. Selfish bastard!"

"He discovered the secret name for God?" I asked.

"Maybe, maybe not. Legend has it that when you invoke the

power behind this name, you actually have the ability to perform miracles."

"Kurzon!" Sarah said aloud, struck with some private insight. "The financier?"

"The same," Bertucci said, "and probably one of the richest men alive. For the last forty years, he's cornered the market on every commodity and stock imaginable. It's as though the man read tomorrow's papers today. See what I mean?"

"And Allison?" Sarah asked.

"Killed in a car accident . . . we think. Never confirmed."

"And my father?" I asked.

"Killed in battle in 1967 in the Six-Day War between Israel and the Arabs. Died a hero of Israel. He's buried on the Mount of Olives, within sight of the Western Wall."

Bertucci signaled the waiter for a refill.

"The world was simpler, easier to understand, John and Sarah. We succeeded. Link after link. Information flowed like oil through a pipeline. We were good. Sure, we kept things complicated, but only if you were looking at it from the outside. Looking from the inside out, it was easy to understand. There were good guys and bad guys, and all the bad guys were on the other side. It made no difference what you did, as long as you did it on our side. Then it was good. Their side, even if they did the same thing, then it was bad. This way, we kept it simple and we knew the rules. But when those crazy nutcakes found those Stones, we didn't know what to do. All of a sudden, there was another side, not subject to the rules. Look at it this way: No one was ready to meet his maker . . . I mean *really* meet his maker!"

The waiter brought another drink for Bertucci, and I joined him. Sarah was still nursing her single glass of wine, which I noticed she'd hardly touched.

"The last time I saw your father, we met in this hotel, in a room upstairs. We met alone. He was an interesting man, your father."

"I'm beginning to find that out," I said.

"I liked him," Bertucci said. "He did his job well. He was even able to divert large sums of cash from a Soviet account in Zurich to one of ours. Never did find out how he did this. He was from Chicago, your father. My wife was born in Chicago. Moved as a little girl. Odd, the things you remember."

Bertucci seemed to drift off into a private world. Was he thinking about his wife?

"He brought with him the latest product from Teheran. Stupid stuff, really. Redundancies. We already had most of it in the cooker. But that's when I found out what was really on his mind. You see, he had another envelope with him—this one," Bertucci said as he took a small white envelope out of his pocket and placed it in the middle of the table.

"These are, in my opinion, the most valuable photographs in the world," he said.

Sarah and I froze in anticipation.

"These are photographs of the Messiah Stones," he said.

Sarah and I looked down at the envelope he'd placed on the table in sheer disbelief. Bertucci was offering us photographic proof of the existence of the Messiah Stones. Was he giving it to us?

"All these years, no one has cared," he said. "No one has

asked, no one has cared. Until Sarah called. Your father knew what he was doing, John. He gave me these photographs and left it up to me to take the next step. You know what? I couldn't get anyone's attention. They didn't want to hear about it! They thought I was crazy."

Bertucci paused.

"They said either the Stones were real, or not real. If they were real, then what we didn't want was a panic on our hands, millions leaving on pilgrimage, giving up their jobs, their homes, who knows what? And if they were not real—no Messiah, no panic at the millennium—then I was a nut. And photographs? Pictures proved nothing. Show us the Stones, they said, which I couldn't. I'll tell you this, boys and girls, it jeopardized my career. Until I shut up about Bill McGowan, and Sarah, and Stones, and a Messiah, and judgment. I had the biggest piece of news in two thousand years, and I couldn't get arrested!"

Bertucci was impassive as he quietly sipped his drink. He puffed at his cigarette and politely blew the smoke off to the side.

"And you know the craziest part of all? They said it was a trick. Take them with you; they belong to you now. In a way, you can say you've inherited them, John."

Sarah reached out and took the envelope. I could see how much it meant to her. As she had with Barbara's album, she delicately picked it up, like a flower.

The envelope was not sealed. She turned it over, opened the flap, and reached in. She removed the photographs, which she then placed in front of us on the table. Three glowing beacons quickly appeared and illuminated our faces as if we were seated around a campfire.

It was beautiful, unbelievable, and at the same time extremely frightening.

"A trick, they said it was a trick, some kind of radioactive dust, like hands on a watch that glow in the dark . . . like a carny's trick! So they had them analyzed in the lab. Four different times. Couldn't find anything, not once. Still, they said it was a trick. They had them translated, the three languages, the Signs, the stories, the whole nine yards. You know what? I couldn't believe it. They gave them back to me, deciding the nut scenario was the safest one. So I had three souvenirs and a hell of a story to tell. Only trouble was, I had no audience."

"You were too early," I said.

"They had no faith," Sarah said.

"They didn't believe in miracles," Bertucci said. "It's not easy, even when you see a miracle, to accept it. I know."

The waiter came over to our table, unasked, and stood next to us, unspeaking, mesmerized by the three luminous objects. He had never seen anything like them before.

"I've worked hard to believe," Bertucci said. "Your father believed, probably from the beginning. He wasn't like the rest of us. He was closer to it somehow. He was caught up in it. I thought he was just another smart young man looking for a career, like the rest of us. But he wasn't. He had a calling, and he answered the call."

"Could I have another glass of wine?" Sarah asked. The waiter slowly retreated to the bar.

"What will you do?" she asked.

"Do? Old soldiers never die, they just disappear, didn't you know that? Tell me one thing, though."

"What's that?" I asked.

"What will *you* do?" Bertucci said.

"We'll find the Stones," Sarah said.

"I wish I could go with you," he said. "It's only a few more years. Then he'll be back, won't he? You know that already, don't you . . . he'll be here in the year 2000, the third millennium. Or maybe he's here already, waiting for the right moment. Is he in us? Is he out there? The Stones foretold his coming. Has he been here before, Sarah? Why were you chosen, Sarah? John? Tell me, please . . . why were you chosen?"

"We were all chosen," I said.

"You know something?" Bertucci said. "The ones you love the most are the ones you hurt the most. And you know how you hurt them the most? You ignore them."

The waiter returned with Sarah's wine. She never drank it. We left Bertucci, wondering if he would ever feel loved.

"HE WAS AFRAID," Sarah said as she sat behind the wheel of our Explorer on the drive back home. "Couldn't you see it?"

"Afraid of what? Of dying?"

"I don't think Joseph Bertucci has ever been afraid of dying. No, I think he's afraid of knowing, of seeing, afraid of what is coming. It's not that he's a murderer, or rapist, or slave trader, it's not that . . . it's just that, well, knowing the truth about the Messiah brings with it a certain responsibility, John. It sets you apart from everyone else. It makes you different, and no one wants to be different. Sure, it's easy to seek out God, but what if you find him? Your whole life takes on a new aspect. Happiness? Okay, but also responsibility. And remember: Bertucci has known all these years and had to live with his knowledge. I wonder what he's done with it? Maybe he was always waiting for tomorrow."

"But he had proof."

"I'm sure he tried to tell people, probably feebly, if his career depended on it. They used to be called Organization Men, and our Mr. Bertucci is one fine example. He who rocks the boat is dropped overboard, understand? Anyway, why should they have believed him?"

"He had the pictures. Seeing is believing, isn't it?"

"Sure, and now we do, and so did your father . . . and God knows who else. But they said it was a trick, remember? Same with the album. People have eyes, but they don't see. Think about it, John: If you had to get people to believe, how would you do it? Miracles? They'd call you Houdini and get you an agent. Truth is, it's difficult if not impossible to make believers out of most people. No, this is not a government caper at all. Bertucci and the rest of them just acted like normal human beings—disbelief, mixed with heavy doses of fear and doubt. Pretty much like the original priests who protected and hid the Stones at the same time. If the truth will set us free, John, then what? Freedom can be terrifying. No, this is about taking a step forward as your father did. Pretty scary stuff when you think about it."

We made the same single pit stop on the ride back. Sarah is an excellent driver, and, honestly, I had had one too many. It also had begun to rain as we headed north into Pennsylvania.

So many thoughts raced through my mind that I couldn't grab hold of any of them and stop it long enough for a closer examination. How had Sarah and I gotten ourselves on this road toward . . . toward where? Where were we going? Were we ready to discover the Messiah? Wasn't this in the same league as myth and superstition? No, I no longer believed it was. I had passed that barrier somewhere in the last week. Everything that was happening was converging up ahead into a single lane of truth . . . the physical existence of a Messiah and his introduction into our lives, which was only a few short years away.

Heading north, the way General Lee and his troops headed north toward a small town in Pennsylvania over a hundred years ago. What had happened to my historical perspective, my academic neutrality, the distance I had so carefully cultivated between events of the past and my view of them? I was too caught up.

I understood what Sarah meant about the fear that comes from knowing. I recalled the biblical story of Moses' being chosen by Jehovah to represent him, to lead his people, to perform miracles, to part seas. Moses declined at first, unwilling to accept the responsibility. He claimed he had a speech impediment and could not play the part of a prophet and messenger of the Lord before Pharaoh. So, too, Jesus, who at the last minute wanted the burden removed from his shoulders, the cup taken from his hand. Was this the same fear? If it was, I was afraid. I was only a spectator in the audience, not a major actor on the stage—and if they were afraid, I was petrified.

We were headed down a road that few had traveled, and none in recent memory. The book on messiahs was supposed to have been closed long ago. Now, all of a sudden, the millennium was rolling around again, and the book was being removed from the shelf of time, dusted off, and set before us.

The photographs of the Stones were safely tucked away in Sarah's bag on the backseat of the Explorer next to Joshua's soccer ball.

These thoughts raced through my mind, out of control. I had an enormous headache, and for the first time that I could remember, I was afraid to close my eyes. I might dream again!

I'm not sure if I eventually dozed off or not. Late in the evening, when we arrived home, we found the boys watching television and the baby-sitter on the phone. My headache was gone.

Everything seemed back to normal, except that we discovered an unexpected guest waiting for us in the living room, seated on the sofa and calmly reading a magazine.

"You are back!" Miss Schmitt said. "Did you have a pleasant time?"

"Yes, yes . . . we did," I said.

I introduced Miss Schmitt to Sarah.

"Good. Well, you are no doubt wondering what brings me here. I have time, I can wait, you have had a long drive. Would you like to freshen up?"

It was like being in the presence of a kind old grandmother who usually knew what you had on your mind before you thought of it yourself. But she was right. I left the room to go upstairs, and Sarah invited her to stay for dinner before I could get back. It's not that I was opposed to asking her, it's just that I wanted some normal quiet in my life again.

The boys had already eaten. I paid the sitter and she left.

"Tell me what you have learned," she said.

I started to tell her about Bertucci and the spies of two generations back, but this only bored her.

"No, no," she said. "What have you *learned*?"

Sarah retrieved her bag and brought it into the living room. The boys followed her, circling Miss Schmitt. Oliver wanted her to take a look at the toy truck he'd just gotten for his birthday.

Sarah removed the envelope and took the pictures out, placing them down on the carpet. For effect, she turned off the lights.

"Wow!" Joshua exclaimed.

"Wow!" Oliver added.

"Wow, indeed!" Miss Schmitt said. "How amazing it is— truly is—when you see it with your own eyes!"

"How'd they do it? Can I touch them? Are they hot? How'd they do it? Can you turn them off?" Joshua asked these questions in a staccato flurry of excitement.

If Oliver could have remembered them all, he would have repeated them. Instead, he merely said, "Why, Daddy?"

"I don't know," I said lamely. "It just is."

I had always prided myself on my ability to explain things to my boys. This time, however, I was at a loss.

"Daddy and I are trying to find out," Sarah said. "Right now, it's time for your bed," she concluded, switching the lights back on and returning the pictures to their envelope.

"May I see them?" Miss Schmitt asked. Sarah handed them to her.

Oliver had forgotten all about the toy truck. He asked the all-purpose question: "But why, Daddy?"

"Because," Sarah answered with the all-purpose answer. The boys moaned and complained, gave us all a kiss, and like "big boys" trundled up the stairs to put themselves to bed. This independence was something new in our household, and seemed to be working.

Oliver turned around on his way up, however, and gave me a parting comment: "You owe me a story, Daddy!"

I promised one soon.

Miss Schmitt joined us for a superb dinner that Sarah whipped up at the last minute. Her best dinners are the unplanned ones, composed of this-and-that leftovers, or "experiments," as she calls them, that she fashions out of whatever is available. Miss Schmitt and I helped slice some of the vegetables and pick the seasonings for the brown rice.

We were busy in the kitchen, working, talking, actually enjoying ourselves. It had been a long day and we were quite hungry. Sarah and Miss Schmitt had hit it off from the start.

"You have a marvelous family," Miss Schmitt said. Then she added in the next breath: "I have never been married. My father wanted me to marry. I think I wanted to marry. There was a young man once, when I was nineteen. It just didn't happen. There were excuses. What I miss most, I think, is children. They complete one's world, do they not? You are very lucky, John and Sarah. Someone must tell you this."

"Thank you," Sarah said, "but you don't have to—"

"Oh, but I do have to, Sarah, and I want to. I want to very much. First, please, can you both call me Martha?"

"Yes, Martha," Sarah said.

"May I tell you something?" Martha asked. "I believe you two have been chosen for a reason. Yes, I do believe this. Of course, your name is on the Stones, and that is reason enough. But perhaps there is more to it. Have you thought so?"

Sarah said, "I think there are others, Martha, others that we have no idea about. The Stones and the globe were not meant only for us. We're just ordinary people. The Messiah will speak to many, I'm sure, just like us."

"Is that what you've learned?" Martha asked.

"I've learned a great deal," Sarah said. "We both have. We have the letters, the photographs. We know the Signs."

"And now?" Martha asked.

"Martha," Sarah said, "it appears from everything we've read—and learned—that the Messiah is coming again in the year 2000. We're convinced of that—my God, how can I say it with such . . . I don't know . . . so matter-of-factly. Do you know what I mean?"

"I think I do," she said.

"But suppose we're too early," Sarah said, "like John's father and the others. Suppose the timing is off, and we go down this road and find nothing. Then what?"

"What harm is there?" Martha said. "And suppose, just suppose, you two have been picked, for some reason—I'll even grant you that there may be others—then can you ever live with yourself if you don't go down this road? Think about that. Being invited and not going. Oh, it's too frightening to imagine!"

We talked well past dinner. After the dessert, Martha disappeared for a few minutes and then returned with a gift she'd hidden in the hall closet.

"I almost forgot," she said. "I brought something special for after dinner."

It was a fine Armagnac, which we savored in the living room.

"You have a rare opportunity," Martha said. "I feel honored to know you. I am so happy you came to see me, John."

"I'm not sure how honored you should be, Martha," Sarah said. "It could turn out to be a wild goose chase. I've been calling it a caper."

"Wild goose? Who knows where the wild goose goes?" Martha asked, quoting the song lyrics.

We all laughed.

Then, in what seemed to be a perfectly logical way, Sarah asked Martha a totally illogical question, but given everything that had happened in the last few days, I wasn't surprised.

"Would you like to join us?" Sarah asked.

"May I volunteer?" Martha said.

The two women smiled at each other.

"Did I tell you what Barbara said?" Sarah asked. "That women are the first to sense the truth. It's our legacy."

"Join us for what?" I said.

"Why, to find the Stones!" Sarah said.

"Oh . . ." I said, nodding in approval, but not seeing the next step.

"The Signs have told us what to do," Martha said. "He will be seen at the Wall, isn't that so?"

"Jerusalem?" I said.

"It is the next logical step," Martha said.

"There is nothing logical about this at all!" I said. "Are you actually suggesting that we fly to Jerusalem?"

"Yes, I am," Martha said, "unless you have a better way to get there."

"Jerusalem?" I repeated, dumbfounded. "When?" I asked.

"I would think as soon as possible. Wouldn't you agree, Sarah?"

Sarah sipped her Armagnac; her cheeks took on a faint glow.

"Some caper!" Sarah said. "Yes, I think we do have to go."

"But we have five years," I said. "He's not supposed to appear until the millennium. That's 2000, not 1995!"

"But he may be here already," Martha said, "and you said yourself that the calendar may be off. Maybe it is early, but maybe it is also late. And I'm an old woman, too old to sit at home and teach while you two go off on such an incredible adventure. And there is something else that we can't forget. Your father told us it must be now. It was 1995 that he specified, was it not? Not 2000, but 1995. Maybe it will take five years to find the Messiah. Maybe there is preparation of some sort. Maybe it's the Stones we must find first."

In my heart, I had to find out if the Stones were real, and where they existed. I remembered the cryptic comment Barbara had made: Could the Stones possibly have been in Poland? And why would they be there? And my father—again my father—was buried in Jerusalem, a hero of Israel. How had this happened?

"So," I said, "it looks like we're going to Jerusalem. May I volunteer, too?"

"But without the boys," Sarah said. "I'll have to leave them with my mother in New York."

"Are you crazy?" I asked.

"Yes," Sarah said.

"Yes," Martha added and lifted her glass to offer a toast.

IT TOOK US a week to arrange all the details. Even though everyone we spoke to thought we had snapped—we didn't tell everyone why we were going, although we'd dropped the cover story about my father's illness in New Mexico—Ruth was confused, but happy he'd improved so quickly—we did say we were off doing research. Sarah and her partner lined up the extra sales help, and the university was understanding. It seems that this had happened before—academics were notorious for their sudden departures—and the department was able to cover the classes. In any case, I convinced the department chairman that our research was historical in nature and could possibly benefit the school in the future, because I was contemplating a book based on the research, although the book that materialized, this one, was not exactly what I'd promised.

In the midst of our decision-making, we'd realized we'd made a new friend in Martha, someone we both immediately liked. She was seventy-six years old but, according to her, in the prime of her life. I have to admit that at first she struck me as a pretty standard academic type—as I was? I really hadn't known her well at all, but had only seen the surface. She had been able to arrange for her departure easily, since she wasn't actually teaching that semester. She had no cat, no dog, no goldfish to care for and was ready, she said, to be adopted into our family.

In the days before we left for New York to drop off the boys, we spent almost every evening with Martha, who would join us for dinner. Each time, she would bring a special dessert, which she'd often prepared herself. The boys loved her.

One night, after dinner, we sat and talked.

"When I was young," she began, "before the prime of my life, I imagined myself a lady at court—don't laugh, I actually did! It is such an old-fashioned idea. People don't think that way any longer. But you must remember that I grew up in the 1920s, in Germany, which then was still very much a nineteenth-century society. Regardless of what you have read, not everybody was jazzing it up. Some subjects were never discussed. Love was romance, not sex. Work was expected of you. Father and mother and family were everything. There was a constancy and consistency to our lives. So, I imagined myself at court, in a queen's chamber! It was another world. Of course, all that changed. When my father and I emigrated to America, he had to start all over again. His English was poor, and at first I spoke none at all. My dreams of the royal court went up in childhood smoke. Girls here in Pennsylvania did not dream of becoming ladies. They wanted to be movie stars, like Barbara Stanwyck and Ginger Rogers. Do little girls dream of being ladies or movie stars now, I wonder?"

"You've had a distinguished career," I said.

"Let me tell you something," she said, as Sarah placed the strudel Martha had made in the microwave to warm it up. "We lost everything in Germany. We left with only two suitcases, a few marks, and two steamship tickets. I was fifteen years old. My father was a man of principle. We were not Jewish, but my father's politics made us outcasts. He couldn't live in Germany anymore. I couldn't understand his decision to leave. He was taking me out of the only world I had ever known. My mother had died giving birth, and I was an only child. He was my father. I respected him, but I truly hated him for this decision. It was only later that I changed."

"What changed you?" Sarah asked.

"Time, my father's death, the war, loneliness . . . mostly loneliness. I know you will find this hard to believe—because you have so much, it is often hard to imagine someone else who has so little—but I lived many lonely years. Then the time passes so quickly, Sarah! I lost myself in my studies. I worked harder than I thought possible. I'll tell you this, if you want to know what I believe. I believe a point arrives in our lives when we must make a choice between our hopes and our fears. If we choose our fears, we choose a living death.

"Please, I want to tell you this . . . I need to tell you." She placed her hand on Sarah's arm, preventing her from speaking. "Do you recall what Thoreau said, that most men lead lives of quiet desperation? I think Thoreau was an optimist. I believe most of us lead lives of absolute desperation—daily, weekly, monthly, in jobs we hate, in homes we detest. Please understand, this is a choice we have made. But if we choose our hopes, we can choose life itself! No one is forcing us; the choice is ours, but it comes suddenly, like a thief in the night!

"I myself have been content, though never really happy. It is such a simple thought: happiness. We know it when we are children, when it takes so little to make us happy. Our lives are complete for an hour, or a day, when we have a toy truck, or a piece of favorite strudel. But when we are older, we begin the search, to question again, the constant search for happiness. Now our worldview has changed too radically. People are in shock. People used to believe in God—no, I withdraw that remark—people *still* believe in God, but now we are confused, we do not know how to express our belief. And if we admit it, we are ridiculed. People want to believe in the person of God, in a physical place called heaven, in a life after death that continues our existence. This must be real to them, not a story to tell children at night, but as real as rain, or the sun, or the strudel. This is what has changed."

"For someone who makes such delicate strudel, you've got a pretty dark view of the world," Sarah said, placing the aromatic, delicate dessert in front of us.

"No," Martha said, "it is a realistic viewpoint, not dark at all. It is not afraid to look at the world and accept it on its own terms. In the end, it grants us a measure of freedom. It lifts the veil from our eyes. People like Stanton, the lawyer you spoke of, or Bertucci, even Barbara Allison, from what you've told me, they are all good people, I have no doubt, but they are fearful people, afraid to make a final leap into the arms of the Eternal. Your father, John, he was not afraid. Do not delude yourselves, for in the final analysis that is what it will take—a leap into the air, into the arms of the Eternal. We are on a high wire, high above the ground, trying to make it from one pole to the other, and there is no turning back. The only way is forward. There is no net. This must be our choice. His arms are wide open and waiting for us to make the jump."

Chapter 5

THE STARS
LOOK DOWN

THE FOLLOWING DAY, all of us—Sarah, Martha, the boys, and I—piled into a rented station wagon for the drive to New York. Sarah had already spoken to her mother and, as she said, "cleared the decks," whatever that meant. Her mother had lived in New York most of her life, and Sarah grew up there. Sarah's parents had divorced when she was a little girl, but, luckily for Sarah, one of her grandfathers had been quite wealthy, and had left a trust for Sarah's mother, who used her inheritance to complete her education, enter medical school, and become a very successful pediatrician.

Anne was now retired, but was still living in the same spacious apartment she'd had all these years on the Upper West Side of Manhattan. From time to time, we'd visited her as a family; she was really the only grandparent the boys ever knew. They called her Nana, as she insisted they do, and they adored her, probably because she spoiled them and gave them everything they wanted, sometimes even before they knew they wanted it.

She and Sarah had worked out a plan to place the boys in a private school until we returned, which, we assured her, would be very, very soon—Sarah said they'd left the time vague in their conversation, but it was "shorter rather than longer," which both she and her mother understood perfectly. Fortunately, since the boys were young, we were able to arrange for their school registration on a monthly basis. Anne's only request was that we return before their high school graduation.

"Just kidding," she said.

When we arrived in New York, we drove straight to Anne's apartment. I found a parking space on the street in New York, not having to pay for a garage, feeling as if I'd beaten the system, if only for a few hours. The station wagon didn't have to be returned until the morning. Martha had made a reservation in a hotel, but we insisted that she stay with us. Anne had a very large apartment, since she had sold her practice and redecorated all her professional space.

We were not scheduled to depart for Jerusalem for another twenty-four hours.

It had snowed in New York about a week before, and we could still see huge spotted and pocked mounds of snow, standing like frozen sentinels among garbage cans and heaps of trash bags. I don't know why, but I've often had the impression when visiting New York of being in the presence of a giant refuse-producing monster that lies hidden somewhere between the canyons of buildings and that day after day is fed his monster food and night after night has his leftovers bagged in black plastic bags that are then arranged like trophies of trash at every corner of the island. Then, out of nowhere, roaring white trucks with vast, open mouths appear and swallow all the trophies. Where they go, nobody knows, or cares.

I realize this is a ridiculous view of what is probably our greatest city, but I can't help it. Whenever I'm on this island, I get the same feeling. And it's gotten worse over the years, to the point where every time I hear a story about drugs, or runaway teenage girls, or urban violence—stories which might in fact have originated in Detroit or Spokane or Tampa—I immediately think of New York, where it must be just as bad, if not a whole lot worse.

When we arrived, it was already late in the afternoon, so we decided to have an early dinner. Anne had an assortment of takeout menus in her kitchen, at least three of which were for Chinese restaurants. One of the saving graces of New York, I'd have to admit, is that anytime of the day or night, seven days a week, food is ready and waiting, only a phone call away. When you live in the boondocks of rural Pennsylvania as we do, you could easily become spoiled in the midst of such a feeding frenzy. In addition, what is even more remarkable, perhaps, is that all the food is good, especially the Chinese dishes, which the boys enjoy a lot.

Anne and Sarah ordered for all of us the usual assortment that later on turns out to be too much food. The boys helped me bring up the remaining suitcases of their clothes and, after dinner, planted themselves in front of the ever-present video games that Nana had bought two years before.

Most of the after-dinner conversation, as it turned out, centered on the boys and their new school. I realized, slowly at first, that for some reason we chose not to talk about Jerusalem—or, as Anne called it earlier that evening, our "little expedition"—or the Messiah Stones themselves. Anne had asked a few questions, of course, but seemed to be satisfied with the general answers we gave her. She actually looked upon our sudden departure as some sort of eccentric reaction to our "quiet life" in Pennsylvania, and also viewed Martha as an aging academic who had nothing better to do than join us on our exploration.

But as I thought more about this, I realized there was very little we could really tell Anne. We were about to take our own next step—I still had very strong doubts and didn't want to take too close a look at what they meant—and it was difficult enough dealing with my own fears. We were grateful to Anne, of course, and could not have left the country without her help, but we were also separating ourselves from her world, as though we knew we were going to a place she couldn't go.

I don't remember very much else about that evening, the last evening we spent in New York. Anne had rented a movie she thought we'd like, but it was something I'd never heard of and took place in China; I could barely read the subtitles on her TV screen in the living room. For all their excitement, the boys were tired and went to bed early. Sarah and I also turned in early. I think Anne and Martha stayed up to catch the news.

I slept soundly.

In the morning, when we were all having breakfast, I was relieved not to have awakened with the burden of another dream. Perhaps my dreaming stage was over. I recalled again that one of the Signs said that the power of dreams would be returned to us, but I still had no real concept of what such a power was. And when had we lost that power? And why would it be returned to us?

But my relief was short-lived and ended when Anne put the radio on.

Like most people, Anne is in the habit of listening to the radio in the morning; but unlike most people, Anne prefers classical music to talk and weather.

"What's that?" I said in surprise.

"What's what?" Anne looked up at me. She was eating a Swiss-type cereal full of nuts and dates and every other healthy miracle you'd never suspect belonged in breakfast cereal.

"The music . . . what's that?"

"Oh, I don't hear it anymore," she said. "I leave it on all day, in the background, FM, very low. It's soothing, John, don't you think so? I always had the music on in the office. Even had a big tank of goldfish. Very calming."

The music was having the opposite effect on me.

"Do you know the piece?" I asked.

"Verdi? Vivaldi? Just guesses; I mix them up all the time," she said.

"Mozart, I think," Martha said.

"Oh," I said, "Mozart . . ." I bit into my rye toast. I must've pronounced the composer's name slowly, in a dreamlike way, for I could see everyone staring at me wondering what I was thinking.

"Just curious," I said, and I could see no one accepted my answer.

"Is everything all right, John?" Sarah asked.

"Oh, yes," I said.

Sarah looked at me, and I could tell that she knew immediately that everything wasn't all right.

"John likes Mozart," Sarah said to everyone by way of explanation. "He's a big fan of classical music." She looked at me with that inquisitive, yet uneasy look in her eye.

I should have recognized the Mozart horn concerto; it was very well known. But that's not what I was thinking about, nor what had frozen me in my chair. As soon as I heard the music, it sparked my memory of the dream I'd had during the night. This dream was very different from the previous dreams I'd had, though equally difficult to explain.

In plain words, I had seen myself standing on the steps of a magnificent double staircase that was built somewhat in the shape of a huge horseshoe, and in the background I could hear Mozart's majestic overture to *Don Giovanni*. Even now, at the breakfast table, I could hear the repeated melodious chords . . . music I'd heard dozens of times over the years, for it was from one of my favorite operas.

The night before, somehow, I'd seen myself standing on the steps of the Grand Staircase of the Paris Opéra, hearing the orchestra as it rehearsed Mozart's music. I knew this for a fact. But as frightening as this was to me, I was even more frightened when I remembered looking up at the ceiling of the famous opera house and instead of seeing what would be expected—the chandeliers, the glow, the opulence—I saw instead the vast, limitless expanse of constellations of stars in the sky. In my dream, the Paris Opéra had no roof! And I had been there—no, that wasn't quite it, I thought as I tried to get a better focus on my feelings, it wasn't that. It was more a feeling that I was *supposed* to be there; I was supposed to stand on the marble steps.

I had been given a direction, a message through the dream medium as I slept, a message to go somewhere. I knew this as certainly as I knew that we had our tickets for the flight to Jerusalem.

But Paris? The Paris Opéra? Was I supposed to go to *France*? We'd actually been there once before, on our honeymoon, but I hadn't thought about it in years.

I sat there absorbing this and probably looked as if I'd swallowed something bitter. But if what had been happening in the past few weeks was difficult to explain in a rational way, this latest dream was off the scale. Instinctively—or maybe to protect my own sanity, or pride, because I strongly suspected I'd be ridiculed—I decided to keep this latest message to myself.

"I'm okay," I finally said. "It's just that everything . . . everything's so new to me."

"It catches up with you," Martha said.

"You look a little pale," Anne said. "Wouldn't you like something? I could give you something."

"Is Daddy sick?" Joshua asked.

"No," Sarah said, "it's just something he ate."

"What?" he asked. She didn't answer him.

Our flight was leaving at eight in the evening from JFK. We had the whole day ahead of us. I was on the edge of an emotional cliff I completely didn't understand, but I knew I had to get out of that apartment. Maybe it was New York that was doing this to me; but I couldn't blame last night's insanity on New York. Whatever it was, it was inside me.

"Let's go out for a while, Sarah," I said. "Let's take a walk. I've got to get out."

"That's a good idea," Anne said.

"Can I come, Daddy?" Joshua asked.

"Me, too?" Oliver jumped in.

"No, Daddy and I are going out alone," Sarah said. "We'll be back soon. Nana has a busy day planned for both of you. Finish your cereal."

Sarah put her arm around me as we walked to the hall closet. "It'll be good to get out," she said. "We never get a chance to walk anymore, especially in a city. We'll forget how unless we practice," she said as she smiled warmly at me.

I wouldn't know what to do without Sarah. She understands my moods, as I hope I understand hers. If you had asked me when I was younger if I believed I'd ever have the kind of love I share with her, I would have said no. How could I have known, never having shared it before? But now at this juncture of my life, she and I were one.

But I wasn't sure if even Sarah would understand what I'd dreamed, because I didn't understand it myself. How fine, I wondered, was the line between sanity and madness, and had I crossed it, not even knowing I had? I hoped not.

We left her mother's apartment and began walking downtown, for no particular reason, except that we always seemed to walk in that direction. Anne lived pretty far uptown, and the few times we'd taken a walk, we always seemed to gravitate toward midtown.

I readily admit that, as probably has been obvious, I have a love/hate relationship with New York. I can't speak for Sarah, of course, but the city does have a dangerous attraction that repels me at the same time. I don't doubt that the city is a historical and artistic and financial center of our planet—but it is also the tragic underbelly of our society. I saw one estimate, for example, that there are upwards of fifty thousand homeless in New York, wanderers who roam the streets every hour of the day and night.

There is also a pace that I see in the city that reminds me of old films, where the director has speeded up the action to show streams of people flowing up and down the streets, like schools of fish in a river heading toward the spawning pools, or armies of ants ceaselessly busy, carrying bits of food and foliage from hill to hill. I imagine the director's hand on the switches marked "Fast" and "Faster" as I see New Yorkers speed through the streets. Where are they going? Why do they have to get there so fast?

I couldn't escape visualizing these images as we started out.

We walked briskly. It had warmed up a bit; the sun was bright. Since it was a Saturday morning, there were actually more people on the street than there would normally be on a weekday morning. Sarah and I picked up the pace as we headed east on Seventy-second Street, then south on Fifth Avenue. We were both wearing sneakers and were physically enjoying ourselves for the first time in many days. The blocks blended one into another as we crossed each succeeding street. For a long time, as we started out, we even held hands as we took strides in unison. But then we gave that up, walking in tandem, but not holding.

"How far should we go?" Sarah asked.

It occurred to me that we'd been walking very fast, somehow in a sense becoming a part of that old-time film and giving it all we had. The drive the previous day had been long and confining, and now we had a chance to use all the energy we'd stored.

I looked up and saw that we'd perhaps come a couple of miles, and were now standing in front of the General Motors Building. People walked back and forth all around us.

"This way," I said.

If you had asked me at that point where I was going, I don't think I would have known. I certainly hadn't known when we'd started out. But as we continued down Fifth Avenue—we both loved to look at the store windows; mall shops could never compare to them, and some still had their Christmas displays—it became apparent to us that I was heading in a definite direction.

Not at first, that is, because I'd tried to put my dream out of my mind, and the streets and sights were so distracting as we walked along. Then again, we didn't speak to each other, not a single word until Sarah asked how far we were going. At that point, I seemed to pick up the pace even more, with Sarah right at my side, as we reached the corner of Forty-second Street and Fifth Avenue. We'd been at this corner a few times before, once when we'd visited Anne and taken the boys to a parade. Now as we stood there, waiting for the light to change,

Sarah turned and looked directly at me, at first without speaking. She was waiting.

Then she said, "Is it your dream, John?"

"I think so," I said.

I didn't wait for the light to change, but quickly turned left and began walking farther east down Forty-second Street. We were walking more slowly now, Sarah right with me, as I carefully scrutinized the stores and the pedestrians. I was looking for a sign of some sort, something I could recognize, to help me along. The people who passed us must've thought we were lost, because I think I looked at each of them, trying to connect someone or something with my dream of the Paris Opéra, of Mozart, of the stars, all of which, I was convinced, had a connection to where we were.

I felt as if we were at the end of a thick rope in a tug-of-war and were being inexorably pulled toward the other end, somewhere I couldn't quite yet see. It wasn't a dream anymore, but a real place at a real time that was very close to us. All we had to do was continue walking and we would know the place when we arrived.

I don't know when she did it, but at some point as we approached Grand Central Station, Sarah placed her arm in mine. I could sense that she was looking at me, while at the same time watching the people and the street for any clues. Finally, we crossed the last street and a long row of taxis as we entered the station.

We'd never been in Grand Central Station before. It did not appear crowded, though I had the impression that on busy weekdays, throngs of people flowed in and out at this central commuter artery.

We passed a newsstand and a large bakery, whose odors of rich cakes and freshly baked loaves of bread and baskets of assorted bagels greeted us as we turned into the main concourse of the station.

There in front of us was a large, circular information booth with an old-fashioned large clock on top of it. Beyond that and against the high wall displayed above the ticket booths was an enormous board that listed all the arriving and departing trains. As we stood there, one section of the display was being updated, each time and place flipping over like a card fanned in a mechanical deck, to reveal a new time and place.

I could feel Sarah's arm in mine as I looked to my left, and to my right. It was then that I understood.

"Here," I said.

To our left, at one end of the main concourse, a small group of young musicians were playing Mozart's famous overture that I'd heard in my sleep the night before. They were boys and girls, their sign said, from a local high school. They couldn't have been more than twelve or thirteen, dressed casually, but playing their instruments with passion and concentration. Though they were young and amateurs, I felt at home listening to their music.

"It's Mozart," I said.

"Yes, I know," Sarah said. "Your dream?"

"Look!" I said, pointing to our right and heading in that direction. There at the other end of the main floor was a huge double staircase, set below magnificent arched windows through which waves of January sunlight bathed the spacious hall. We walked toward the staircase and stopped before it. It was exactly as I had dreamed it.

All I could do was sit down on the bottom marble step to my right. Sarah sat down beside me. No one bothered us or asked us to move. Except for the music that filled the station, it was very quiet.

Sarah waited without speaking, but I knew what she was thinking. I then told her what I had dreamed and how frightened I was.

"It's hard to understand, John, I know, but it's happening. For some reason, you were meant to come here today."

"No, *we* were meant to come here. We were invited."

"What do we do now?"

"I think we wait," I said. "It's not over yet."

It was about ten in the morning. We sat on the steps and waited. Since I still had no idea what we were waiting for, we watched everyone and everything.

"Perhaps," Sarah said, "perhaps we're supposed to take a train, one of those trains over there."

"I don't think so."

"What happened in your dream when you were standing on the steps? What did you do?"

"I'm trying to remember."

"Is it the music?"

"No, I don't think so."

"Then what?"

"I don't know."

"Does it have to do with one of the Signs?"

"I don't know."

We sat on the steps for almost an hour, waiting, uncertain, wondering. A number of groups came and went, tourists mainly in twos and threes, teenagers also, and a few people running to make their trains. The sound of the flipping flaps on the huge board overhead became familiar to us, like the regular ticking of a clock. Now and then we were approached by some ragged man with a cup in his hand, and one in particular who had a pathetic story about how he'd lost his wallet and needed just one more dollar to buy a ticket to get home. We were approached a few times. Once, a police officer appeared almost out of nowhere and chased the beggar off. Sarah, however, had given the man who needed the dollar some money.

"He also had a mother," she said. I didn't say anything.

"There has to be a reason why we're here," I said. "It's all so specific. It's this waiting that's so frustrating. It's hard to be patient."

"I think we're doing a good job, John. It's not as though we've had a lot of practice at this. This may have started out as a caper, but now we don't know who's after who!"

"Dammit!" I said, standing up and placing my hands on my hips. "I'm here! I've done my part: Why can't he do his?"

"Who, John?"

"I don't know!" I said.

I don't know why I was so angry or what I meant exactly. But I was angry at myself, angry at everything. I was doing all that was expected of me. I had left my job to travel halfway across the world on what amounted to a mixture of blind faith and miraculous evidence. I'd taken my children out of school and left them with their grandmother. I'd listened to virtual strangers recount events that happened decades ago but could affect the rest of my life. I'd even begun to reexamine my relationship with my father, a man I'd hated for many years, to the point where I thought I'd grown to love and respect him . . . and now I'd arrived where I was asked to be and I was kept waiting!

I knew it was my pride again, my sense of independence, my ego asserting itself. Sure, I wanted to be the center of attraction in what was turning out to be something absolutely extraordinary, but what I couldn't stand was the thought of becoming just another of those faceless, speeded-up robots that skidded across the station floor on their way . . . on their way to somewhere unimportant!

I was seeing a new side of my personality that scared me, that I didn't like. It was frail and thin and it bristled against my skin. Sarah stood up; she also seemed at a loss.

"Maybe we should just go home," I said.

"To my mother's?"

"No, I mean home, to where we belong. Maybe we should just call the whole thing off," I said with a sigh.

The young musicians had stopped playing and were taking a break. They had brought snacks along with them and hot drinks in thermos bottles. People we assumed to be parents of some of the children stepped forward from the audience that had formed in a semicircle around the musicians and now mingled with the players.

Traffic had picked up a bit since Sarah and I had arrived, but, paradoxically, the more people who filled the station on their way to their trains, the more anonymous each one of them seemed. I was no longer watching individuals pass by; rather, I was back in my usual New York mode, seeing only crowds of soulless shapes.

Was it possible that I'd imagined the whole thing, simply because we'd once been to the Paris Opéra and enjoyed the music? Or—and this last thought struck me like a slap on my face I didn't expect—was this only doubt, the human failing that plagues our spirits like an internal virus?

Whether it was doubt or not, I wasn't allowed much time to form an opinion. Standing before us—where had she come from?—was another of those beggars, those homeless, those faceless, that wander the streets of New York like mice trapped in a maze with no exit.

She was dressed in jeans, a black leather jacket, and the thick black shoes that are so popular on campus. She wore a red woolen ski hat and a dirty white scarf around her neck. It was hard to tell her age—probably not more than forty, even though she looked much older. Her skin was very pale and she had a fresh bruise on her right cheek. Now and then, with her tongue, she nursed a cut lip that was a day or two old. She walked purposefully away from the clock—where I had to assume she'd been standing, though I hadn't seen her—and walked directly over to us.

"You're from out of town," she said. We didn't answer her. "I can tell when people are from out of town. They have a certain look."

She smiled at us, nursing her lip. Sarah opened her bag and was about to remove a dollar bill.

"We're leaving," I said, "so why don't you go somewhere else?"

"John, please," Sarah said.

"Oh, it's all right," the woman said. "It's just that I give tours here in Grand Central Station, and you looked like you were waiting, and I thought maybe you'd like to have a tour."

"We're leaving," I said again, "and we don't want a tour."

"I'm really an excellent guide. I've been doing this for some time. It's not an official tour—I mean, I'm not part of the station here, they have their own tours, Wednesdays and Fridays at twelve-thirty, I think. They're very good. Mine are, well, special, but very interesting. And you looked like you were waiting."

"Perhaps . . ." Sarah began to say, holding the money out toward the woman.

"Oh, it's free, Sarah, no charge at all," the woman said. "You can put your money away, it's no good here."

At first, I assumed she'd overheard Sarah's name.

"Today," she continued, "I'm here for you, Sarah, and you, John, for this tour. It'll really be enjoyable, since this is your first visit to Grand Central Station. Where you're standing, John, is where I usually begin the tour. On the staircase."

"How . . . ?" I tried to form some other words, but gave up.

"How did I know your names? Ask me at the end of the tour."

From that moment until it ended, the woman became the focus of everything Sarah and I saw and heard in that vast hall. Although we had many questions that we thought of as she spoke, we were for the most part silent, her captive audience.

"This," she said, "is the Grand Staircase that you're standing on. It was designed after the more famous one in the Paris Opéra. These steps are marble. This is one of my favorite places in the station. I've spent many hours here, John and Sarah, with people like you, always on their way to somewhere. Faraway places. Come," she said pleasantly, "let me show you the clock."

Sarah and I followed the woman to the information booth in the middle of the hall. No one seemed to take notice of us as we walked behind her.

"Isn't it fantastic!" she said. "It's a four-sided clock, made of brass. Some nights, when I have late tours, I can literally see it glisten."

The woman stood in front of the clock and looked up at it. Sarah moved closer to her.

"What is your name?" Sarah asked.

"My name is Beverly," she said. She looked at both of us. "Don't be frightened. I'm here to help you, to guide you. I'm really an excellent guide."

I thought of so many things to ask, but didn't ask any of them.

"What happened to your lip and your cheek? Can we do something?" Sarah asked.

"No, no, there's nothing that can be done. I'm not hurt; it's just the way I look. Looks can be so deceiving, can't they? We judge other people by how they look, isn't that right? Please," she said, "take a moment, this is an important section of the tour, please, look up." She pointed to the ceiling.

We looked up, and I felt momentarily dizzy. Sarah grabbed my arm to steady me.

"It's all right, John," Beverly said. "It happens to a lot of people."

I couldn't believe my eyes—the proof in my eyes and the absolute conviction at that moment in time, the certainty beyond doubt, that I was in the presence of a special being. For there on the ceiling was precisely what I had seen in my dream.

"It's a mural," Beverly began, "of more than twenty-five hundred stars of the zodiac. You might recognize some of the constellations. Isn't it incredible? I've seen it so many times, but always marvel at it. Just look up and see the stars, here in the middle of Grand Central Station. I can tell you that people are amazed by what's just above their heads in the most un-likely places, if they'd just take the time to stop and look. You know what it is, really? It's a sign that they're not alone, that there's much more to life than what can be found down here."

I looked at Beverly and tried to fathom everything I was see-ing and hearing; but I felt that she was much more than she appeared to be, that though I could hear what she was saying, I really couldn't grasp it all. And there was something else, some-thing that I had never felt before, which convinced me that she was more than just an ordinary person. I've thought long and hard how to describe this feeling, because even though I abso-lutely knew the truth as I stood in her presence, I also realized it would be difficult to convince others, since they had not been there. It was as though someone had flipped an internal switch in my soul and, in the darkness, the light had gone on. I heard the click and I could see.

"Try not to understand too much too quickly, John," she said, "at least on this part of the tour. Later on, in Jerusalem, you will have a much more qualified guide who will direct you. He will show you what you need to see. Here, in New York, you and Sarah have been given a chance to make a small stop along the way, to refresh yourself, to cast your doubts away. Think of it like this: The stars look down on the entire world, not just on Jerusalem, or any other single location on this planet. The Creator's beauty shines through every corner of the world, into every darkness where light is needed. Each spot of earth is sanctified by the Creator and will be blessed in the end. Soon each spot will be reclaimed as it was in the beginning. What I am telling you is old news, really. It's the working of a clock, the playing out of a covenant. Everything is connected to everything else and always has been. Everything counts. Everything has consequences. There is nothing new under the sun, not for people, not for the earth. There is only Good and there is Evil. Life and Death. What is promised and what is given. This is an old story, so don't look for new insights into the human heart, new blueprints to remake the old world. People don't change, sad to say. But you know this already, don't you?"

Sarah held out her hand. Beverly took it and held it in her own.

"Ah," Beverly said, "smell the bread and the cake! Can you smell them?" she asked as she turned her head toward the bakery.

"But the Stones," I said, "the Stones will change everything, won't they? Won't it all change when we find the Stones? Won't it all change when the Messiah arrives?"

"Yes, everything will change when the Messiah arrives.

When that day comes, both for those who welcome it and for the others, who . . . well, for the others, we won't speak of them today; that's for another time. Today, I've been sent to bring you a message, John and Sarah, and especially you, John. You will find the Stones in Jerusalem, and you and Sarah will be given an assignment once you find them. Have no more fear or doubts. Do you understand?"

I said, "Yes."

Sarah said the same.

"Come," Beverly said, "we'll finish the tour. This is the best part, why I've been sent to you, why your father left you your inheritance, the letters, your search for the Stones. I hope I can answer all of your questions in the time we have. I was delayed, you see. There are others, John. But first . . ."

She began to walk toward the Grand Staircase again, with us right next to her. She didn't go up the staircase, though, but instead walked around it, and we then found ourselves at the bakery. There she took a few dollars out of her leather jacket and bought a loaf of bread, which she first had the clerk slice.

"It's a special bread," she said, as we walked back toward the front of the staircase. Beverly took out a slice for each of us, which we ate. It was delicious.

"It's a special bread, Jewish, called challah, which is used for their Sabbath. It's rich, made with eggs, rolled in braids. Isn't it delicious?"

"Are you Jewish?" I asked.

"No," she said, "but I never miss a chance to buy this bread."

All three of us ate the challah. Beverly nursed her lip as she ate her slice. I felt sorry for her; it must've been troubling her.

"Life has many sides," she said. "If you have two loaves of bread, sell one and buy a lily. Have you ever heard that?"

"No," I said.

"It's a beautiful thought. We need joy in our lives, not just bread."

"Can we get something for your lip?" Sarah asked again. "There must be a pharmacy—"

"No, no, there's nothing to be done. It never heals. My cheek is always bruised. I'm one of the faceless here in New York, except when I give these tours, sort of an unofficial guide. You've seen me before, John, though you've never wanted to see me. I'm not pleasant to see, I suppose. I frighten people. But I like my work, especially when I get to break bread with two people as fortunate as you. Yes, John, you will be given another guide in Jerusalem—that is an appointment you must keep. Because these are special times, just before the end of days, and you are a special person, not because of anything you've done, but because of your father and what he did. He is the one who started you on this search for the Stones, but also on the search for your true self, for who you are as a human being."

"Are others chosen?" I said.

"Many," Beverly said. "Many have been called. Some never go, like Barbara and Bertucci. Hearing is not enough, it is only the beginning. Doing is the hard part. Everyone knows fear and doubt; it is the human condition."

"Beverly, can you tell us who you really are?" Sarah asked.

Beverly looked at her with love and compassion in her eyes.

"I have been telling you," she said. "Make no mistake: the Kingdom of God is within you and you will find it. You will be present at the final victory, and you will know the Messiah through love and through man. Remember, John—you will know because you will see."

"I don't understand," I said.

"Everything," Beverly said, "everything is connected to everything else. From the beginning of days to the end of days—and beyond the end of days to the mind of the Creator—everything is connected to everything else. Stanton, Barbara, Martha, and all you are about to learn—and the Stones—are of the same fabric, and the fabric is sewn as an act of love. Love for you, love for us, love for us all. It's that simple, and has always been that simple. Why look for complicated answers when the simple ones are best? No blueprints for sudden changes, no gurus and shamans. The laws of the world are immutable and set, until the end. Until that time, remember the fabric and the act of love."

Beverly stopped speaking. I waited, but she remained silent. Was she waiting for me?

"Good and Evil," I said, "and the Stones, and the Messiah, and Jerusalem . . . who will be there, Beverly? You promised you'd tell us who you are."

Beverly took another slice of challah out of the plastic bag, folded it in half, and took a bite.

"No, John, I promised I'd tell you how I knew your names. I have been telling you who I am. Understand, I don't like to keep secrets—it's really not in my nature. It's just that I can reveal only so much. Learning comes from the doing, do you understand?"

"How did you know our names?" Sarah asked.

"I've heard you use them."

"You mean here, in the station?" I asked.

"No, before, in Pennsylvania, other places, other times. As one of the Signs tells us, the Messiah will live among us from the beginning of days to the end of days. You've already seen how that is done. But also, with him, there are others as well, think of us as helpers, assistants who perform certain functions. Messengers, if you will, a spirit on your shoulder to help you find yourself."

"You mean you're an angel?" I said.

"Would it be easier for you to believe if I said yes?" Beverly asked.

"No," Sarah said quickly. "Let us believe on our own."

Beverly smiled at Sarah.

"You're a very lucky man, John," she said, "and you are too, Sarah. Remember New York and its people and those of us with cups in our hands. Until the Messiah arrives, we wander in search of comfort. When you find the Stones, you will understand. You will see the final victory to come."

Beverly then unzipped one of the many zippered pockets of her leather jacket and removed something which she held clasped in her fist.

"The Stones," she said, "are only a confirmation of the truth of the Creator and the Messiah's mission. I think you've seen by now that the Messiah has appeared in more than one place, in more than one time, and that is how it was meant to be. At the end of days, remember New York, which you have seen on your way to Jerusalem. For here, too, as well as in all other places under the stars, the end will come. This, too, is a dry and thirsty land. Here, too, is a wall. Here, too, there will be the light. Until that time, remember to love and to welcome the stranger in your presence. And to remember your tour, I'd like to give you a souvenir. You won't find this for sale in any of the local shops, or anywhere else. It's imported from very far away. Here," she said and handed it to me.

It was a keychain, the kind that we've all seen countless times before, about three inches long. At one end was a ring about the size of a coin for keys. At the other was a round ball, somewhat like a miniature basketball, but a globe of the world instead, onto which had been carved the names "John and Sarah" on one side, and on the other was a small stone chip that looked as if it had been broken off a larger slab or tablet. I held it in my hand, staring down at it, and slowly closed my fingers around it. I then looked up at Beverly.

We were seated again on the Grand Staircase with Beverly standing in front of us. She had finished the slice of challah and stood there smiling at us, nursing her cut lip. Seconds passed, perhaps a full minute, and then I found myself taking a dollar out of my wallet and giving it to her.

"You're from out of town," she said. "I can tell when people are from out of town; they have a certain look. Thanks," she said, and stuffed the dollar in her jeans pocket.

"Here, take this also," Sarah said as she extended the bag of challah to her.

"Oh, no," Beverly said, "I can't accept that. That's for you and John; it's your food."

During our encounter with Beverly, the young musicians had apparently finished their snack, and they were now playing again. I recognized the music as Bach. He was also one of my favorite composers.

As Sarah and I sat on the marble steps, the woman with whom we'd been talking all this while began walking back toward the rear of the Grand Staircase in the direction of the bakery. Quickly, we stood up to follow her, but when we turned the corner, she wasn't there. There we stood, looking at each other, facing a young girl behind the counter, who asked us what we wanted.

"She was a tour guide," Sarah said to me, "and the tour was over."

She was gone.

IF SARAH AND I had any lingering doubts before our— encounter? meeting?—with Beverly, they had vanished. We now knew for certain that we had to go to Jerusalem. But we also knew something equally important: that though it was our mission to take this trip, Jerusalem was not the only place that would be of significance when the Messiah arrived. Every city, including New York, would be the center of attention. Of course, we could see the logic of this now, now that we'd met Beverly.

And I'd learned something else as well that I was only beginning to sense: that, yes, we would find the Stones somehow, and, yes, I would come to understand much more about my father, but I would also find the truth of the Creator in myself, and this would begin through helping other people. Through charity, through the homeless, through deeds and not just thoughts. The anticipation of this made me feel very good inside. Suddenly, even New York appeared different to me. I saw the people who passed us now as individuals, each one a unique signature of the Creator that would never be duplicated.

Like the faces of the slaves in the ship, each person was distinct. "Think of it," I said to Sarah, as we walked around to the other side of the staircase again and sat down, expressing my thoughts out loud. "All of these people, so many of them, and yet each one is different, absolutely unique. Billions and billions without duplication. It's a miracle, isn't it?"

"It happens every day around us," she said, "if only we'd stop and look. Isn't that right?"

"I do feel lucky, Sarah, for so many reasons."

"I wish we could see her again," she said.

"Perhaps we will."

"Who do you think she was?"

"She was Beverly," I said, "that's who she was. A tour guide. She's probably still here in a way, with us. We can't know everything at once, remember?"

I gave Sarah the keychain to hold. She turned the globe around and around and looked at it as though it were a precious jewel she'd just discovered. The young musicians continued to play at the other end of the hall. The huge windows behind and above us practically glittered as the noonday light entered through them and bathed the enormous cavern in brightness.

"You know," she said, entwining her arm in mine, "I've been calling this a caper, and in a way it is. But in another way, it's really no mystery at all. The truth is so simple, it's been staring us in the face since the beginning. Love one another before time runs out. Love one another and you will find God, here inside yourself, where you, too, have been touched by God. It's the key," Sarah said, holding her souvenir in the palm of her hand.

We stood up and started to leave Grand Central Station. As we headed up the ramp toward Forty-second Street, we turned back once more and looked at the gleaming brass clock atop the information booth. Beverly had said she lived here in Grand Central Station. I wondered how she'd gotten her cut lip and the bruise on her cheek. Where could she live here? Was there somewhere down below, down on the many tracks, where people like her came out of the cold and the night?

I knew I was only glimpsing a part of what she meant, but I couldn't help but think about her. I knew I would pray to see her again, and even as I thought this, I wasn't bothered by the idea. Prayer had never been a part of my life before, but now it was here, like my dreams, just one more line of communication with what existed beyond and outside of my own consciousness. I was not the be-all and the end-all of creation. I was only a part of it. And there was something else, I knew, that was very important, which I began to see as we left the station and started walking back to Anne's apartment.

As an academic, I had as one of my central concerns the individual's role in history. I understood, of course, that people could influence their destinies only to a limited extent—that other forces, greater than their own, also controlled them. It was the old debate of Nature vs. Nurture: How much of who we are is in our genes, and how much in our school, our friends, our environment?

But now I understood I had missed a vital link in this chain of thought—and that link was the inescapable connection between the past and the present, and therefore the future. Some things were in the cards waiting to happen. I still didn't believe in the total dominance of Fate, as though some blind, thoughtless process ruled over us, but now I could see that there was an order to existence, a clock of sorts, that operated the basic movements, that set the ground rules for the stars above and the people below.

And these rules didn't change from season to season. They were simple, known, and uncomplicated rules of Life and Death, Good and Evil, Past and Future. And the one central, binding thread that held the fabric together was the concept of the Creator—no, I was beyond that—no, it was God! Not a concept, not an idea, but a physical reality that created the clock, wound its movements, and, if necessary, repaired it.

I realized, too, that like all clocks, this one also told time, and it now told the world that the time was near when the Messiah would arrive to stop the clock. We would have had our chance to live, to work, to feed the needy and the homeless, to welcome the stranger in our midst, and now that opportunity would be gone forever. The clock would stop and the time would be 2000.

I needed to find the Stones.

As we walked back to the apartment, I saw New York differently, as I had seen the tree differently outside Martha's office. He would be here, too, as he would be in Jerusalem, as he would be in all places. Perhaps he was here already, as Beverly was, waiting for the hands of the clock to complete their tireless revolution.

Beverly had asked us to remember New York. I knew I would.

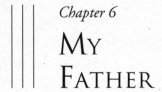

Chapter 6

My
Father

THAT EVENING, Sarah and Martha and I boarded El Al flight 8 departing from New York's JFK. Approximately ten and a half hours later we arrived at Tel Aviv's Ben Gurion Airport. We felt we had left the boys in safe hands with Anne in New York. The boys were actually happy to be with their grandmother, who, on occasion, liked to quote the old joke about why grandparents and grandchildren get along so well—because they have a common enemy.

It was just a short ride to our hotel in Jerusalem. Outside the hotel, a young boy was selling rides on a camel, which he had tied to a pole.

This was Sarah's and my first trip to Israel, though we'd been abroad often, usually to Europe. Martha, however, had been there before, but as it turned out she didn't inform us of this fact until we were well on our way and thousands of feet up in the air.

"Why keep it a secret?" I asked.

"Would it have mattered?" she said. "It was a long time ago, almost in another life. Maybe someday I'll tell you about it."

I knew there was a great deal about Martha we didn't know, and perhaps would never know.

We were tired after our long flight and decided to make it a short evening, but it took me a long time to fall asleep, not just because of jet lag. The sunset that appeared outside our window bathed the horizon in a golden arc. The sun seemed so close, much closer than I had ever seen it before. I lay on my side and watched its slow descent. I was an explorer on a foreign planet observing a natural phenomenon that didn't exist back on my home terrain. At my back, I could hear Sarah, sound asleep, breathing heavily. I didn't allow myself to fade off until I knew that she was asleep. It was my responsibility to protect her. We'd come this far together.

But I was not asleep, though my eyes were closed. I was in a tranquil twilight—warm, serene, attuned to the slightest sounds in the air. A voice within me said I was in Jerusalem, the Golden City, the City of Peace, the City of David.

It was a voice not unlike one in a dream, but not exactly in a dream. It was a voice guiding me to see something.

My eyes closed, my body prone, I looked down on a hill in full bloom, covered with the abundant succulence of olive trees. Then, to one side, I could see a golden gate facing the hill. I could hear the faint echo of cheering crowds as they witnessed the entrance of a visitor through the magnificent double doors into the holy city of Jerusalem. I could hear the cheers grow fainter down through the passage of the centuries. But it was still there, though faint, like a thumbprint in the dust.

I saw the huge gate sealed with bricks to prevent the passage of any other visitor. Alone and afraid, I looked down to see a gathering of lepers in front of the Golden Gate.

The lepers were huddled and seated in the cooler shade. They were removing their layered bandages, one after the other. They unwound the wraps around their arms, their faces, their legs. They would wash these bandages and replace them with clean ones. Two urns filled with water stood ready by their side.

This was a ritual of the lepers, the unclean, the unwanted. They waited at the Golden Gate through the centuries, waited for the Messiah, who would appear here and cure them.

Among them was a particular leper, the same, yet different. He was standing erect, not seated, and was slightly in front of the others and off to one side. He, too, unwrapped his ban-dages, but only one at a time. He would wash this single ban-dage, wait for it to dry in the sun, and replace it before he would remove a second one and then repeat the process. Only one bandage at a time, for this leper did not want to be caught unprepared. He must be ready at a moment's notice, in case he was called. This leper, unrecognized by the others, was the Messiah.

The Jews believed he would have been summoned long ago had they simply obeyed all the laws of two Sabbaths in a row. But this had not happened yet. The Christians believed he had already arrived, awaiting as they did his eventual return. The Muslims longed for him as well, and revered him as guided by the Creator.

"How long must I suffer like this? How long?" the leper asked in a plaintive voice, lifting his eyes toward the heavens.

The other lepers had learned to disregard him. Often they scorned him as foolish.

I fell asleep beside Sarah.

BEFORE LEAVING FOR Israel, I had done a bit of research. I had learned that the Israelis have a computerized database listing everybody living in the country. Israel is a small country, so this was no great problem. Los Angeles and New York City each have much larger populations than the whole of this tiny enclave—half orange grove, half desert. In addition, the Israelis have included the names of other individuals, dead or alive, who have contributed in some way to the prosperity of this embattled country. It was through access to this database that I was able to locate the name of William P. McGowan, my father.

According to their information, my father was buried in the Jewish cemetery on the Mount of Olives, as we'd been told by Bertucci. As next of kin, my mother's name was listed, as well as her old address in Chicago.

Armed with this information, I was determined to get to the bottom of my father's disappearance. After all I'd learned, I wasn't sure it would make complete sense to me, not on an everyday level. But I was not on an everyday level anymore, was I? How would I know how to separate the wheat from the chaff? I was still trying to absorb my vision—was it a vision, or a dream, or a fantasy?—of the leper of the night before. I was on very unsure footing and afraid to slip. But I had to find out about my father. Maybe because of some unresolved issues buried deep in my subconscious, I needed to do this alone, without Sarah or Martha at my side. This was a part of the journey I needed to take alone. Besides, they wanted to visit the Wall.

"He might show up," Sarah said.

"No, he won't," I said jokingly. "He'll want us all together, won't he?"

It was early when I arrived at the municipal office building whose address I'd gotten back in New York. I also had the name of a counselor who was assigned to help me. His name was Yehuda, and he looked barely old enough to shave.

"I am a volunteer, Professor," he said in answer to my question, in English with only the slightest trace of an accent. "I'm studying biology and will probably continue on with my studies toward a degree in medicine. Genealogy is a hobby of mine, so I come here two days a week. Where is your college in Pennsylvania, Professor?"

I told him where it was located.

"I've been to New York and Florida, but not to your neck of the woods. Have you been to Florida, to Disney World?"

"Once. Your English is excellent."

"Thank you. Many Israelis speak English. Now, how can I help you?"

I gave him the information I had from the database. It checked out on his screen.

"You got this in New York?" he asked.

"Yes."

"It's correct. He is buried on the Mount of Olives. Are you Jewish?"

"No."

"Was he Jewish?"

"No," I said.

"Oh," Yehuda said.

"Did you want to add something?" I said, sensing a hesitation on his part.

"No, it's just unusual. The Mount of Olives is for Jews. It's a Jewish cemetery."

Yehuda looked at me.

"For Jews," he repeated, as if I didn't understand.

"He was my father," I said, "but he was not Jewish."

"He must've had some powerful friends," Yehuda said. "Are you sure? There would have to be papers signed, a rabbi would probably be present, maybe other officials. This is a very famous, special cemetery, Mr. McGowan. Not easy to get into, even for Jews. And this database you refer to, well, it's not exactly a database. It's more like a computerized telephone directory, and because the country is really so small, we're able to locate people easily. But you say he wasn't Jewish, is that right?"

"He was a Christian, Methodist, I think. From Chicago. I mean I'm positive, about both."

"I understand," Yehuda said. "Well, however he did it, he's there. The why is another story. Mount of Olives Cemetery in Jerusalem. Do you know how to get there?"

"I'll find out. But is there anything else you can tell me? For example, he had a friend when he lived here. His name was Ari, but that wasn't his real name. He worked for the Mossad, the intelligence service."

Yehuda looked at me without expression.

"It's a complicated story," I said.

"I'm sure it is, Professor. But Ari, well, it's a Hebrew name like John or Bill in English, very common, and if it's not his real name, and if he worked for the Mossad . . . how long ago did you say, forty years?"

"Forty years."

"I'd say your chances are zero, or close to it. I could direct you to their office here in Jerusalem. It's not far from here. Possibly they'll find him in their records. Would you mind if I asked you a question, Professor?"

"Not at all."

"Did you like Disney World?"

I thanked Yehuda and in about ten minutes found myself seated in front of another twenty-year-old. Her name was Leora. She was a brunette with a captivating smile and short-cropped hair. She was in uniform. I was glad to see that she didn't smoke. It was difficult to spend five minutes in Israel without being locked in an office with a smoker, or having to walk through a cloud of cigarette smoke on a street or in the hallway.

In the next fifteen minutes, Leora managed to tell me her entire life story and express her desire to return to school to become a hairdresser. She was completing her compulsory military obligation.

"You have a famous father, Mr. McGowan. He is a hero of Israel."

"How do you know?" I asked.

"It says so here," she said and pointed to the screen on her desk computer. "He was killed in the battle for the Old City in '67."

"The Old City?"

"Jerusalem, this city. In the '67 War, your father died fighting the Jordanians. His unit was the first to liberate Jerusalem. Didn't you know this already?"

I sat there and stared at the computer screen. What I took to be Hebrew letters were lined up in columns, and on one line I could decipher my father's name in English, with a series of numbers above and below it.

"Yes, I knew," I said, lying and telling the truth at the same time. "Of course I knew."

"Would you like a printout of this information? It would be no problem."

"Yes, a printout . . . please, thank you."

I sat on the chair next to her desk and waited for her to return.

"There is something else here that you might want to see," she said. "See? It is the name of the person who arranged for his burial. He is buried on the Mount of Olives. Are you Jewish?"

"Yes," I said, not wanting to go through all of it again.

"McGowan is a Jewish name?"

Leora handed me the printout. I thanked her and left her office. An old woman was sitting on the chair outside, apparently waiting to see Leora. Her face was lined with age and her clothes were worn. I wondered why she was there.

Outside, on a bench, I looked down at the printout. Leora had given me a copy in English. The person who was named as contact in the category "Burial" was Dan "Ari" Ravin. His address was also given, in Jerusalem.

I immediately took a taxi to the location. In the car, my heart pounded against the sides of my chest. It scared me. I was trying to control my expectations, but was doing a bad job of it. So much of these past weeks had revolved around my father and his life, and my own emotions about him—some expressed, some I was just unearthing for the first time. In one way, I felt like an interloper, a voyeur sneaking around the corner for a peek into a scene that was denied to me.

But hadn't I been invited, by him? Hadn't he set this whole thing in motion? Was it his way of ensuring immortality?

Yes, I had done historical research in the past, but this was not the same at all. This was different. It was like watching a movie of my own life, but without me in it, even though I could make out the themes and players that would control my destiny. I had always hated my father, hated him for so long I hardly remembered the reason, yet I could dredge it up if confronted. How could I not have hated him? I had never understood my mother, who had not once had a bad word to say about him. To me, though, he had been a blot in my life, an embarrassing fact I conveniently neglected to mention whenever I spoke of my childhood. And I saw to it that I almost never did.

But over the last few days and weeks, I had changed, and I knew it. I no longer felt hatred. More than anything, I was confused. I felt fearful. I felt ready to love.

The driver spoke a broken English, but was compelled to give me a running description of the neighborhood. He had a sister in New Jersey. Did I know New Jersey? He would give me her address. He told me we were driving through what used to be called the Russian Compound near the Jaffa Road. According to him, Czar Alexander II had bought this area as a refuge for Russian pilgrims in the nineteenth century. He pointed out the Russian Cathedral to our right, with Mount Scopus looming in the distance. Today the area was mostly the property of the Israeli government, with law courts, police offices, and even a medical school. Perhaps this would be Yehuda's school sometime soon.

Most of the buildings shared the façade of gray Jerusalem stone, giving them the appearance of older, venerated edifices. But the building in front of us, where we had stopped, was modern in appearance, a nine- or ten-story apartment building that could've been located in any city in the United States, or even in Europe. A small grocery store was on the street level next to it. A sign for Coca-Cola in Hebrew greeted its patrons on its front door.

"This is your building. Do you know the floor?"

I told the driver I'd be waiting. He gave me the address of his sister in New Jersey.

"In case you ever in New Jersey," he said.

I was able to locate the manager in the basement. He, too, spoke English, and yes, he said, there was a Mr. Ravin who was a tenant here, in number 770. He did not think Mr. Ravin was home, though, but if I liked I could wait in the lobby or, better still, in the manager's apartment.

I thought it might calm me down to bring some humor into the situation, so I asked him if he had a sister in New Jersey.

"No," he said, "in Baltimore. How did you know?"

I thanked him for his hospitality and chose to wait in the lobby. I didn't feel much like talking.

I remained seated in the lobby all day. I thought of calling the hotel and leaving word for Sarah and Martha, but I had no idea how long I'd be, so I didn't.

The Jerusalem evening was brilliant in its intensity. The globe in the sky seemed closer than ever. I gazed out at the horizon through the lobby window and suddenly realized it was not the sun at all I was observing, but the moon. My thoughts had wandered again and I was not processing correctly. I was disoriented in this ancient City of David.

The building manager twice visited me as I sat in his lobby, once bringing me a glass of tea. The hours passed quickly. People came and went during the day and early evening. None of them, however, turned out to be Dan Ravin.

A blue-green halo descended over the city. The streetlamps glittered. The buildings were gray and white. Silence.

As soon as he came through the lobby door, I knew it was Ari. I said his name.

He looked at me and said nothing at first. Then, "You are?" he asked.

"I'm John McGowan, Bill's son."

He stood frozen at the door, one hand holding his keys and the other clenched around a bag of groceries. Between his lips, dangling as smoke rose in a snakelike line into his eyes, was an unfiltered cigarette. Luckies, I guessed.

"You are Bill McGowan's son," he said, not asking at all, but confirming a statement.

I had interrupted a ritual he had obviously practiced thousands of times before—the door, the key, the cigarette momentarily dangled between his lips—but as he stood immobile at the entrance, the smoke began to annoy him.

"Here, let me help you with this," I said, taking hold of the bag of groceries. We then took the elevator up to his apartment. It was quiet as we walked down the narrow hall. So far, he had said nothing else.

Ari was a big man, much taller than I. He walked with a presence, his back straight, taking long strides. As we entered his apartment, I thought about Sarah and Martha again. It had grown late and they'd be concerned.

He had been reluctant to give up his bag of groceries, I felt, so I handed them back to him as soon as the door was closed behind us.

"Have you been waiting long?"

"All afternoon."

"All afternoon? Why didn't you call me? I wish I had known you were here. I would've come right over."

"I should call my wife. She's at the hotel and probably worried."

"Of course, of course."

Ari helped me with the telephone call. Sarah and Martha had not returned yet. I left Ari's phone number and a message for them to call me when they got back.

"It's hard for me to believe that you are here, that I am seeing Bill's son."

"It's also hard for me," I said.

"But I am not surprised. You look like him, you know."

Stanton had said the same thing; I looked like a man I'd never met. It was strange to have people point this out to me, as though I were walking in the shadow of a ghost, or had a double who would occasionally make appearances in my behalf.

"He was a great man," Ari said. "But where are my manners? Would you like something to eat, to drink? Have you had dinner?"

"Whatever you have."

"Wine? Do you drink wine?"

"Sure."

He excused himself, and I watched him choose a bottle of wine from a well-stocked rack next to the bookcase. He returned with a corkscrew and two wineglasses.

"Beaujolais-Villages," he said. "Very pleasant and becoming more and more popular. I hope you like it."

Ari poured two glasses of wine and raised his in toast. I did the same.

"*L'chayim!*" he said. "To life!"

"To life!" I answered as we touched glasses and sipped our wine. I nodded in appreciation. It was an excellent wine.

"I'm glad you like it, John. It tastes all the better in your company."

Ari walked over to the stereo and placed a CD in the tray. He pressed a few buttons, and in a moment I could make out the dulcet tones of Bach.

"Glenn Gould," he said. "Brand-new on CD. He died years ago, but he is still my favorite. This, I think, is his best. It's *The*

Well-Tempered Clavier. They just made a new film about him. He died when he was only fifty, you know. Too young. Your father also appreciated Bach. I even have some of his old records here. Books, too."

So not only did I look like my father, but he and I shared a love for classical music. The fruit doesn't fall far from the tree—an old cliché that seemed to have been coined for us. I wondered what else we had in common.

"Thank you," I said, "but they belong to you."

"In case you want them, they're here."

Perhaps the wine was casting its spell on me, or maybe it was because I had been sitting quietly in the lobby all afternoon, but I immediately launched into a recitation of everything that had happened from the day I received Stanton's letter. I had not brought the letters with me, or the photographs, or the souvenir Beverly had given us—all of these were in our hotel room—but it hardly mattered. Ari knew everything about the Stones, about Stanton, about Bertucci.

"It was not my position to interfere. It was your father who decided what was to be done. He merely confided in me."

We sat in a comfortable room in two leather chairs, opposite each other.

"Beautiful music, isn't it?" he said.

"Ari, could you tell me . . . could you . . ." I hardly knew where to begin.

"You must have so many questions, John. How much do you want to know?"

"Everything," I said.

"Oh, that is so much! I don't know if I can help you. We only know what we have lived, isn't that correct? Tell me, what do you do?"

"I'm a history professor; I teach."

"Isn't that interesting!" he said with genuine interest. "I suppose I have become philosophical in my old age. I love history, the past."

"Everything," I repeated. "I must know everything."

"Typically American, if you'll forgive me. Americans want everything, and always quickly. I wonder why you are all in so much of a hurry. You should take more time to relax, drink some wine, eat some food that didn't get cooked in a microwave. Yes, you want to know everything. Well, then, let us start with America, a country that has always enjoyed peace at home. When I travel to the States I am always amazed by how free you are. No soldiers, no Uzis, no checkpoints. Here it is a different story. You go to the market, you see soldiers. You go to the movies to escape for two hours, you see soldiers. At the bus station, at the synagogues, at the mosques. And you wonder where the war is. And the soldiers are always young, these boys and girls, babies really. People die. They are blown up. So start with that if you want to know everything."

Ari walked over to the bureau and removed a framed photograph that rested there.

"Here, look at this. The story begins with this."

It was a picture of a much younger Ari on the beach, looking robust and content. With him were a woman and two small boys. It was the picture of a happy family.

"You are a teacher, of history you say. So you know, you

understand, this land and its people. We are the birthplace of civilization. Humanity was born here. God spoke here. He gave us his laws and his light, here, not far from where we sit. Thousands of years ago, in the dawn, one cold morning, he spoke to us, separating the night from the day. His presence still fills this land.

"But the birth, like every birth, has an afterbirth, and like every afterbirth, this one is filled with blood. In this land, the center of the universe to the poets, there is blood, always blood. What you are looking at, in that photograph we took on the beach, is my wife and our two small boys. They were blown up one day, shopping in a market. Nine other people were killed, including two Arabs. It was estimated that there were enough explosives in the car to kill each person three times. Body parts were blown into the air. Some were never found."

I sat back in my chair and stared at the faces in the picture.

"I do not tell you these things to shock you, John. I tell you because you want to understand. Everything, you said. Then first you must understand how we feel, what we have lost. Then, again, you can never really understand at all, not everything, not unless you are a Jew, or . . . unless you have been touched by God. I believe your father was touched by God."

"I'm sorry," I said.

"Don't be sorry; just understand."

"We also have two boys."

"Then you are very lucky. It was originally a Greek idea: immortality through your children. Logical, like everything Greek. Have you been to Greece?"

"I'm not logical anymore. I used to be."

"Logic has its place, like anything else, but you must know where to use it and when."

"How was my father touched by God?"

Ari opened a fresh pack of Luckies and offered me one.

"I don't smoke," I said.

"Like your father again," he said.

I put the picture down.

"I'm glad you're here, John. You should know. But remember—you're in Israel now, and things here happen upside down sometimes. You'll get used to it. Even our language is backwards. We consider it the correct way, of course."

Ari closed his eyes tightly and rubbed his forehead roughly with his fist, seemingly trying to loosen some memories of the past.

"Bill was part of a group that had decided to suppress the Messiah Stones, in one way or another. Americans, Israelis, even an Englishman. An assorted mix of professional spies, bureaucrats, academics, bone hunters, young tigers like me and Bertucci. It was a lucky blunder, really, though there had been rumors of something—up there in Shiloh, finding that first block. It was quite a mystery, I can tell you. Imagine if you can—an archaeology dig created as a cover for espionage—and what do you think happens? They find something! And not just some old bones or shopping lists, but an earthquake of a discovery that actually has a message for our time! Something like a bottle thrown out to sea at one end of the earth, and centuries later it floats ashore at the other end. Can you imagine the consternation? Yes, they were thrilled—but scared as hell!"

"Why? Why was everybody so scared?"

"Why? Because they believed the Stones, that's why! What it said, you understand, was like a volcano. The Stones had been delivered to Moses by Jehovah, but kept secret by the generations of priests. I can't say if they were right or wrong, but I am sure they thought people were not ready to hear this news. It would have been like a license to steal. You understand?"

"So they hid them?"

"Yes. I saw the Stones, John, when my father found them. They were wonderful. There are no words to describe our reaction, in Hebrew or English. They glowed like small suns. But more important was how we felt in their presence. You knew—right there—in your mind, and in your soul, that you were part of creation. It was like something clicked in you, very instinctive. You could hear in your mind, like an old song, played over and over in your childhood, you could hear the voice of the Eternal, your Creator. You knew, and this knowledge made you happy at the same time it frightened you. My father said he felt like a bird on a branch hearing for the first time the song of other birds. It confirmed his existence. You see?

"But these other men, not your father, these other men had answers for everything, except this new fact. They could not explain what was there in front of their eyes—a contradiction of nature! There was no radioactivity, and they knew it. This was a creation of the living God. You either accepted it or you didn't. Your father, he accepted it from the outset. Like me, like my father. It had nothing to do with being Jewish, or Christian, or anything else. Religions only confuse.

"You see, my mother was Jewish, and I was raised by her. But in my blood, mixed with the wandering Jew, is the wandering Bedouin. A one-night stand in the desert years ago, between two people so very different, yet so much alike. And I am the result. So I have been different from the day I was born. From that day, I have been both an occupant and a stranger in my own home. It is not easy to explain; it is not easy to understand. We are the Catholic Irish who live up in the north."

"How was my father different?"

"He wanted to see God. He was not frightened."

The Bach in the background grew intense. I hadn't heard this classic rendition for many years.

"Bill went back to the States and tried to persuade the group in Washington to bring the Stones to the United States for safety. He took photographs of them. He lobbied here in Israel. He had visions of the Messiah, even drew pictures."

"We've seen them—the album," I said.

"They were absolutely incredible. He took the album with him back to the States on one of his trips. But it was no use—it was not on their agenda, as we now say. So they decided to bury it, bureaucratically, what had been buried in reality for two thousand years. But fate or the hand of God intervened, and the Stones disappeared. No one knows where or how. That is the real mystery. My father believed to his dying day that they were called back by God. Or used by God to save us from ourselves. My father thought this world did not deserve them, so God chose to take them back."

"What do you believe, Ari?"

"I believe they are here, somewhere, waiting for the right day. Maybe they're helping us right now—who knows?"

I remembered Barbara's theory and told him.

"Poland? An interesting idea. I will have to think about that."

"Tell me," I said, "what do you mean, he wanted to see God?"

"Just as I said. Bill believed in the Stones and the coming of the Messiah. He wanted to see him, more than anything . . . more than to be with his family. Please don't take this badly. He was a man obsessed with his discovery. His wife, your mother, I'm not sure exactly, but I think she preferred to stay home. I can understand. But he wanted to be here, on the scene, in case . . . well, in case he showed up. Maybe he'll be early; maybe he couldn't wait. Who knows when the year 2000 really is? You know the parable of the wealthy man who confronted Jesus?"

I vaguely remembered; it had been years since I'd heard these stories.

"This was a rich man who was searching for heaven, and he wanted to know what it would take to get there. Isn't this what we all want? Jesus told him to give everything he owned to the poor and follow him. The rich man couldn't—the price was too high. Well, it was easier for Bill McGowan. Maybe because he wasn't rich, but I know how much he missed you. So he decided to make a new life for himself in Israel. He became a citizen, joined the army, lived up north in a kibbutz right on the border. And waited. And waited. Then, in '67, he was in the first group to liberate the Old City of Jerusalem. I was with him."

Ari slumped in his chair, looking away from me. This was difficult for him, I could see. But I could also see that he was determined to continue.

"In my life, I have had two great losses. One was my wife and children. The other was your father. He was like a brother, but more than a brother. You are born with a brother, but this was by choice. Your father was a man I chose to love. I would have given my life for him. He was touched by God. Do you believe in God, John?"

That same question, over and over.

"Tell me how he died, Ari."

"He died at the Wall. Our unit saw the brunt of the fighting with the Jordanians. Now we have peace, but this peace did not come cheaply. It was purchased house by house in hand-to-hand combat. Very bloody. This was not only a war, it was a battle for Jerusalem—our city, the city that was denied to us, stolen from us by the Romans, the British, the Jordanians—it was our home, where our Temple lived and where our God was worshiped. It was our soul.

"Bill McGowan believed he would see the Messiah when he entered Jerusalem. He truly believed this. As the battle progressed, we fought our way toward the Wall with incredible ferocity. Our unit was the first in, did I tell you that? As we approached and saw it in the distance—I was next to your father—a sniper bullet pierced his neck just beneath his chin strap, here." Ari touched the spot on his neck. "His aorta had been severed, and there was nothing we could do. He couldn't speak, but was only able to hold out a hand and point toward the Wall. Two of us carried him down to the Wall and lifted him so he could touch the stone. Bill McGowan was the first citizen of a Jewish nation to touch the Wall in two thousand years, and he wasn't even Jewish."

I picked the photograph up again and looked at the younger Ari and his family. I thought of Sarah and Joshua and Oliver. I was lucky, and I knew it. For the first time, I was sorry that my father had never lived to see how lucky I was.

"What I will tell you next, John, is difficult to accept."

The woman and the boys looked up at me from the flat surface of space and time, captured on a piece of paper in the form of a photograph. Did they still exist somewhere, beyond this temporal image?

"I have never completely understood what happened next. I do not even now. Maybe you will. But if I shut my eyes, even today, I can still see it. You will recall what I told you, that two of us carried your father to the Wall, where he died. That is true. There were two of us. The other man was also a soldier in our unit, but I had never seen him before that day. He suddenly appeared at your father's side just as he was shot, kneeling next to him on the ground. It was he who understood your father's gesture to be taken to the Wall. And at the Wall, it was he who placed your father's hand on the stone. And then he spoke to your father only two words, in Hebrew. These words were . . . in English, they translate to mean 'For you.' Then your father died and this soldier closed his eyes. He kneeled down and removed your father's helmet and placed a kiss on his forehead.

"I have never fully accepted what happened next, because I cannot explain it. But I was a witness and will be to the day I die. After kissing him, the soldier folded your father's lifeless body in his arms. All at once, the bleeding stopped and the soldier—and this is the only way I can describe it in words—the soldier was absorbed, pulled into the body of your father. The soldier disappeared and became one with your father . . . the same flesh with your father. I saw it. That is what I meant when I said he was touched by God."

Ari was a big man, but for the moment seemed much smaller as he sat in the chair with his glass in his hand.

"Tomorrow, I will show you his grave on the Mount of Olives. You must see it for yourself."

"Who was he, my father?" I asked.

"He was just a man, like you or me. Don't think otherwise, John. But for some reason, there was a light over his head. An interesting story . . . yes? Hard to believe?"

"It is for you, and you saw it. This is all new to me."

Ari lifted his glass.

"*L'chayim!*" he said.

"*L'chayim!*" I answered.

The Mount of Olives is diagonally opposite the Golden Gate, one of the ancient entrances to the city, and within sight of its bricked porticos. There, in row after row, the dead await the coming of the Messiah, who according to ancient tradition will enter Jerusalem through the golden doors. Those buried here will be the first to be resurrected.

This is an ancient Jewish cemetery. In the Christian tradition, the area is equally venerated, but has significantly different connotations. In this tradition, this area is a part of the general location which in Hebrew is called Golgotha, or in Latin Calvary, where the crucifixion of Jesus took place. But though there may be doubt about a specific location for Golgotha, most agree that Jesus made his triumphal entry into Jerusalem from this very Mount of Olives.

The Mount is really a hill, like countless hills the world over. But like almost every square inch of earth in Jerusalem, or indeed all of the Holy Land, it is contested land and, depending on who is telling the story, a different land for different traditions. Even the Jews, who have only relatively recently regained control of this corner of the globe for the first time in thousands of years, have divisions within their own ranks. Some Orthodox Jews, for example, view the present Israeli state as a usurping power which will be cast aside when the Messiah arrives and establishes the true Kingdom of Jehovah—for only he, the Messiah, is authorized to reestablish the authentic Jewish homeland, not the Zionists, whom they consider a secular, political movement without a theological franchise.

From 1948 to 1967, under the Jordanians, the Mount of Olives, which was then also this same Jewish cemetery, suffered repeated desecration of the Jewish graves. The Jordanians even located a huge hotel on the summit of the slope within plain sight of the holy burial ground.

On the far side of the Mount, with a clear view of the Judean Desert and the hills of Edom across the Jordan, Palm Sunday processions to Jerusalem begin. Tradition holds that Jesus ascended to heaven from this location. All around, surrounded by names that have become synonymous with the telling of his story, are churches and gardens and crests of hills that bear witness to the unique history of these few acres. In one alone, the Garden of Gethsemane, at the base of the hill, the olive groves have been established to be two thousand years old, typical of the growth on the Mount. The follower who betrayed Jesus may have hanged himself from one of these trees. The Romans may have used some of these trees to help construct the huge siege machines employed in the destruction of Jerusalem. That is the reason, according to legend, that the Mount is so rocky and bare even thousands of years later. Tradition also holds that with the resurrection of the dead at the final coming of the Messiah, the Mount of Olives will bloom once again, radiant in its full beauty.

THE NEXT DAY, as I stood in the cemetery that morning, with Sarah, Martha, and Ari at my side, I could not help but summon up these images in my mind, images of the centuries, of the dead, of the faith in the promise of the apocalyptic salvation that transcends mortality. In front of us were the graves—rectangular shapes, covered in stone, flat surfaces, some rounded at the top like arched windows, above-ground slabs of marble facing upward to the heavens. These were sarcophagi, stone coffins displayed as monuments, miniature mausoleums bearing inscriptions that were weathered and worn by countless storms. I could see layers of moss and mold that had thrived on many of these stony surfaces, shrouding the inscriptions beneath like worn passages in well-thumbed sacred texts.

I couldn't read any of the inscriptions, as they were either in

Hebrew or, as Ari pointed out, Yiddish, the European language of the Jewish diaspora. Still, a few of these burial chambers were not ancient, but relatively new, cut with sharper edges, the stones dark and clean, chiseled with contemporary steel. On these, as on their more ancient neighbors, was the universal Star of David. Here, too, small stones had been placed on the edges of the graves, indicating a recent visit by a relative or friend.

"It is an ancient practice," Martha said, "probably not Jewish in origin, but belonging to the tribes of the desert. You must picture a burial in the sand, where the winds are constant, blowing everything in their path. So you gather many rocks or stones together to cover the body, keep it safe from the elements, or even the occasional bird or marauder. A kind of cairn in Scotland, stones set up in a heap along the road to show a marker. Like a road sign. But here, more like a safe. And now, a calling card. So goes the world."

We had all met for breakfast earlier in the hotel. The previous evening, upon my return, I had updated Sarah and Martha on my conversation with Ari. At breakfast, Ari was a genial host, keeping the conversation focused mostly on food and the weather. I had not had an opportunity to question him further about my father or the Stones.

Now, as we stood on the Mount of Olives, in the midst of so much history, I wondered aloud about something that had plagued me most of the night.

"Ari, who was he, in your opinion, the other soldier, the one who helped you carry my father to the Wall?"

"Your father is over toward this end," he said by way of response. "Come."

We followed the path between the rising terraced steps of the hill, and the rows of stone boxes one after the other. Up in the distance, I could see the glittering façade of the Golden Gate, just slightly higher than the walls that surrounded it.

Like the others, my father's tombstone lay flat on the surface of the ground, but it was small in comparison to many others. Its inscription was in English. Sarah read the words aloud:

> *The Lord God will wipe away tears*
> *. . . and the rebuke of his people*
> *shall he take away.*
>
> *The dead man shall live . . . and the*
> *earth shall cast out the dead.*
> *In that day . . . ye shall be gathered*
> *one by one . . . and shall worship*
> *the Lord in the holy mount of Jerusalem.*

Under these verses was carved an outline of a menorah, a seven-branched candelabra that lifted up seven cups of oil. Next to this carving, also in English, were the two words "For you." At the bottom, together, a Star of David faced a cross.

"The inscription is from Isaiah, of course," Ari said, "and very famous. You will find it on many of the tombstones in this cemetery. In many languages. The last two words are special, for him alone."

"And the star and the cross?" Martha asked.

"Ah, that was my idea," Ari said. "A kind of insurance. It seemed appropriate. It is so cold up here. You would think this was such a desirable location to be buried. There are so many more beautiful cemeteries. But this place is more: It is really a waiting room. Isn't it wonderful, to believe so strongly, to know that your existence in this world is only one chapter in a much larger book? I don't honestly know the answer to your question, John, who that person was. He was so young. He looked like so many of us, tall and thin, unshaven, eager. A soldier. What I saw happen is obviously impossible, so I must not have seen it. It was a . . . what is the word?"

"Hallucination?" Martha said.

"Yes, hallucination, we can say that. But I did see it. That is all I can say. Let's go home," Ari said. "It's so cold here, and I want to share a theory with you. Maybe I can answer your question. I also want you to meet someone." Ari had brought some flowers, which he placed at the foot of the grave.

When we returned to Ari's apartment, we found a magnificent lunch all prepared for us. Ari had invited a friend of his to join us, and it was she who had created this meal, which was more of a feast. The main course was grilled slices of lamb, bathed in a delicate sauce and spiced by her own recipe. On either side of the lamb, we were served sumptuous vegetables and desserts, including the best-tasting eggplant I had ever had. She must've been working at preparing this all morning.

"Not really," she said. "It's from the other night. We enjoy eating."

Her name was Helen Davis, and judging by the way they were at ease with each other, I surmised that Ari and Helen were more than just friends. Helen lived in the same building and told us she was a translator for the Ministry of Agriculture.

"Where did you learn to speak English so well?" I asked.

"In San Francisco. I went to school there. But I'm not an English translator. I'm in charge of the Russian desk."

"You're Russian?" I asked, aware of the many Russian immigrants to Israel, and hearing an accent I could not quite place.

"I was born in Sweden," she said.

"Oh, you're Swedish?"

"No, Hungarian actually," she said. We all laughed. "My parents were placed in Sweden for two months after the war, where I was born, before we made *aliya*—before we emigrated to Israel. Our generation wandered over the planet, and there were many stops along the way. Picking up a language was as easy as catching cold."

Ari and Helen were generous hosts. We had the best meal I could remember in a long while. The tomatoes actually tasted like tomatoes! Even Ari's cigarette smoke didn't annoy me as much as it normally would have.

"Your father was an unusual man," he said. "I want to share a theory about him. Helen has heard this before, but she doesn't think much of it."

Helen laughed. She was tall and blue-eyed, and wore her light brown hair cut short. She wore no makeup, at least that I could tell. Like Ari, she was in her sixties, but seemed younger.

"There are too many legends and too many theories in this part of the world," she said. "This is the main obstacle to peace. Who could imagine that so many wars could be fought over so little land, and most of it desert! Is there gold here? Diamonds? Not even oil!" She laughed as she served the food.

"So you don't believe . . . ?" Sarah began.

"In God? Which God? The Jewish God? The Christian God? The God of Islam? To which God do you refer?"

"Aren't they all the same God?" Martha remarked.

"Not from the way the followers behave," she said.

"Is that God's fault?" Sarah asked.

"Ask Ari," Helen said, trying to get off the spot. "He's the expert, not me."

I watched Ari carefully during this brief exchange between the women. He knew how to remain silent.

"How was my father unusual?" I couldn't help but ask.

"My theory? In truth, it's not my theory at all, but founded on another of those legends Helen finds so disagreeable. But I like it. It's a connection with the Eternal. When you get older, you find time to think—is this so strange?

"Supposedly, in every generation," Ari continued, "there are a number of special souls in the world. Call them special people, blessed or touched by God. Some say there are ten, some say as many as thirty-six. These are souls that have reached the highest level of perfection, closer to God. Very mystical, you understand. But the reason these souls have been placed in mortal beings is the point I want to make. It seems that after God destroyed the world with the flood, he saw that in his anger he had destroyed his most precious creation. These were innocent children. He could abide the destruction of wicked men and women, whole cities, the destruction of animals, trees, flowers, fish, the birds of flight . . . he could abide all of this destruction, but he could not abide the death of innocent children, the boys and girls and infants who reflected his own, pure image.

"So, in order to avoid the temptation—in a moment of anger—of ever destroying the world again and with it killing the children—for he knew he would be angry again, that his mercy would be constantly tested—to prevent this, he allowed a certain number of perfect souls to inhabit mortals in each generation. He knew he would never destroy the world as long as these souls were among the living. Tradition also says that the angels protested this decision, arguing that this made mankind invulnerable to their folly. But the Lord prevailed, and in each succeeding generation from the time of the flood until now, these perfect souls have lived among us, scattered around the world. Black, white, yellow, all varieties."

Helen asked us to sit down to eat.

"He believes your father was one of the perfect souls in our generation," she said.

We began our meal in silence. Ari didn't say anything else. Helen poured some wine in each of our glasses.

I didn't know what to make of his remarks. Ari was obviously educated, a man of the world, not someone who lightly believed in ghosts. From what I could gather, he'd been a part of the world of international politics, strategies and spies and plots, a soldier in at least one war, and I suspected I was being told only a small part of what he'd been through. As a historian, I had studied men like this for years, and they fascinated me—how they used their power, their control, their ability to manipulate the flow of events. But in all of my study, I had never actually met such a man, and, moreover, one who combined equal amounts of the practical and the mystical in his personality.

"You mean," I said, "you believe my father was some kind

of saint, one of those perfect souls in a sort of symbolic way
. . . not a literal fact, isn't that what you mean?"

Ari lifted his eyes to stare directly at me.

"No," he said, "I believe it is a literal fact. Why do you find
this so hard to accept, John?"

"I'm not a mystic," I said. Up to that point, Sarah and I had
not told anyone about our encounter with Beverly. It was still
too fresh an experience for us, and too much outside the normal reference points we human beings readily accept. But this
appeared to be as good a time as any, even though we might be
ridiculed.

I looked at Sarah, and she guessed what I was thinking. "Go
ahead," she said. "Tell them."

I related the events as I remembered them.

"Another guide . . . you'll meet another guide here in Jerusalem?" Helen asked.

"Yes," I said.

"I gave up gurus long ago," she said. "In San Francisco, in
the sixties, there were more gurus than cops. Everyone knew
one. That woman you met in New York, John, I hate to say it,
was probably a con artist. You gave her money, didn't you?
You can't be too careful in New York."

We were silent as we ate.

"I am not a mystic either," Ari said. "I don't even have a
religion. I don't attend services on religious holidays. I don't
burn candles. I don't pray. Not even for my family. My mother
was a Jew, my father was not. But I have described to you
events I witnessed, like war, the same thing. Isn't that why you
are here, to learn everything?"

"Everything," I said, remembering. "Who was the soldier, Ari, the one with my father?"

"I told you what I saw, as you have told us what happened to you, but I also told you I have not ever fully accepted it. Everything in my experience tells me that what I saw could not possibly have happened. Yet it did happen. It was no trick, no mistake. I can still see it. You know what, John? It scared me most of all."

"He believes the soldier was the Messiah," Helen said, "in one of his lives, or an angel."

I tried to visualize again the scene in front of the Wall. Three soldiers, one bleeding to death, one appearing out of nowhere to succor his fallen comrade. It was clear to me, in detail, like a painting on a museum wall, but hard to imagine in reality.

"Why would he be an Israeli soldier?" I asked.

"Why not?" Martha said. "Reason must be a handmaiden to faith. Don't you see?"

"What was he doing then? What did he mean when he said 'For you'?" I asked.

"For almost thirty years, I've struggled with that question," Ari said. "Who can really know?"

"Children know," Sarah said.

"Yes, they do," Ari said. "I understand what you mean. We lose our sense of wonder and innocence, we forget how to believe. We grow up, we think we're gaining on the world, but we honestly lose the truth we are born with. Only when we die do we get back this wisdom."

"I thought you weren't a religious man?" I asked.

"He's not," Helen said.

"She loves to poke fun at me," Ari said. "I let her do it."

"Please continue," Sarah said.

"I believe," Ari said, "he was among us to join your father in death, to have a victory over death."

"But he died!" I said.

"He died in this world, but can we say that he is truly dead forever?"

"What else, Ari?" Martha asked.

"It was also a sacrifice at the Wall. One life for another, as in the Temple days."

"But he didn't save him!" I repeated.

"Didn't he?" Ari said.

"But a human sacrifice?" Martha asked. "Which tradition is this? Jewish or Christian? And wasn't human sacrifice banned by the Jews? They only killed birds, pigeons, goats, in the Temple. Cruel, yes, but never people."

"I didn't say my theory follows a religious creed or tradition, one or the other. I am not a subscriber to these beliefs. I am only telling you what I felt as I stood there."

"Anything else?" Sarah asked.

"I also believe it was a miracle . . . for me to be a witness, so I could tell it to you . . . to you, John, and Sarah, and Martha, and even to you, Helen, my darling unbeliever!"

Ari lifted his glass of wine.

"L'chayim!" he said.

I drank the wine.

Chapter 7

AT THE
WALL

MY FATHER HAD CHOSEN to follow his God, even if it meant giving up his wife and his son. Whatever happened in his life, I was only permitted to see events in pieces, in parts, as though my father were in a room and I found myself on the other side of a closed, thick door. I could put my hand on the doorknob and try to turn it, but it wouldn't turn. There was no keyhole, only a narrow slit between the door and the jamb, and if I pressed my face right up against it, I could see into the room— but only in sections. First this corner, then the next. My father passed from one part of the room to another, and as he passed, I saw his movements. But the light was faint and I was a small boy at the door.

I could call out to my father to open it, to let me in, to turn the doorknob on the other side so I could join him, but he either could not hear me—the door was thick, encrusted with brass—or chose to ignore me. Was he alone in the room? Were there other voices? Was that the shadow of a second person I could see that fell against the floor, or was it the fluttering of the curtains hanging over the window?

I could stand on my toes and stretch as high as I could to see to the farthest side of the room. My father stood between two windows through which light passed into the room. The windows were high and narrow, with square glass panels that ran like a checkerboard up and down. At the top, rounded in a semicircle, the panels arched under the ceiling. Between the pair of windows, behind my father, was a shelf of books, itself high and wide. Each book stood out to reveal its spine in bright colors—reds and greens and violets—but these colors were pushed back into each volume by the light that streamed through the windows. My father didn't turn around to witness this. He faced forward, looking across the room in the direction of the locked door, in my direction. I didn't think he could see me.

And I was afraid—afraid he would never see me, afraid he did not know I was at the door, afraid he could not hear my child's voice calling him from the other side. This was a fear I had always known, deep inside me, and would not go away of its own volition. It was a fear I could taste, and the taste was dry and bitter. I could feel it in the tips of my fingers, which were numb and cold. Most of all, it was a fear I sensed behind my eyes, which burned as though in the grip of a fever. In my eyes, as I saw him, I feared I would never see him again, and this fear, this was the fear of death, his death and then my own.

My father had left me as a child, and then I knew that I would die. The door was closed. How much of a man's life can you ever know?

I awoke and heard Sarah's steady breathing in bed next to me. The fear in my dream—was it only a dream?—was still with me, this fear of death. It was then I knew how I had lied to myself and to others. I knew how much my father's disappearance had meant to me and how it had taught me to be afraid. Now the fear was back, and I could taste it again. It spoke to me and lifted my lids, not allowing me to sleep. It spoke to me of my mother.

Why had I turned away?

I was nineteen when my mother died. She had lung cancer. She started smoking when she was thirteen. To her credit, she stopped smoking eight years before her death, but it was not soon enough. When her illness began, it was first misdiagnosed as a back problem. She did have a back problem, but the pain this time was much more intense than she remembered. And, worse still, she started losing weight. But she had often lost weight, as she was constantly on diets. Her doctor assured her that it was her back, but to be on the safe side, he recommended X rays. These were taken and proved negative. Later, when it was properly diagnosed, he said the cancer had been hidden and too small to detect, and that's why the X rays had come back negative. But it was nobody's fault, the doctor said.

When it was correctly diagnosed, we were with her in the hospital. Her family was there, people I saw infrequently and did not care about. They arrived in time to hear the bad news. Her doctor said it didn't look good, it was in a bad spot, it could be serious—everything but the truth in plain words. He didn't even look at her, but at one of her sisters instead. He talked about her as though she were invisible, not even in the room.

She was in bed, her bright, beautiful hair still radiant in her sickness. Her arms were wedded to translucent plastic tubes that dripped liquid into her veins. She was very pale.

She turned to the doctor, courageously.

"Are you saying I could die?"

"Yes, that's what I'm saying."

He wanted to get this over with.

"In a month?" she calmly said.

"It's possible," he said, now looking at her for the first time. He was an oncologist and had many cancer patients like my mother.

No one spoke.

"I'm sorry," he said, and left the hospital room.

There was nothing to be done but wait. I turned away and never really looked at her again. Why had I turned away? Was I afraid of death? Five weeks later, she was dead. I couldn't cry at her funeral and hadn't cried for her all these years . . . until I awoke in Jerusalem and began to quietly sob in bed, waking Sarah.

"I'm afraid," I said, with teary eyes. I think I frightened Sarah.

"Of what?"

"What we'll find."

"It's been hanging over us since the beginning, John. Let's hope we can handle it."

"Not out there, but in us, in ourselves. Life is so short, Sarah, we don't ever get enough time to get ready, to understand what to do with this gift we're given. I've denied too many things. I don't know where to pick up the pieces. I feel helpless."

"Was it another dream?"

"I think so . . . I'm not sure anymore."

I told Sarah about my dream, trying to see my father in the locked room.

"Things are happening too fast," she said. "Too much too soon. It's being put right before our eyes, and it's blinding us. I also couldn't sleep. Our world has been shaken, John. A short while ago we were on steady ground. Now this earthquake, and it's shattered. The clock is ticking, as you said. I don't know what to think. I don't know if the world will really end in a few years; maybe it won't. Maybe we have no conception of what the end really means. We can only see things through our own eyes, and maybe that's not enough. Will we die? You and me? Our marriage, our children, our love? Is that what it means?

"I don't believe God created us all to just end it, just like that, in a twinkling of the eye. There must be something better to look forward to. What does one of the Signs promise, that he'll remove our knowledge of Good and Evil? Then we'll be innocent again, like children, won't we? Imagine, like children again! It's a beautiful thought. But I can see why they were all afraid. We should be the most afraid, I guess—we're closer to it. I'm also still afraid, even after Beverly, I can't help it, afraid of what will happen. I keep thinking about those mass suicides you read about from time to time, in Africa, in Switzerland— end-of-the-world crazies who take a pill. No wonder they tried to hide the discovery of the Stones. Who could handle it?"

"I feel guilty," I said. "I never cried for my mother."

"I know—you were talking in your sleep."

My mother had needed me those last few weeks of her life. I

was only nineteen, but I knew how depressed she was. But I couldn't look at her, dying, silent in bed, tied to those plastic tubes and bottles that hung overhead like parts of a machine that dehumanized her. So I hardly visited, preferring to stay away. Part of it also, I'm sure, was my ego, my pride again, unwilling to accept another loss, another parent who was about to leave me. I would rather be in charge, choose the time and place myself for how our relationship would end. It was a way for me to keep control of the situation. But, in the last analysis, she died without me at her bedside, alone, surrounded by a few relatives and anonymous nurses.

Beverly's lip was cut and her cheek was bruised and now, thousands of miles away, I felt such remorse and pity for her I could feel the tears well in my eyes. And I remembered my mother, and was ashamed I had not shown greater love.

I held Sarah close to me in bed.

We met Martha for breakfast downstairs in the coffee shop. Sarah and Martha had visited the Wall the day before, when I had located Ari. Now I was ready to join them at the Wall. Ari and Helen had promised to meet us there by noon. We didn't have a definite plan for the afternoon or evening, except that we knew we would remain together.

I felt as though I were descending a staircase into a catacomb of ghosts and skeletons. Perfect reason had abandoned me. No longer completely objective, I awaited the day like a wanderer lost in the desert, wondering what lay ahead.

I HAD SEEN photographs of the Wall in brochures and guide-books. In fact, I had been doing quite a bit of reading since this all started, about Jerusalem and its history, as well as the history of the region. I had learned a long time ago how tricky photographs could be, how distorted an image of reality could be conveyed through a picture. I once wrote a paper on the assassination of President Kennedy, comparing the political climate of the time to those of other presidential assassinations. In doing the research, I paid a visit to Dealey Plaza in Dallas. At the time, I was a true believer in the conspiracy theory that the Mafia and the CIA had combined to murder JFK. It was plain to me that one lone nut could simply not have accomplished the deed.

Until I stood in Dealey Plaza and looked up at the sixth-floor window of the Texas School Book Depository building, that is. What immediately struck me was how low the window was. This was no huge, expansive plaza, surrounded by tall buildings, as I had always imagined—based on the photographs we all saw. This was instead a small, self-contained square, in full view of a window that was not very high, in a building that was itself not too tall. I imagined Oswald up there with his rifle and I had no doubt he would get his man. It was not a difficult shot.

I had the same impression the first time I visited Rome and stood gazing down at the old city of Imperial Rome. Here was the Roman Senate and the other buildings. Here was the Arch of Titus, commemorating his victory over the Jews. Here under my feet was a paved Roman road, and still visible were the parallel grooved lines of chariot wheels, carved into the granite over the centuries, silent scars that remained to the present day. And what struck me then was a similar impression: How small and tightly compressed everything was! All of Imperial Rome, the heart of the Empire that ruled the civilized world, was contained in a handful of acres that comprised little more than downtown Philadelphia. The magnificent Arch of Titus? Dozens of other arches around the world were much bigger. All of Imperial Rome's capital looked like the façade of a movie set.

I mention these impressions by way of contrast.

When we approached the Wall—we were walking down, from above—I had the opposite reaction. What I saw displayed before me, I felt, was the remnant of an incredible wonder of the ancient world. I had read that the Wall was only a portion of an outer wall, but it seemed enormous to me nevertheless. I could imagine in my mind's eye a splendid temple, glittering in the sun, bustling with crowds. But whatever I had expected, this was more.

As I looked down, the plaza in front of the Wall was split into two parts. A short fence divided the space, two-thirds reserved for men in prayer, and one-third for women. This was a reflection of the Orthodox Jewish influence in Jerusalem, since, in their practice, men and women had to be separated during prayer. And even on this cold January day, I could see groups praying at the Wall, both men and women, even children.

But praying is too vague a word—adoration would be better. A young boy stood and prayed erect, then genuflected and kissed the Wall. Small boys of six or seven sat on chairs lined up in front of the Wall, facing it, prayer books in their hands. Their curled sidelocks dangled around their ears as they swayed back and forth to the internal rhythm of their prayers. Their hands were gloved as they turned the pages of their books with some difficulty, for it was a cold day.

These were among the visitors to the Wall, a scarred façade that stood as the silent reminder of a lost war and a devastated nation. I recalled one story, almost a footnote, I had recently read. In it, a Roman soldier stood on top of one part of the Temple wall and urinated down into the holy perimeter. According to the author, this was the final calumny which ignited the Jews' revolt—and led to their eventual defeat. Looking down, I could see the top of the Wall and tried to imagine that Roman soldier. Had his violation occurred on this Western portion, the façade that remains, or had it been somewhere else?

"I still can't get over it," Martha said.

"Let's get down there," Sarah said.

We walked down into the plaza. I wondered about the graves nearby on the Mount of Olives and who in addition to my father was buried there. I looked up at the Dome of the Rock as it gleamed in the bright sunlight, its golden hood resplendent in all its glory. Here was the one site that inflamed passions more than any other in Jerusalem, or the world for that matter. For here was the Temple Mount, the sacred rock on which Abraham, father of two nations, prepared his beloved son, Isaac, for sacrifice. Here was the same sacred rock from which Mohammed was believed to have ascended to heaven mounted on his magical steed. And here, too, beneath the glistening tiles and quotations from the Koran, were the curved pillars at the top of the steps leading inside, from which scales would be hung on Judgment Day to weigh and separate the good and evil souls of mankind for all eternity. Such was the poetry of Islam.

So much history, so much faith, in so little space!

It was overwhelming. As we drew closer, we sensed that there was much to discover, but had no idea how real our expectations might become. I now understood the strength there was in faith, in belief beyond reason, beyond understanding. In knowing.

Sarah and Martha had been to the Wall the day before and seemed to be drawn to the women's side at the fence. A cluster of women prayed off to one side. Another group, smaller, stood at the opposite end. Each group faced the Wall. But toward the back and nearer to us, there was one woman who stood alone.

It was difficult to see her face at first, or tell how old she was. But she was young, probably not yet thirty. She wore a full-length gray winter coat and a kerchief over her head. Like some of the other women, she had what appeared to be a prayer book in her hands, unopened. She wore no gloves. She was turned slightly toward us, and I could see her lips move as she intoned the words of a prayer. Then we moved closer to her. The woman continued to pray, the words long ago memorized and a permanent part of her consciousness.

Sarah and Martha had moved forward and stood next to her. I was farther back. Then the woman turned and offered them the book.

"It's good to see you again," she said.

"Thank you," Sarah said, accepting the book.

"I hope we are not late," Martha said.

"No," the woman said.

"Let me introduce you to my husband," Sarah said, as they walked in my direction.

Her name was Lillian Berger, and she was an American. She'd met Sarah and Martha the day before at the Wall, but only briefly.

"It's not as busy today," she said to Sarah. "Sometimes it's like this—there's no telling one day to the next. I feel better when I hold the book. You may find it helpful, too."

"I'm sorry," Sarah said, "it's just that . . . well, I'm not Jewish."

"Neither am I," Lillian said. "There are many of us out here who aren't Jewish. They leave us alone. It's really open to anyone, like a church, if you don't disturb them. It's their Temple, isn't it?"

"But if you're not Jewish," Sarah began, "why . . . ?" She let her question go unfinished as she raised her hand up toward the Wall.

"Well, it is a beautiful place." Lillian didn't elaborate on her comment.

I interjected myself in the conversation by stepping forward.

"I understand you teach," she said to me. "I have a cousin who teaches history in Austin. In high school. My husband—"

Lillian halted in midsentence, wrapping her arms around her body as though she was suddenly cold—had I seen someone else do this recently? Sarah returned the book. Lillian gripped it so hard that I could see her knuckles turn white.

"It is a cold day," Martha said. "We were just wondering if

you would like to join us for a cup of coffee, that is . . . if you are finished?"

I wasn't sure what Martha was doing. As I looked at Lillian, I couldn't decide if she was cold or frightened, or both, or something else I couldn't decipher. Her drab coat, her kerchief, indicated a person who cared little about her appearance. Yet there was another quality I saw—an energy that existed beneath the surface.

"It is cold," she said with a laugh. "Thanks! I think I would like to sit for a while."

We found a small café within a short walking distance of the plaza. Lillian kept her coat on when we were seated.

"Did you say you were from Atlanta?" Sarah asked.

"I was born there. My folks moved south just before I was born. Some of the cousins are in Texas."

"Have you been here long? Yesterday, I think you said you were a 'permanent tourist.' That sounded pretty long."

"It's just my way of expressing myself. It's been six months, or seven. I'm not sure."

A southern accent still rested beneath her remarks like soft grass under a picnic blanket. It was pleasant to hear, especially so far away from the warmth of her region, in the middle of this polyglot country.

"Are you studying here?" Martha said.

"Why?" Lillian asked, somewhat surprised.

"Six months just seems long . . . that's all," Sarah said.

"No, I'm not a student. Not working either. This is such good coffee. The coffee in Israel is much better than at home. I do miss the doughnuts, though."

I could see Sarah and Martha were caught up in this woman, especially Martha, who listened very carefully, as though she were waiting for something. But she kept quiet, waiting.

The coffee was excellent, and all of a sudden I also missed the doughnuts. The power of suggestion? We wrapped our hands around the warm mugs. Finally, Martha reached for the book Lillian had placed on the table beside her.

"May I?" she asked.

Martha picked it up before Lillian could answer.

"I also teach," Martha said. Then, flipping through the pages, she said: "It's blank! It's one of those blank books."

"It's a diary, actually," Lillian said. "I bought it just before I left for the Holy Land. Kind of a prop at the Wall. I thought you might want to use it, too. It helps me."

"What an interesting way to pray," Martha said. "Your prayers are from your heart, aren't they? You do not need the words."

"Words get in the way," she said. "They're not my words anyway."

"Six months," Sarah said. "Do you like it here?"

"Yes. And you? Tourists?"

"It's kind of hard to explain," I said.

"Honest explanations are usually the best," Lillian said. "Simple answers sometimes seem complicated, only because we make them complicated. This is a complicated country because people keep it that way. It's the distance that keeps them apart that complicates things."

"We're doing research," I said.

"Research? That says a lot, and nothing."

"There's more to it," Sarah said.

"There always is."

I hadn't noticed before how strikingly beautiful Lillian was. She did nothing to accentuate her features, but as I took the time to look closely, I could see their beauty. She had reddish-brown hair that she wore at shoulder length. Her hands were amazing—each finger delicate and long, relaxed and pink with life now that she was no longer cold. She had deep brown eyes that looked right at you without hesitation when she spoke. Her voice was alive.

I felt I'd been rude, cutting her off, not responding politely. Was it because of the lilt in her voice? Did I harbor some sort of unconscious prejudice against people with southern accents? I hoped not.

"Well," I said, "it's much more than research. We're looking into the history of some relics which were discovered here, in Shiloh actually, about forty years ago. My father was a member of an archaeological team. He—"

"The Messiah Stones?" Lillian asked.

Martha slapped her hand over her mouth in a gesture of shock and surprise, something I hadn't seen anyone do in a very long time. Sarah opened her eyes wide with equal surprise. I—practically stunned beyond belief—somehow continued to speak.

"—made the discovery, which has brought us to Israel."

"The Messiah Stones," Lillian repeated. "I realized you were looking for them when I met Sarah and Martha yesterday at the Wall."

"But how?" I asked.

"I've seen them . . . seen you . . . for almost a year, standing there. Two women joined by a man, one woman with bright red hair. I could've identified you all in a lineup. It's a simple explanation, but also complicated, John."

"But how?" Martha said. "How did you know this? I have heard about things like this, but never—"

"I don't know how, or even why, really. All I can tell you is that this is an important day for me. I knew it the moment I woke up. For a whole year, I've had no one to talk to, no one who would listen and believe me. But now you three are here. I feel as though I've found my friends. I'll have something to put in the diary now."

"Lillian, lately we've been thinking . . . well, almost as if we've been actors in a script that's been ordained for us," Sarah said. "Does this mean anything to you?"

"Chosen?" she said.

"Would anyone like another coffee?" I asked.

"It's like waking up from a dream," Lillian said, "but there are so many parts of the dream, it's so complicated, you don't know where to pick up the thread."

I knew the feeling very well.

The waiter arrived and refilled our mugs. The café was practically empty, except for a group of nuns at a table near the entrance and a young couple at the other end. Each table, including ours, was decorated with a red candle stuck in the mouth of a beer bottle. The candles were not lit. Next to each bottle, in identical wire baskets, were mounds of huge, fragrant oranges.

"I'm married," Lillian said. "I've been married for six years, and we have a darling little girl. Her name is Katie. She's five. We're not a religious family at all. We went to church when I was a child, I can remember that. But it was no big deal. Just something we did, like the museum, or taking a vacation. Everybody did it. You know, I remember going to church, but I hardly remember talking about God in any serious way at all. It was mostly prayers in a book, words that didn't mean much. Words do get in the way, so I use a blank book. Until about a year ago, when it changed."

As we listened to Lillian, I tried to recall the dreams I had recently had—dreams that had become more than passing brainwaves in the night and that had taken on realities that lasted into the day. I was convinced that these dreams had a meaning for me in my life. Call them messages, or visions from another world, I was sure they were more than psychological wish fantasies to pass the night away. Now as I listened to Lillian, I was more convinced than ever that I, too, was on the receiving end of some vitally important communication. I am not a psychologist or psychiatrist, and I've never tried to look for complex meaning where simple explanations would do— wasn't it Freud himself who said that sometimes a cigar is only a cigar?

But in the face of evidence that demands new thinking, it would be the epitome of narrow-mindedness for me to reject the proof because it contradicted my beliefs. Here before me was such evidence: a person who had made contact with us on some level that defied normal explanations. Like Beverly—or the photographs of the Stones that glowed, or the album we'd left with Barbara—Lillian was a revelation, a confirmation that

Sarah and I were not alone, that there were others like us, perhaps many others, who were following their own paths to the door of the Creator. I wondered: Was she the more powerful guide Beverly had promised? In any case, she was a person we all felt drawn to. We had much in common.

"It was a Sunday night about a week after Christmas," Lillian said. "I worked in a hospital. I'm a nurse, actually a supervisor. I'd been up till about one A.M. getting some work done for an early presentation Monday morning. I was so tired I fell asleep before my head hit the pillow.

"The dream always begins the same way. I've had it now so many times. But the first time, that night, it was the most vivid, and also the most frightening. Have you ever had a dream that was so vivid you knew it wasn't a dream? Does that make any sense? So real you felt as if you were on the outside looking in on a movie—a real movie? So real you could smell things, or touch them and tell whatever is hot or cold?"

Lillian and I had been having the same kind of dreams—not the same dream, but the same kind of intense experience. Was this the way it would happen, the way we would be contacted, spoken to by the Messiah, or were these our own voices, reflecting what we wanted to hear? We were now living in the months and years right before his coming. Was there something in the air, some change to the human atmosphere, that was preparing us, some new formulation in the mix of elements that attuned us to the message? Was he getting us ready? The Bible was replete with dreams, and so were ancient cultures. Perhaps it was beginning all over again, starting with dreams.

"Tell us your dream, Lillian," Sarah said. "Please." Lillian smiled. I could sense that she was happy.

"I am in a field," Lillian began again, "a beautiful field of tall grass. It is a bright, sunny day. I am walking through the field. My feet are bare. The grass is cool and very soft. The earth is warm. I can smell the green life beneath my feet. It is the smell of grass, and it is a green smell. I know that I am experiencing the color green in a way I have never appreciated it before. All my senses now accept the color green—I can now understand, feel, what it means to be green. This is very, very exhilarating, but also scary.

"I feel the sun on my bare arms, the warmth of the sun, but even more, the beauty and comfort of the sun. Its warmth and comfort have a texture I can feel, a fine, soft velvety texture which I now perceive for the first time. It reminds me of a soft cashmere sweater Mother wore when she cuddled me in her arms. It is warmth, but it also feeds me with life. I know this is the way a plant must feel, absorbing the energy of the sun as it grows taller toward the light. All of this I feel for the first time as I walk through the grass. I am astounded that I have never noticed any of this before."

We listened to Lillian recount her dream, and knew instantly that it was not a dream at all. She was there in the tall grass, walking through it, taking us with her in her journey.

We could see it in her eyes and we knew it was the truth.

"The field is in a clearing, and as I walk on, I reach a slight elevation and can now see the edge of the forest. The trees beckon to me, and I walk toward them. As I come closer, I can see a gap between two of the trees, as though an entrance has been provided for me. I don't know why, but I am afraid to pass through this entrance. I know—I understand—it was made especially for me, it is my personal entrance. The field itself is my field. But I am still afraid. But I know I was born to enter between the trees. I know this in my blood, and though I am afraid, I must continue walking.

"This sun is so warm on my bare arms! I feel it and it comforts me. It is with me and part of me. Do you feel it? The sun helps me, it feeds me with energy and sustains me as I approach the entrance. Then, without knowing how, I am there: I have passed through the gap into its arms, between the trees, and I am in the Garden.

"I am in the Garden."

I stared at Lillian's face as she recounted her story, but mostly at her eyes—fantastic, absorbing eyes that took us in.

"This is the Garden, the special place I could not see from the field. I know this is the first Garden, the home from which everything springs. I see all life before me: birds, animals, the fish in the streams. Every creature is in harmony with the balance of its life. Calm, all is calm. I am only an observer, but I also know I am home. I look up at the sun. It is brilliant with light, but I do not look away. I can look at it directly without pain, or fear. I am one with the sun."

Lillian pressed the warm coffee mug between the palms of her hands. It rested on the table in front of her. She brought it closer.

"I am no longer afraid. Though I am surrounded by animals of all kinds, I show no fear, because they have no fear. This is the Garden for all of us.

"As I walk deeper into the Garden, I can see two trees at the center. I know what these trees are, and I walk away from them. These trees are not meant for me; I am enjoined by some force outside of myself to avoid these trees. But I can have anything else in the Garden. I know this. Can you smell the colors? See them—they are beyond description. Each flower is an original.

"Then I see her for the first time—the woman. A beautiful young woman of about twenty. She is walking in the Garden. She is nude. She stops and stares at one of the two trees in the middle of the Garden. She stares at it a long time without moving. 'What is she thinking?' I ask myself, but there is no way to know what she is thinking. She turns her head this way, then that way, thinking. She doesn't seem to be frightened, just curious. But she frightens me. I don't want her to stare at the tree! She must go away—the tree is not for her!

"Then I see her turn her head even more to one side as though listening to a voice. What does she hear? What is the voice saying? The woman listens to someone I can't hear. She approaches closer to the tree. The tree is alive. It pulls back from the woman's outstretched arm, bending its trunk, pulling branch and leaves away from her as if swept and arched by a powerful wind—a hurricane!—in this calm, peaceful Garden. But the woman continues to approach, to reach her hand out, taking two steps closer, tilting her head, listening to the silent sounds.

"She is at the tree. The tree can bend no more. Reaching out and high, she plucks a fruit from a branch—it is not easy, she must pull hard, even now the tree refuses to give up its fruit—

but having secured it with a snap, she holds it in her two hands and turns it around and around to observe all its sides.

"She doesn't see me. I'm only an observer. But I am there, in plain sight, a witness to what she has done."

I looked at Lillian's eyes—bright brown eyes, luminous with their light. I could see her as she saw herself in that place, a witness to this primal scene. As she told her story, her eyes moved ever so slightly. What did she see now? Where was she looking?

"There is another person in the Garden, someone else besides me, watching this woman. But this other person isn't only an observer. This person is a participant. This person also calls the Garden home.

"It is a man, vigorous in his youth. His skin is smooth and tight. His body reveals a perfection of power taut under the skin. He too is nude. He watches the woman—has been watching her. For how long? I don't know; I've only just seen him.

"The woman doesn't see the man. She is still inspecting the fruit in her hands. Up to now, this prize has been only something she has seen from a distance. She has longed for it, but it has been denied to her. She turns it around and around, backing away from the tree, which now regains its erect position. Again she tilts her head, again listening to that silent melody or message that only she can hear. Why is her spirit so restless? She is not concerned with the man who stands watching her. I can see him. He is silent, but not moving toward her. There is no expression on his face. He only watches. 'Is he curious?' I wonder.

"The woman's breasts are full and firm, and she begins to breathe heavily standing in the Garden. Then, having heard what she has heard, she brings the fruit to her mouth and places it between her lips, biting hard into its side. The sound of her bite snaps the calm air of the Garden—perhaps it echoes beyond the Garden into the stillness of the field on the other side of the trees. It is the sound of an explosion! All at once, the woman staggers, dropping the fruit, staggering back until she falls!

"Oh, I know what I have seen in my dream . . . and I can't stop my heart from racing . . . it is racing so fast I can feel it pulse up into my neck and beat its drum!"

Lillian's hands shook as she lifted her mug to her lips to sip her coffee. Sarah helped her steady herself by holding on to her elbow. Martha moved her chair closer to Lillian's.

She continued. "The woman is on the ground, crying softly, the fruit dropped at her side. The man has been watching all this time. He is her husband. He too lives in this wonderful Garden. He too has seen the fruit from a distance, always a distance. But now he approaches his wife and helps her to her feet. He loves her. I can see him touch her face with tenderness and wipe away her tears. But he is confused. He has never seen tears before. He touches her tears with the tip of his finger, then places his finger in his mouth.

"This is the man the woman loves. I can see her love in her eyes. The man is the center of her universe. She was made to be with him. She is his flesh and blood. Her bones are his bones. Her joy, his joy; her sorrow, his sorrow. They must know things together in order to love each other. But now she knows more than the man. She is still with him, but also apart from him. She is beyond him. She knows this now. She has the power of knowledge of Good and Evil . . . and this brings her loneliness, because he is not with her. She must share her knowledge with him; he must lose his innocence with her. So she picks up the fruit and offers it to him. She wants him to taste its power. She implores him. Without hesitating, he bites into it—and once more I hear the snap and the shock of the explosion—and once more the fruit is dropped as this time it is the man who staggers and falls to the ground.

"I am the observer. I see what they have done. She extends her hand to him, and he gets up. They see that they are naked, and they begin searching for broad leaves.

"I wonder if they see me. They stand together, weeping, moaning like animals, sobbing into their cupped hands. Suddenly, they turn. They can hear footsteps approaching, familiar footsteps. It is their Master, who is out walking in his Garden. The man is called. He tries to hide. He is discovered, he can't hide, there is nowhere to hide or run. I can't watch the scene that is played out! The man is banished, cast out of the Garden, along with the woman. They are thrown out of their home by their Master, who is very angry. I am an observer, but I cannot see the Master, who is hidden beyond the tree. I can only hear the voice, the angry voice that like the roar of the wind pushes the man and the woman toward the gap in the trees.

"They are swept away from me toward the edge of the Garden. They stop for a moment at the entrance and turn to take one last look at their home, which they will never see again. I can see the sorrow in their faces, the pain for themselves and the countless generations to come.

"The Master's angry voice sweeps them through the gap and into the outer field. Then a flaming sword descends from the sun, spinning through space, and bars the entrance to the Garden. From now on, it will not be possible to enter or exit the Garden this way. I can no longer see the man and the woman, only the back of a rotating, flaming sword.

"I alone remain in the Garden. I and the Master, who knows I am there. I am not frightened anymore, or ever again. I am happy, filled with incredible joy and gladness. I know I am to go to Jerusalem, to be at the Wall, to wait for two women and a man and to tell them my dream. I know this as well as I know the shape of my own face in a mirror. And I also know I will meet someone else. Soon."

Lillian had a radiant smile on her face. Martha and Sarah, sitting on either side of her, each held one of her hands.

"I've been in Jerusalem waiting for you, but also waiting for the Messiah, who will come in the year 2000. He may already be here, waiting like me. I am not the only one here. I've seen others at the Wall, Jews and non-Jews, also waiting. There really is nothing to say when you know the simple truth—everything else becomes so trivial, you just want to be here. It's where you belong when you know. I told my husband what I saw, what I dreamed. And it got very hard at home. I didn't know what to do; my husband is a difficult man, he needed proof. I had none to give him. Then my mother died after a prolonged illness. She could've helped me, but she was gone. I love my husband and Katie, but I had no choice—I had to get to Jerusalem, I knew it. My dream compelled me. Can you understand that? I hope so, because it's the only way I can explain it. My husband wouldn't go. I felt very guilty, leaving them. But I had no choice. Please, you must understand. . . ." Lillian sobbed softly.

I did understand, all too well. Lillian had approached the same fork in the road my father had come to years before. Had he tried to tell someone? My mother?

"It's better now," Lillian said. "I was alone before, but now you're here."

"How many times have you had this . . . vision?" Sarah asked.

"I don't know. Many times. It's made me strong."

"But how did you know about the Stones?" I asked.

Lillian wiped her eyes with a tissue Martha gave her.

"I've only told you one of the dreams I have," she said. "There are other versions of it. In one of them, the man and the woman stop at the entrance to the Garden just before they are expelled. There they see three glowing Stones on their left and two Tablets on their right. These had been given to them by their Master. I see them lift these onto the back of a donkey and depart with them out of the Garden. The Stones and Tablets shine with their own light, the light of the Master's creation. The Master allows them to leave with these possessions. On the three Stones, the Messiah Stones, I can see what is written. The words are foreign, but I understand, and at the bottom of each I see the name 'McGowan.' Lastly, the man picks up a perfectly round stone globe and carries it under his arm as he leads the woman, the animal, and their sacred objects out into the field."

"It says 'Sarah' on the globe, doesn't it?" I said.

"No," she answered. "It says 'Lillian.' "

"We can only see part of the story," Martha said. "We are never allowed to see the rest."

"I don't think it matters how much of it we see," Sarah said, "as long as we see *some* part of it."

"Yes," Lillian said, "but I'm no longer afraid. Isn't that enough?"

"Contrary to what we may have heard on TV or seen in the movies, space is not the final frontier," Martha said.

"I know," Lillian said. "It's death, isn't it?"

"It is death," Martha said. "Death indeed. Death was introduced in the Garden and will only be finally vanquished when the Messiah arrives. It is what all the stories are about. The supernatural words, the power of miracles, the ability to avert disaster in times of great peril—all of it is a way to conquer death, to slay the fear of death. Is that not the final miracle? Someone who has the power to confer life after death? Just imagine if it were possible to do it, to have such power. Not merely to cure disease, but create life, to invoke the secret name of the Creator and part seas, make birds out of thin air, make water drip from dry stones, and, above all else, put the spark of life into the ash of dead flesh."

"It'll happen," Lillian said. "I know it."

"Maybe we do not need to ever know the whole story," Martha said. "Maybe we can imagine the whole from only a piece, like completing the DNA chain even if we do not possess every single cell. Perhaps. The Jews have a legend which they would tell at times of impending doom. It did not help them this last time, in their greatest crisis. But it shows the truth of what Lillian has found, I think."

"Can you tell it, Martha?" Sarah asked.

Martha said, "It begins with a rabbi or holy man who, in times of great peril for his people, would leave the city and go out into the woods to kindle a fire and intone the secret name of God in prayer. This would save his people and avert disaster. In the time of the prophets, this was how tragedy was avoided. But as the years passed, times changed. In the next generation, the people grew further away from the Creator. Then, in another crisis, another holy man went out to the forest to kindle the fire and intone the sacred name. Though he had forgotten the prayer, it was enough to save his people. In the next generation, a succeeding rabbi knew the location in the forest, but didn't know the secret name or the prayer. So he merely kindled the fire. But that was sufficient for his generation. Finally, in our generation, we have forgotten the location in the forest, we have lost the ability to kindle a fire, we do not remember the secret name for God, nor do we know the prayer—all of it is now lost in the mist of legend. Yet, we still have the story itself to tell, and hope that the story itself will be enough to avert the greatest calamities."

"Something will happen, soon, very soon," Lillian said. "Everything is connected to everything else. Nothing happens without a reason. It seems so simple, doesn't it? Why do we have such a hard time accepting the truth?"

"Because truth has been filtered for us, mixed with flavors

and additives, and we can't even taste it anymore," Sarah said. "Whose truth would you like? The Jews'? The Christians'? Islam's? The Hindus'?"

"But isn't there just one universal truth? If God is God, wouldn't he be everyone's God, regardless of who recognizes him or not, regardless of how he's been interpreted?"

"Of course, John," Sarah said. "The problem is not with God, it's with his creations—us!"

"Maybe we have been chosen to help get it right this time," Martha said. "More than chance is at work here. Don't you sense we are close to something? Tell me, Lillian, in your dream, what color, what race, are the man and woman?"

"Color?" Lillian asked, thinking. "I really don't know. I can't see them that way. I never thought of that before. I can see them clearly, but they have no race, not one race. Is that possible?"

"And yet you describe colors so vividly," Martha said.

"Yes, the colors are real."

"And the Stones," Martha said, "why are the Signs of the Messiah in three languages, like a theological Rosetta Stone?— you remember, the stone Napoleon's troops found in Egypt that has allowed us to interpret hieroglyphics because it has a version in Greek. Why Hebrew? Why Aramaic? Why Latin? It is as though everyone must read it, in all languages, so we can all know. It is not meant for just one group, or one race, it is meant for us all. There are no sacred languages, except the word itself, which is the Creator's.

"Think of it: Does not religion set us apart more than anything else? It is the great divider. 'My way is better than your way, better than his way,' et cetera. The wars of centuries are fought for such ridiculous reasons. I can attest to that! I can see their flags. The crusaders of all religions who preach the unique, the purifying, the one and only. Believe me, I have spent my life studying religion, and I have learned only two things with absolute certainty: First, all religions are the same in their basic desire to reunite us with our Creator, and second, religion and faith are as separate as night and day. Never confuse religion with faith, or the ultimate truth, which is within us. What we see in our churches are the productions of our own imaginations. But what you have experienced, Lillian, will never be found inside the approved margins of official dogma. Yes, you are not afraid, and that makes all the difference!"

I felt fortunate to have met these women. It was true that they shared some spiritual communion which I didn't have to the same degree. In our age of political correctness—of anti-sexism, feminism, and blind obedience to salute the creed of absolute equality of political rights—we've lost our sense of understanding that people are different, that there are certain qualities unique only to some. I'd recently read an article of new scientific data which showed that men and women use their brains differently, for example. Now I had come to this conclusion: that the women in my life were superior to me in their spiritual qualities. Could I dare express this viewpoint out loud? Would championing this special sensitivity of women be construed as a throwback to a time of discrimination, when women were relegated to a station in life somewhere below the superior, rational pinnacle of mighty man?

I would keep these thoughts to myself and somehow hope to

attain their higher level of sensitivity. I knew it was also necessary to keep my own spiritual antennae stretched as far as possible, not only to listen to what I heard, but to understand. I had traveled a great distance, but there was still far to go.

Sarah reminded us that Ari and Helen would be meeting us at the Wall. Since it was almost noon, Lillian suggested that this would be an even better time to be there. We paid and left the café. When we got to the Wall, I could see what Lillian meant. The entire plaza was now filled with crowds of people, perhaps a hundred or more, with others arriving as we approached.

People were praying their afternoon prayers, Lillian explained, facing the Wall and chanting the verses and phrases that had been handed down through the ages. Though the Temple no longer existed, there was a spirit alive among its acolytes that was almost tangible. I envied these people. To be so certain, to have the ultimate knowledge deep inside their hearts, and to be secure in that knowledge, and not afraid! This was no existential philosophy I was seeing displayed in front of my eyes—this was instead a personal express train to the Creator.

In fact, it had become a tradition over the centuries after the destruction of the Temple for supplicants at the Wall to write prayerful requests on small pieces of paper and stuff them in the narrow crevices between the huge blocks. These were pleas, no doubt, of every description, messages from mankind sent directly to the attention of the Almighty: for health, wealth, wisdom, but most of all for happiness. How many of these had been answered? Who was it who said that the two greatest tragedies in life are, first, not getting what you want and, second, getting it?

These were not my people, however. I had little in common with these men who wore long black robes and black hats, whose long, shaggy beards swayed as they prayed and chanted in a frenzy of devotion. The words alone were only a part of their love and obedience—their entire bodies participated in the act.

Others, too, were there. Younger men, soldiers and civilians, many unlike these adjutants of adoration. These others were billboards of modernity—their clothing could have been mine, their sneakers and jeans my own, their clean, shaven faces reflections of mine. But they, too, chanted and genuflected, echoing the words of afternoon prayer.

Then I realized I was focusing on everything that separated people, the outward differences in clothes and appearance, rather than what connects us all, the common fabric, the simple truth of a common heritage. It was so difficult to get beyond the self, the ego.

I thought: Were the prayers designed to benefit their God, or themselves? Does God need the prayers of his followers, or do his followers need the prayers to acknowledge their love for God?

Are prayers one way of not ignoring the Creator's existence?

I was becoming enmeshed in ideas and concepts that before had literally never entered my mind. I was like some shipwrecked survivor drifting on a raft in the middle of the ocean. Alongside, a huge ocean liner appears. A Jacob's ladder is dropped overboard, its many steps loose and swaying in the ocean breeze. I start to climb, but find it difficult. It is a rope ladder, true, but it is also a web, accepting each of my steps, each grasp of my hand, then giving way to one side and then the other, not allowing me to climb directly up, but pulling me to one side, then the other, against my will. Why was I having so much trouble understanding? Lillian had made the leap, as my father had. What was holding me back? How could I break free and make the climb? Could I do it alone, or did I need help?

It was an age-old question, really: If God had wanted us to perceive him, why did he make it so difficult? Or did he? Isn't he visible in each leaf, in each thumbprint, each shell on the beach? Then why do we have so much trouble picking up these shells?

If there was a path for me up the ladder, it would not be an easy one, but it would not be up to me alone. I could see that I would need help. And I would take it.

Here I found myself in a land on the brink of real peace for the first time in modern times. Wasn't this one of the major prerequisites for the return of the Messiah? Was he here, among this crowd, waiting for the ink to dry on the last and final peace treaty? How soon would the millennium arrive?

Sarah had brought along with her the photographs of the Messiah Stones. She took them out of her bag and showed them to Lillian. The three women stood looking down at the illuminated images without speaking. Were these the same Stones Lillian had seen in her visions? Even in the well-lighted plaza, the light from the pictures burned as brighter candles in the darkness.

I was standing at the rear of the section reserved for the men, and then I moved forward, deeper into the area reserved for prayer. This was not a temple, or a church, or a cathedral at all, but simply the façade of a destroyed, ancient symbol of worship, a shrine that had once sheltered animal sacrifices, where blood ran down the marble, where living creatures were slaughtered for the benefit of their Creator. I tried to imagine such scenes as must have taken place on the other side of the Wall. I tried to imagine the thoughts of the supplicants, of the priests, of others in attendance. I tried to imagine their faces and their hands as they wielded their knives. I tried to see the terror in the eyes of the doomed goat as it awaited the cut of the blade.

I couldn't see it. It was beyond the wall of time. Thousands of years and too much of the world separated me from the blood on the ancient stone, and from the bloodless plaza where I now stood. How was a man of the twentieth century to see inside the chambers of the first?

There, off to the side, the women were gathered, circled around the radiant photographs like warriors around a fire. And I—equally in need, equally cold outside the circle of fire—found myself still hesitant.

The men in front of me bowed and prayed. I could only see their backs. Above us, reaching high into the sky, the blocks of stone rested one atop the other. The stuffed paper messages were nestled in the spaces between them. Here and there, grass had taken root on this ageless surface, much like the life that had sprung up on the cold slabs resting on the Mount of Olives.

I had made the journey to Jerusalem and found myself at the Wall. The sounds around me were foreign and strange, rhythms I had not ever heard before, guttural chants that seemed to come from some deep well within. Were these the same frequencies that quickened the life force in the first man and woman, that resounded down the corridors of empty space, that collided into the molecules of existence to explode into life . . . when out of nowhere, the universe rippled into the morning and the evening of the first day?

Were these those sounds?

Will these be the sounds we hear when the Messiah arrives to summon the faithful and trumpet his kingdom? And when we hear these sounds, will we be afraid, or will the peace that surpasses understanding grip us like protective parents holding our hands as we pass through darkened tunnels?

What was happening to me?

This strange place was taking hold of me in a way I did not understand. The Wall itself seemed to brighten. I was an explorer, and now I had made my discovery—of what? It was a discovery that lay on the other side of the Wall, I knew that much. But it was also a discovery about myself, as a man, a son, and also as one of the many in devotion at the Wall.

I discovered there was a part of me that was trying to escape the boundaries I had built for myself, to reach out and up toward a larger meaning for my life. This was a frightening discovery, but it also gave me joy. I lacked the words to express this feeling properly. I lacked—and I sensed this to the bottom of my soul—the humility that would allow me to express my discovery to others, as Lillian had, unself-consciously. My ego was like a weight around my neck. How could I possibly remove it?

To gain my freedom, I had to give up my freedom.

I had also discovered another truth, one that blossomed in my consciousness in an instant of childlike insight: that progress is an illusion, a sleight of hand, a fabrication in a magician's laboratory. It is like a new construction of tall, modern buildings of glass and steel, electronic marvels that connect us to each other at the press of a button, or the sound of a voice, that warm us in winter and cool us in summer, that sway gently in the high winds a hundred stories above the ground . . . and yet, and yet, these soulless structures are built over hidden treasures, simpler homes, prouder edifices that once fed our beings with the wonder and joy of the universe. Today, we can live longer, but the joy is less, for we are alone in our old age. We are offered a greater abundance of food, but the taste is bland, and the crust is heavy. We can choose the sex of our children, but love is lost in our lives and we go to bed eager for affection. Above all, we can shoot rockets to the moon and beyond, plant our steps on the sands of Mars, listen to the winds as they sweep across the endless vistas of Venus . . . but the voice of the Creator is unheard in the land, lost, muted in the deep well of progress, buried in the dark, distant, forgotten Garden.

"The Lord is One," says the ancient text, and the words entered my mind like welcomed guests in the storm. Was this another discovery I was yet to make? Was this the secret to the heart of Jerusalem, this temple that had given refuge to so many searchers in times past?

In a sense, I realized, I needed to get to the other side of the Wall. On the other side, even if it existed only in memory, was the figure of the Messiah, cast like a giant shadow across the marbled floor of time. There also existed the Stones, salvaged by the first man and woman in their banishment and a long exile. The Stones were universal and whole, unfiltered through the sands of time, the ultimate symbol of our happiness and joy. There, on the other side of the Wall, I knew the Messiah waited like a bridegroom for his bride. He waited for all.

He waited for me.

I pictured the photographs of the Messiah Stones as I had last seen them, glowing like beacons in the night. It all came back to the Stones, those stubborn remnants of a hope that refused to die, Tablets that remained buried like time capsules from the Creator, to be unearthed at the ringing of the chimes.

Were the chimes ringing? Were they ringing for me here at the Wall?

I had not started out on this road wanting anything special, nor had I especially sought the road in the first place. From the day I was contacted by the old lawyer, however, I had hoped it wouldn't come to this—to knowing for certain. Perhaps this was my greatest fear—to know, and yet to be on this side of the Wall. If the chimes were ringing for me, they were also ringing for each of us, alive or dead. They were ringing to announce the Messiah, who was ready to enter our lives and change our world forever. Yes, it all came back to the Stones, three Tablets that told the same story, in three different languages. We had photographs to prove their existence. Who took the pictures? Had they died believing?

—

BUT AS I stood there, I begin to see something else.

I am drawn up. I am passed through the Wall. My eyes are closed and I am on the other side.

What I see are the Stones themselves—not pictures of the Stones. They are real, glowing with their inner fire, alive with their promise.

I see them and I know what they are, why they are there: I understand their function. They are like giant dishes, transmitters that beam out their constant message to a receiver outside of our world. Someday soon, the receiver will respond to the call and return with a message to our home base, to our lives. The return message will be the Messiah.

Then I am taken up again, up . . . to view one more spectacle.

I am drawn above the lights of cities into the whirl of clouds, into the constant night that covers the globe. I am transported on invisible wings, carried in flight on the air, which guides me with its own intelligence. I am taken up, floated high and into the distance. Passing beneath me are seven huge eagles that fly in formation out toward the shore. Their shadows can be seen wide and dark on the sands below.

The eagles fill me with wonder and joy. I see the magnificent spread of their wings and how easily they soar beneath me. These are eagles, yet they fly perfectly in formation.

The sun rises above the horizon. It is large and red and living, moving in slow motion to its inner clock. Its life and light fill the earth and sky with the promise of a new day, a miracle of creation that I witness. I have never seen this before. Is this my world? Where have I been not to have noticed this? Here is splendor beyond imagination. I feel like applauding!

But I am taken farther and farther, deeper and deeper into this world—this world that is mine, yet is not mine. Like the eagles beneath my sight, I am heading for a destination beyond the forest, which now comes closer into view.

I don't want to see it! I refuse!

My body aches this time . . . yet, I know I must look. It is there, and it will erase any lingering doubts or fears that I still have.

It is the flaming, revolving sword that blocks the entrance to the Garden. So it is there that I am being taken—the Garden!

But it isn't possible!

I can see the sword, flaming and turning, creating a whirlwind of fire impossible to breach. There are the cherubim who wield the sword, beautiful yet frightening creatures that are half child and half bird. They have been placed at the entrance to the Garden to prevent passage—my passage, someone else's?

The sword revolves on its own axis, yet is visible and distinct within the circle of flames. The cherubim look up and see me, but are helpless to delay my descent. They must remain at the entrance, constantly vigilant, turning, chained to the entrance. I, however, have been freed to soar above and over their terrifying gate.

I pass over the terrible scene and enter the Garden.

I am where I belong. I hear the music of the spheres. I see the peace of the animals. I smell the living colors of the chrysanthemums. And there, in the middle of the Garden, are the two trees: One of Good and Evil and one of Life. I am forbidden to eat of the fruit of these trees, especially of the Tree of Life, for on that day I, too, would conquer death and become like God.

Why am I being shown this scene?

I descend and set foot in the Garden. For the first time, I feel complete. This is my home. These plants are mine. These animals belong to me. They halt in their tracks, stop their grazing, lift their heads, and freeze in recognition of a man in their midst. But they do not flee from me; instead, they return to their eating, heads down, unconcerned and unafraid in the Garden. There is the lion, there is the lamb.

It is neither day nor night, but sometime in between. No wind, only the sound of the animals as they graze and pass one another.

A bird in flight.

I am hungry and pick up a fruit that has fallen from a pear tree. It is the best food I have ever tasted. I see dates and olives, and I eat them. I am in no rush. I want the time to pass slowly. I want to feel the joy of the Garden, to know the touch of each leaf as it gently brushes against my skin. I want to take in each view, as a lover first seeing his beloved.

I cannot believe it exists for me, as it existed for Lillian.

Then I hear footsteps approaching. Someone is walking in the Garden. I am afraid to imagine who it might be. He calls to me and I answer.

It is the Messiah walking in the Garden. I cannot see his face, but I know who it is. He is the centerpiece of my vision. He is making his presence known to me. He is telling me he is pleased that I have come to Jerusalem to find his Stones. He is telling me that my search is nearly complete, that his day has nearly come.

He tells me not to be afraid, to wait and to watch. I am being shown the Garden to know that all will be well in the end.

"The Garden is for you," he says. "Death is not the end; it is only the beginning."

I HAD COME so far in so short a time.

I now opened my eyes again. I was back at the Wall surrounded by people. In front of me, the men prayed. Above their heads, I fixed my gaze on a huge block of Temple stone, massive in its majesty. Without moving, I sensed I could touch its surface, feel its texture, kiss it from a distance. It was a door or a window through which I had passed. The Temple in front of me, which had been destroyed two thousand years ago, was now rebuilt and within me. I knew this.

The sounds around me slowly died away, and what remained was a faint hum in my ears. A buzz: men at prayer . . . the women . . . the glowing photographs . . . both an ancient and modern mosaic of sound and color framed by a single block.

Then the stone itself above my eyes appeared to move.

I closed my eyes, then opened them. A tall man stood next to me.

"Would you like a guide?" he asked.

Chapter 8

The Messiah Stones

HE WAS YOUNG, about thirty, perhaps a few years younger or older. He was tall and thin, but not gaunt. His hair was thick and dark; his eyes were brown. He wore a navy-blue jacket buttoned up the middle that seemed one size too small. For a moment, he reminded me of a sailor. He wore no hat, but over his shoulder, strapped to his back, he carried a backpack, the kind that I'd seen thousands of times around campus, but this one much larger. It looked like something you'd want if you went camping or touring. Jutting out from the bottom of it at its sides, I could see what looked like a large spoon, or it may have been a small shovel. It was hard to tell. I then realized that his jacket was not too small at all, it just looked that way, pulled in tight by the pressure of the strap around his waist that secured the backpack to his body.

He wore brown hiking boots. I had a similar pair myself, although I did no hiking.

He stood next to me, at my right. He was a bit taller than I was, so I had to look up into his face. I've thought long and hard about how to describe his face and his features, especially the slight smile I could detect, but it is difficult. It's not that I don't remember what he looked like, because I do; it's simply that when I looked directly at him, and he at me, I found myself fixing almost exclusively on his eyes.

His dark brown eyes were deep and warm and seemed to freeze me in my place as I stood next to him. They were not threatening eyes, but nevertheless were commanding. I found it extremely hard to look directly into his eyes, but at the same time could not look away. Then I became self-conscious at what I was doing, feeling that I was intruding on his privacy by peering too deeply into his eyes. But I was not afraid. For the first time since Stanton had contacted me—even beyond what I had felt in Beverly's presence—fear was not among my mix of emotions. I think he sensed this in me, that I was completely at ease.

But I didn't know what to say, or how to answer him. He had spoken first and asked a simple question. He seemed to be waiting for a reply. Then I said something that just came to me, completely unrehearsed, something I'd probably said before to total strangers, but not since I was a child, looking for a friend in the playground. It was something I'd said to children my own age.

"My name is John," I said simply.

"I'm happy to meet you, John," he replied. "My name is Simon." He extended his hand, and I shook it.

"Simon," I said.

"Yes," he said.

"I'm happy to meet you," I said and smiled.

He waited, then he spoke again. "Would you like a guide?" I'd forgotten that he'd asked the question.

"Yes! Oh, yes!" I said. "Yes, very much! But there are others here, too."

"You're in a group," he said.

"There are four of us, with two others coming. Six," I said, somewhat nervously telling him the obvious arithmetic.

"Yes," he said. "I saw you before, talking. I was standing over there, just off to the side, waiting for someone just like you, John. As we say, you're from out of town. You have that look about you."

I remembered what Beverly had said in New York; Simon was echoing her comment.

"Simon?"

"Yes?"

"Was it you we were supposed to meet in Jerusalem?" I asked. "Are you—?"

"Yes," he said simply. "If you want me, I'm here. You must have many questions, as always, John. I hope I can answer all of them for you. How much do you want to know?"

I looked directly into his eyes, then had to look away.

"Everything?" he asked. "That is so much."

Simon had read my thoughts, and I felt embarrassed, not so much because he'd intruded on my privacy, but because my answer was so naive, and also so greedy. What right had I to know everything, to be shown everything, to understand everything? Again, I felt like a child, eyes wide with desire, so needy and so helpless.

I don't know why, but I extended my hand again and touched his arm, confirming again what my eyes and senses were telling me, that he was a physical reality. He didn't seem to mind when I touched him.

"Is this a dream?" I asked. "Who are you, Simon?"

He smiled and appeared to slightly shift the weight of the pack that rested on his back.

"Shouldn't we include the others, John, the others in your group? I hope you're ready to do some walking."

"Tell me, Simon, please!"

I must've sounded like an idiot, speaking to him that way. Yet I didn't feel embarrassed at all, just utterly absorbed in a deep longing and curiosity.

"I am who you want me to be, John. It's as simple as that. My name is Simon and I'm a guide here at the Wall, in Jerusalem. We have other guides, here too, but also in other cities. You met one of us before, in New York. She told me to be expecting you."

"But," I began, "there has to be so much more to it than that, Simon. You know me, you understand me, you understand . . ."

"John, I know I'm very happy to meet you, and I can see you feel the same. But you're a stranger here, and there is so much history surrounding us, so much to see."

"I don't want history!"

"You will do yourself a disservice if you don't start at the beginning. That's why I've come to meet you, to be your guide. Can you see that?"

"How far do we have to go? How far back?"

"That depends," he said, "on how far forward you want to go."

"I'm lost," I said. "I don't understand anything."

"That is a beginning, John, for now we know where you are. It will help in your assignment."

Then I remembered why I'd come to Jerusalem: for the Stones, for my father. Simon understood my thoughts.

"Yes," he said, "we will find the Stones. We will bring them here from where they have been these past forty years."

"At the Wall?" I asked.

"Not far."

"And my father?"

"Do you want to find your father, John?"

I didn't quite understand Simon's question. My father was dead.

"Yes," I said. "I want to find my father."

"Then don't look for him among the dead," he said. "Look for him among the Stones. And in yourself."

During our conversation, without my realizing it, the women had walked over to us. I wasn't sure how much they'd overheard. Sarah was standing next to me, with Martha and Lillian beside her. Honestly, I didn't want to acknowledge them at all—I wanted to keep talking to Simon. I wanted him all to myself. Everything he said seemed to raise other questions in my mind. On one level, I understood him; on another, it was as though he were speaking a foreign language. Ever since we'd left New York, I'd known in my heart that we'd be encountering something, someone. Now I was being told to start at the beginning again, far back, if I wanted to go forward.

Perhaps, it occurred to me, the beginning and the end were the same.

"My name is Simon," he said to the women. His voice and presence gave us a sense of security.

The women said nothing. Sarah took my hand and held it in hers. Lillian clenched the black book. It was Martha who spoke. She was still holding the photographs of the Stones, which I could see glowing in her palm like burning embers.

"We want to go all the way forward," Martha said, "as far as you can take us. We have come a long way to meet you, Simon. I am Martha."

Simon turned to the others.

"And I am Sarah."

"My name is Lillian."

He then turned to Martha once more. "You've been to Jerusalem before," he said to her.

I now remembered that Martha had mentioned that she'd once been to Jerusalem and had promised to tell us about it, although she hadn't.

"Yes," she said, "before." She had a faraway look in her eyes.

"Like a frog placed in boiling water, the truth comes slowly," Simon said. "And death is frightening, but not the end. If you want to go all the way forward, Martha, then you need to tell us where you have been. God has sent you a boat and it's time you got in, isn't it?"

Martha had tears in her eyes. For the first time since I'd gotten to know her better, she seemed less confident somehow, less in control of herself. Simon had touched a nerve that was not only very alive in this woman, but very much on the surface of her soul. Although we were standing in a small circle at the Wall, surrounded on all sides by groups of people, the din of their voices seemed to fade as we all looked at Martha. Her hair, as always, was in a neat bun; her glasses dangled on the gold chain around her neck. She spoke calmly, her manner unaffected, completely open.

"It was for a child," she said. "After . . . after my father and I left Germany, we came to America. All these years . . . my studies, my books, my students . . . all these years. I am ashamed."

Tears streaked down her cheeks, but she ignored them. No one said anything. We waited.

"Once," she said, looking at Sarah and Lillian, "after the war, while I was still young, I read that there were many orphans who needed parents. Refugees from Europe. Survivors from the camps. I had always wanted children in this life. I could have been a good mother. And there were so many who had needy eyes and open hearts. So I took a trip to the Holy Land and made inquiries. There were so many children to choose from, so many. I couldn't believe it. I could have adopted one, a particular little girl, she was so beautiful, only five. I remember her so well. There isn't a night that goes by that I don't see her before I fall asleep. And I would have been permitted to return to Pennsylvania with her had I so wished, even though I had no husband. They were so needy. But . . . how can I explain? I was afraid at the last minute, to risk, to love. Please," she said, removing her glasses from around her neck, folding them, and placing them in her coat pocket, and turning again toward Simon, "why was I afraid?"

Simon looked at her thoughtfully.

"We are who we are," he said. "Each life is precious and unique. We cannot go back, Martha, but we can start from where we are. God has promised that in the end, except for a few, we will know happiness. So begin a new beginning today, take a risk, extend your hand. Believe me, there are many who want to take it."

"How?" she asked.

He said, "There is still time, but I will tell this to each of you: There is not much time. Everyone is given chances in this life—the doors are always open to those who wish to enter. The truth is simple: Love your God, love your neighbor as yourself. But first, you must love yourself and not be buried in the past. You are who you are in each life. Human society does not change. The rules of creation have been fixed in the foundation of the universe. There is Good and there is Evil, and there is Death. Don't look for secret potions or magic pills. Look instead to the poor and the needy, the homeless, the survivor, the orphan child in your midst. When you help one of these, you help yourself."

I'd been totally absorbed in Simon and did not realize that Ari and Helen had arrived. It was Simon who turned to them.

"I am Simon," he said and shook hands with Helen, who had a puzzled expression on her face as she looked at Martha, who was wiping away her tears with a tissue.

"Is something wrong?" Helen asked.

But if Helen had a puzzled expression on her face, Ari was completely transfixed. He stared at Simon. His mouth was slightly open, in what Sarah often called "my dumb look." But Ari didn't look dumb; he looked shocked, and it was not easy to shock Ari, since there was little in this world he had not seen. Then again, perhaps what he was seeing was from somewhere else.

Simon shifted the weight on his back and seemed to flex his shoulders. He hadn't removed the pack, and we'd been standing there for quite some time. He turned from Helen to Ari.

"It's nice to see you again, Ari," he said. "We were just about to begin the tour. It's been many years since you've seen the Stones. I'm glad you're here."

Ari didn't move. He then slowly extended his hand, and Simon took it. Then he said, "It's him, the second man, John, the one I told you about, the one who helped me carry your father to the Wall. It's him!"

"Come," Simon said, "let's walk up to the Mount. We've gotten way ahead of ourselves. The tour normally begins up there. Come."

As we followed Simon up toward the Mount of Olives—he was walking quickly, even with the pack on his back—Sarah and I were closest to him. It had begun to get windy and colder as we made the journey from the Western Wall to the ancient cemetery. The midday sun was high in the sky. I could see a long, dark shadow separate the Mount from the golden resplendence of the Dome of the Rock and the Old City. It was a surreal landscape of light and dark, of day and night, in the middle of a bright afternoon. Sarah's red hair took on added radiance as it blew in the wind.

"Why were we chosen? Tell us, Simon," she asked cautiously, as we walked.

"Don't be afraid, Sarah," he said. "Nothing bad will happen here today."

"I'm not afraid," she said.

"I know that." He paused. "Many are chosen, not just you and John. And many more will be chosen in the next few years. The world was made for these people. It is the simple truth: You have love, you share love, you love one another. Even the homeless have to stop wandering, don't they, Sarah? Even the homeless have mothers. You have charity, as well. So you have the greatest of blessings. There are no secrets. Everything is connected to everything else. And there is another reason why you and John were chosen."

"My father?" I asked.

"Yes, your father, John. Ari was right: Bill McGowan was one of the elect, the perfect souls that the Creator lets visit this world in each generation, to protect it from destruction, until the day comes."

"For the Messiah? For judgment?" I asked.

"Yes," he said, "for that. For you."

"Are you the Messiah, Simon?" I asked.

Everyone heard my question, and almost on cue, we stopped walking as Simon addressed us.

"No," he said, "I am not the Messiah. I am a messenger who has come to deliver the Stones into your hands for safekeeping, and to give you another assignment. You have been permitted to glimpse the Messiah today, John, at the Wall, in your vision of the Garden. He awaits everyone there, as it says in the Stones. Come."

We continued walking toward the Mount. I noticed that

Martha was having difficulty keeping up. Simon noticed, too, and slowed down.

"I'm sorry," he said. "I was walking too fast. Sometimes I forget. Let's rest for a few minutes."

"Oh, I'm just an old woman!" Martha said. It was the first maudlin comment I'd ever heard her make. It seemed out of character.

"Your happiness is still to come," he said to her.

As we stopped along the way, I realized something else about Simon which hadn't been obvious at first. Although we all were impressed by his presence, and especially his eyes and voice, there was another quality about him that was hard to put into a single word, but the word that came closest, I suppose, was silence. He was silent most of the time, and only spoke to us when we approached him with a question, expressed or unexpressed.

Helen, as well, had been uncharacteristically quiet since she'd arrived. She walked along, next to Ari, and had no difficulty keeping up. Like Simon, she was tall and thin, with her hair cropped in a boyish cut. But there was nothing boyish about Helen, who had a warm, feminine charm about her.

And it was Helen who broke the silence.

"Do you mean to say," she began, "that you are taking us to—I don't know how to put this—to find the Messiah Stones? That you know where they are? Is that what you're saying?"

Simon didn't hesitate. "Yes," he said.

"Well, that would be something, wouldn't it?" Helen then looked at Ari as if to confirm she'd just asked an important, perhaps tricky question. She folded her arms across her chest. Was she being defiant, stubborn?

Ari stepped forward, taking her by the arm. He seemed to be trying to move her away from Simon.

"I think we're all eager to learn where the Stones are," she said. "I'm just asking out loud what we're all thinking."

"Helen," Sarah said, "you don't have to believe—"

"I'm not saying I don't believe," Helen said. "It's really not a question of faith. Mr. Simon seems like a very nice person; I'm not quarreling with that. But I'll have to be honest with all of you. Ari and I are very familiar with everything around here—we've been here many times before, you know—I mean, if you want a tour. Stories and such are harmless enough, but let's not pretend that there really are Messiah Stones, or that the Messiah will arrive, and that the world will end in the year 2000. I don't want to hurt anyone's feelings, but people have had these ideas for thousands of years, and, well, so far the sun still comes up every morning. It's okay to be good, to love your neighbor as yourself, to feed the hungry. . . ."

Simon had started walking again toward the Mount while Helen was still speaking. We followed him. I hadn't realized before just how close the Wall was to the old cemetery. I was reminded once more of Rome and the close proximity of the important buildings. There must have been a special feeling of brotherhood and security in those days, when people were nearer to each other, separated at most by the distance animals could travel in a few hours. We've lost that sense of nearness and security in our time; distances have become challenges to overcome and now separate people.

Helen had stopped speaking. Simon didn't seem overly concerned with her doubts and criticisms. I understood what she was saying, though, having traveled down her road myself in these past few days. I could see that doubts were a necessary stage in our development as human beings. I wondered what it would take to make believers out of most people, what degree of proof would be necessary. We had in our possession photographs of the Stones, we had seen the incredible beauty and horror of Barbara's album, we had met Beverly and Simon, who were clearly extraordinary beings beyond simple explanations, and yet there was someone among us who still didn't believe in the inevitability of the Stones and the Messiah. Was it human pride, or an inflated sense of our own importance, or was it that stiff-necked, rational attitude we'd developed in the last few hundred years? Perhaps human beings were beyond total belief in the Creator. Perhaps a faith large enough to fill a mustard seed was just too much for us.

Jesus had seen how fickle his disciples could be, how he would be denied by them in his hour of greatest trial, even as they professed their unquenchable faith. Their denial must have given him enormous pain. Moses, too, atop his own mountain, conversing with God, having displayed for his people the miraculous power of Jehovah as he led them out of bondage to God's holy mountain to receive his Laws—Moses, too, descended only to find them worshiping a golden calf, an idol, a figment of their human imaginations. What was it in the human condition that refused to take the final leap of faith?

Simon had taken us to the Mount of Olives cemetery, where the dead await the coming of the Messiah on the Day of Judgment. A long, dark shadow still separated this quiet resting place from the golden expanse beneath us. I looked down from where we had come and held Sarah's hand.

We followed Simon as he walked between the slabs of flat stones that bore their inscriptions in strange languages. Soon I realized where he was taking us. There, beneath us, was Bill McGowan's grave. The chrysanthemums that Ari had placed there the day before fluttered in the wind. I read the epitaph from Isaiah to myself. It was cold.

Ari picked up a small stone and, following the custom, placed it on the edge of my father's tombstone. Martha and Lillian did the same. As I watched them do this, I saw Simon unstrap his backpack and remove it. He seemed to be struggling just a bit; it must've been much heavier than I'd guessed.

"Can I help you?" Ari asked.

"Yes, thank you, Ari," he said. Both men placed the pack on the ground next to my father's grave. Simon then bent down and unzippered a separate pouch on the bottom and removed what did turn out to be a small shovel. He then reached around the pack to the other side and pulled the largest zipper all the way around. When he lifted one side of the pack open, we could see what he had been carrying all along.

"It's earth," he said in answer to our unverbalized question. "From the Garden. It's pure. It has not been cursed."

He then began to shovel the earth over the flat tombstone at my father's grave. This didn't take him very long, but Simon did it slowly, almost neatly, carefully scooping each shovelful and bringing it over the slab, then turning the shovel to one side to let the earth fall. Before long, he was finished, and he stood up. He walked some paces away, and we followed and waited with him. A neat mound of earth covered the grave. It was dark brown and seemed very rich.

It had been getting colder up to that point, but as I now realized, it was warmer. The wind also seemed to have calmed down. Everything appeared calm around us, as though we were on a small, secluded island set off from the mainland. I could still see the Golden Gate and the Dome of the Rock in the distance, but now they seemed miles away.

All at once, I felt a slight trembling in the earth. It grew stronger. Sarah squeezed my hand harder. Ari and Helen held each other, as did Martha and Lillian. We had no idea what to expect. For the first time that day, I was afraid of the unknown.

Simon looked at us and said, "The final victory is over death."

There were six of us there that day who had been brought to that spot by Simon. What we saw next changed us forever.

The trembling stopped. A brilliant, funnellike shaft of light, unlike anything I'd ever seen before, shot out from the grave as if a tremendous beacon down below had been suddenly turned on and the door above opened, so that the light could escape. The shaft of light was steady and strong and rose up and out into the sky, narrow at the bottom and wider as it got higher, like a funnel. The light itself was almost visible, and I remember feeling it might have a texture as well, so that if you touched it, you could feel it.

It also appeared warm and had a certain glow. As we marveled at it, I could see each of us was not only fascinated and awed by it, but also attracted to it, as though we were a part of it and had known it before. If we'd felt some momentary fear at the trembling of the earth, it was gone. Now, more than anything, we felt comfort and security, knowing that we were in the company of something that could only bring us happiness.

"This is the light," Simon began, "that God created at the beginning of time. It is the primal light which will reveal to all the coming of the Messiah. It is the light of redemption, of the covenant, and of the Stones. It is the light of victory over death. It is for each of you and for everyone in these final days."

Then, appearing in the shaft of light, rising up and held in suspension in midair as though buoyed from below by an invisible force, bathed in the glow of light and perhaps twenty feet in the air above, I saw a man who I knew immediately was my father. People had been correct: He did look like me, or, rather, I looked like him. He was smiling down at me, calm, his eyes focused first on me and then on Sarah. I knew in my heart that I loved him and that someday we would be together again. I knew that he had found God and fulfilled his mission. But, more than anything, I was grateful to have had the blessing of being shown my father.

I also knew, beyond the shadow of any future doubt that might surface, that the resurrection of the dead will occur, that life does not end with the final breath we take on earth.

And yet, even as I was being given the gift of proof of the divine plan, even as I witnessed the miracle of my father's appearance, I thought the scene being enacted was only for me. But it wasn't.

Ari was a big man, but now he cried. And as he cried, I could see a smile on his face.

"It's them," Ari said. "My wife and my boys. It's them, in the Light. I see them."

Ari said this as I saw my father, and no one but my father. He spoke out loud, unself-conscious, free.

"Exactly as I remember them," he said.

As I turned to Ari, I noticed Martha with her arm extended toward the Light. She seemed to want to take a step forward.

"No," Simon said to her. "Just look."

"It is my father," Martha said. "My own father. He's looking at me. He loves me. I want to hold him!"

"No," Simon said.

Next to Martha, Lillian had gotten down on her knees. Her hands were cupped in supplication in front of her.

"My mother," she said. "My mother!"

I wanted so much to keep looking at my father, but my attention was pulled away by the others, who, each in turn, had acknowledged what they were witnessing. I realized I was in the midst of a modern-day miracle I would not be able to contain, that someday I would have to tell the story of what was happening in front of our eyes. Each of us had seen the living proof of redemption, and we were still alive ourselves, on this side of our human wall.

I looked up again at my father and felt Sarah squeeze my hand even harder, so much that I pulled it away. The expression on her face was beyond description, beyond words. No smile, no tears, just her eyes that seemed huge as they focused on something in the center of the light above us.

"Tommy?" she asked. "Is it Tommy? Tommy? Tommy?"

She repeated her brother's name over and over. She'd been eight or nine when he was killed in a motorcycle accident when he was only nineteen. The tragedy had destroyed her parents' marriage. So the last time she had seen him was as a little girl, years ago. And as she called out to him now, on the Mount of Olives, she was almost that little girl once again in her voice.

"Tommy? Tommy?"

I cried that day for Tommy and for my father.

The light was caressing, all around us. It had a certain heat, but did not burn. I felt it on every part of my body and on my face.

Everyone had spoken except Helen. Helen stood off to the side a few feet from Ari. She, too, looked up at the light above us.

"It has always been a question of faith, Helen," Simon said. "If you can deny your own eyes, then you can deny the truth. If you can accept what you see, you will know God. You have been given a great gift."

Helen said nothing, but just looked up at the light.

There was silence again in this small sea of calm that Simon had created for us. Some time passed, as he allowed each of us to spend precious minutes in the presence of our loved ones. I studied my father even more closely and realized how young he looked. He said nothing, but just moved his gaze from me to Sarah and back again. I wondered if the others had similar experiences. Then, just briefly, he lifted his right hand and waved to me. Was it a wave of greeting or farewell? I couldn't tell.

I don't know how much time elapsed, but just as quickly as

the funnel of light had appeared, it vanished, as did my father. In its place, resting on the earth above his grave, were three tablets of rock that glowed with an inner fire.

Before us, at our feet, were the Messiah Stones.

They were just as Dr. Allison and my father had described in their letter of forty years before, each in a different language and about three feet square. At the bottom of each, I could read the name "McGowan." Beside the Stones, arranged in a circle, were six globes about the size of basketballs. I knew that there was one for each of us standing there that day.

I looked over at Simon. He understood my question.

"Yes," he said.

With his permission, I then walked over to the Stones and touched one. It was warm, but it didn't burn my hand. Sarah joined me, as did the others. All of us, except Helen, touched the Stones.

Simon came over to us.

"There are no secrets under heaven for those who search for truth," he said. "These Stones are for all people, as the Messiah of whom they speak will also be for all people. There are many lands that are dry and thirsty. There are many walls in this world that separate neighbors, and parents from children. There is much darkness in the world, where the light is needed. And there is Evil. The Stones protect as well as promise. They were brought from the ancient city of Shiloh and placed beneath the ovens of death in Poland, where they have been these forty years. Now they are home, in Jerusalem. You have been given a great gift and have been permitted to see what it will be like at the end of days. You now have the responsibility of knowing. There is no returning this gift. The Stones are for you.

"John, your task is to build a house for the Stones here in Jerusalem, where people of all faiths can see them and marvel at God's gift. This is your special task, for you and Sarah, with one more. You will write the story of the Messiah Stones, the story for all to read. For understand, the days grow short. Soon the Golden Gate will open here in Jerusalem, and also in every corner of the world. The truth is simple: Follow your heart and be not afraid."

With that, he walked over to Helen and placed something in her hand, then started down the hill away from us. We stood there in a group and watched him leave. He walked away without saying another word. When we could not make him out anymore, we turned to Helen. She opened her hand. In it, she held a keychain with a tiny globe at one end. On one side of it, we saw a small chip which might have been broken off from a larger block, and on the other, carved in golden relief, was the name "Helen."

She began to cry. The tour was over.

I don't know how long we remained at my father's grave. In all honesty, without Simon we weren't sure what to do next. Somehow, it had also gotten much later than I imagined, and it was cold again. The Stones remained in front of us, glowing. The globes, as well, rested exactly where they had appeared. We were still trying to absorb everything that had happened. I, for one, kept staring at what was now empty, blank space above my father's grave, half hoping that the light would appear again. I imagined that the others had similar thoughts. I could still see the image of my father in my mind's eye, as I can to this day. It has been burned there forever.

Simon's backpack and shovel lay on the ground. They, too, had remained, artifacts of a sort. I began to think: There were still many unanswered questions in my mind.

I now had enough faith to fill a mustard seed. With it, I walked over to the Messiah Stones and touched one. It had been carved by the hand of the Creator at the dawn of time, and now I could feel its warmth on my skin.

Helen came over to me and handed me the souvenir Simon had given her.

"We have the key," she said. "Come, help me, there's so much to do! It's time to begin!"

And so we began, all of us.

Afterword

ABOUT TWO MONTHS AGO, I received a phone call from Jerusalem. I had been hoping to receive word one way or another either from somewhere in the United States or from somewhere else. As it turned out, it was from somewhere else, but not much of a surprise. If I had been a younger man, I might have made the trip with them.

It wasn't John McGowan who called, but Sarah, his wife. I've never met her, but now I felt I knew her better than I've known most people in my long life. She informed me that she and John had decided to relocate to Israel, for reasons, she said, which I would understand later, since—to quote her exactly, which is what I am trained to do—I was "the spark that lit the fire."

I assured her I was only fulfilling my fiduciary responsibility as Bill McGowan's attorney, but I don't think she believed me. She seemed to think there was much more to it, that in a way I was part of a grander scheme that connected in some way with the doings of the Almighty and his appointed Messiah.

Perhaps Sarah was right; then again, maybe I'm just an old man enjoying his last few cigars.

I told Sarah, be that as it may, I was very interested in everything that had happened in Jerusalem, and before—indeed, everything that had happened from the day I first contacted her husband, or even back to that day years ago when I was hired by Bill McGowan. "Have no fear," she said, somewhat happily, I should report. "John is busy writing everything down, word for word, as if lives depended on it. And maybe they do. He's been at it these two months here in a small apartment we've rented in Jerusalem. You'll understand later, I hope, what's happened to all of us here and what we're doing. Don't be surprised, but we found the Stones, with a little help, I should add. The real surprise, I suppose, is that the Stones are not the end of the story, but really the beginning. We've been given a job to do. I just don't know where we'll get the money. My mother will help—she's here now with the boys. But it'll take much more than we have. I sold my share of the bookstore. You know, as it turned out, we got parts in the biggest caper of them all! Anyhow, we've thought about you often, and we did say that prayer."

It was nice of her to contact me. I have a surprise for her, and for John, which I'm saving. You see, like her husband, I'm also a conservative sort of fellow, and never really needed all that money Bill McGowan gave me. So I invested it. It's a very considerable sum now, forty years later—enough, I hope, for a spectacular building to house the Messiah Stones. They deserve nothing less.

Then, about a month ago, I received a manuscript from Jerusalem. With it was the following note:

Jerusalem
April 1995

Dear Mr. Stanton,

Been meaning to write to you, but honestly have
not had the chance until now. Sarah once said that
people don't write letters anymore, but I think I'll
start a trend. It's old-fashioned and I like it that
way.

After you read the enclosed manuscript, I'd appreciate your opinion. Can you help me find a publisher? I hope you'll agree that we've had the most
incredible experience. I know we've gone through
this for a reason.

You may come to believe that I've been out in the
desert sun too long, or that late in my life I've
caught the religion flu. I assure you, neither is the
case. I know this because I've found the truth, and
it's inside me, just as it was promised. I'm not afraid
anymore.

Also, for other reasons.

Those reasons are Martha, Lillian, Ari, and
Helen. (When you read the manuscript, you'll understand what I'm about to tell you.) Martha retired
from teaching and now devotes herself full-time to

working with troubled children in Philadelphia. In a way, I wish I could be with her. I know what it's like to be lost and confused as a child. Lillian has returned to her family in Atlanta and is a nurse in the AIDS ward of her hospital. Ari and I and Sarah now spend all of our time planning the building to house the Stones. They are magnificent; I hope you can see them one day. You don't have to believe, but I warn you, there is something contagious about them.

The surprising thing is that Helen has turned out to be the most inspired member of our group. She still won't tell us what she saw on the Mount. I will say this, though: She's working on the project as if there were no tomorrow.

Well, there you have it, a Tale for Our Times.

Thanks for everything, especially the "call."

John McGowan

P.S. Don't be a stranger; life is definitely short. Visit. (If you do, let me know when we can expect you. I'd like you to make a stop first in New York's Grand Central Station. There's someone there I want you to meet who is always hungry.)

Which is exactly what I intend to do—tomorrow.

James Frederick Stanton

Barbara Benig

ABOUT THE AUTHOR

IRVING BENIG is married and the father of two children. He has traveled widely. *The Messiah Stones* is his first novel.